# BYRON

George Gordon Byron was born on 22 January 1788. He inherited the barony in 1798. He went to school in Dulwich, and then in 1801 to Harrow. In 1805 he went up to Trinity College, Cambridge, later gaining a reputation in London for his startling good looks and extravagant behaviour. His first collection of poems, *Hours of Idleness* (1807), was not well received, but with the publication of the first two cantos of 'Childe Harold's Pilgrimage' (1812) he became famous overnight. In 1815 he married the heiress Arabella Milbanke, but they were separated after a year. Byron shocked society by the rumoured relationship with his half-sister, Augusta, and in 1816 he left England. He eventually settled in Italy, where he lived for some time with Teresa, Countess Guiccioli. He supported Italian revolutionary movements and in 1823 he left for Greece to fight in its struggle for independence, but he contracted a fever and died at Missolonghi in 1824.

Byron's contemporary popularity was largely based on his romantic works, but his satires such as 'Beppo' (1818), 'The Vision of Judgement' (1822) and 'Don Juan' (1819–24) represent his most sophisticated and accomplished writing. He had a great influence on the Romantic movement, and the Byronic hero was a prototype frequently imitated in European literature.

# Byron

*Poems*

Selected by A. S. B. Glover

PENGUIN BOOKS

PENGUIN BOOKS

Published by the Penguin Group
Penguin Books Ltd, 27 Wrights Lane, London W8 5TZ, England
Viking Penguin, a division of Penguin Books USA Inc.
375 Hudson Street, New York, New York 10014, USA
Penguin Books Australia Ltd, Ringwood, Victoria, Australia
Penguin Books Canada Ltd, 2801 John Street, Markham, Ontario, Canada L3R 1B4
Penguin Books (NZ) Ltd, 182–190 Wairau Road, Auckland 10, New Zealand

Penguin Books Ltd, Registered Offices: Harmondsworth, Middlesex, England

This selection first published 1954
7 9 10 8

Copyright 1954 by Penguin Books Ltd
All rights reserved

Printed in England by Clays Ltd, St Ives plc
Set in Monotype Bell

# CONTENTS

# INTRODUCTION

BYRON's life and work is like a book which seems at first sight to be dominated by its highly coloured plates. First there is the standard portrait – a magnificently turbaned profile posed against a stormy sky – Byron dressed up as a Byronic Hero. Then comes a picture of Newstead Abbey, a suitably 'Gothic' retreat for Byron and his friends, sitting up late in 'friars' dresses, drinking burgundy, claret, champagne, and what not out of the *skull-cup'*. Byron is seen at Cambridge, sharing his college rooms with a bear; and on his entry into society – the pale *homme fatale* of the drawing-rooms : 'mad, bad, and dangerous to know'. Women come into the picture : Annabella Milbanke, whom he so unaccountably and unfortunately married; Caroline Lamb, who made a public scandal of her love for him; Augusta Leigh, his half-sister, with whom he was more in love than with any other woman, and one of whose many children he considered to be his.

Byron is next seen leaving England on account of the moral indignation aroused by his private life. The scene shifts to the Mediterranean. The colours become brighter: Byron swimming the Hellespont; Byron travelling through Italy with the Countess Guiccioli, and a caravan of monkeys, dogs, and peacocks; finally, Byron dead in the cause of Greek liberation. 'My God,' wrote Jane Welsh to Thomas Carlyle, 'if they had said that the sun or the moon was gone out of the heavens, it could not have struck me with the idea of a more awful and dreary blank in the creation than the words, "Byron is dead!"'

That was how Byron appeared to the majority of his contemporaries : as a luminary, a dynamic force. His works were translated into all the languages of Europe, the literary scene was thronged with 'Byronic' young poets, and the progeny of his Heroes multiplied yearly.

Today the flamboyant aspects of his personality have not only ceased to dazzle, they even tend to detract from our appreciation of Byron's work, seeming to be simply the successful poses of a man playing to the gallery of his own day. They do not, however, represent the whole of Byron. He had many other facets. He was an aristocrat who rebelled against social injustice; a man who not only spoke about liberty but worked for it; an affectionate and loyal friend; an immensely lively correspondent; a trenchant satirist.

Byron was born in 1788. His early childhood was spent in Scotland in an atmosphere of disorder and poverty, dominated by an hysterical mother and a dissolute nurse. These years left their legacy of nervous insecurity, only partly concealed by the aristocratic façade provided by his title and his handsome patrician features. In 1800 he went to Harrow and in 1805 to Trinity College, Cambridge. Unlike Milton and Wordsworth, Byron did not regard his studies at Cambridge as part of the discipline essential to becoming a great poet. He did not draft out plans for any new English epic or record the progress of a poet's mind. He made friends, went to parties, and swam at Grantchester:

We have several parties here, and this evening a large assortment of jockeys, gamblers, boxers, authors, parsons, and poets, sup with me,—a precious mixture but they go on well together; and for me, I am a *spice* of everything . . .

But he goes on to say that he has 380 lines of a satire written and that his published verses have just been 'praised to the skies' in one review and 'abused greatly' in another.

In 1807, when this letter was written, Byron had brought out two volumes of poetry: *Hours of Idleness* and *Poems on Various Occasions*. The interest of these early poems is largely biographical. Though they showed that Byron wrote verse with great facility, they did not seem to hold out much promise for the future. Yet the very next year he wrote a lyric, 'When we two parted in silence and tears' (p. 32), which had all the qualities of his best work in this kind. It is quite simple both in thought and expression, but beneath the quiet rhythm there is a strong current of feeling.

The satire also mentioned above was 'English Bards and

Scotch Reviewers'. It was Byron's first long poem. Byron was a great admirer both of Dryden and of Pope, and saw himself as their successor, the satirist of the English literary scene. The poetasters of Grub Street were replaced as the butts of satire by the 'troubadours' of the Lake District, Wordsworth, Coleridge, and Southey. Byron's attack has vitality and punch, though it has nothing of the polish and subtlety of Pope's mature work. Today the part of the work which deals with the Scotch reviewers is of limited interest, as the subjects of the satire are little read, but what Byron writes of Wordsworth and Coleridge (p. 58) provides a refreshing antidote to a too solemn regard for these poets. Byron was not, however, a discriminating judge of literature; his pronouncements on it are often no more than sweeping generalizations of little value, and taken as a whole his criticism of Wordsworth, Coleridge, and Keats was singularly lacking in perception.

In 1817 Byron, now living in London, published the first two cantos of 'Childe Harold's Pilgrimage'. His name was made: he awoke to find his book on every table and 'to be made the greatest fuss of'. A contemporary commented: 'Language can hardly exaggerate the folly that prevailed in 1817, when waltzing and Lord Byron came into fashion.' His readers identified him with his hero and watched for like symptoms of melancholy.

> Yet oft-times in his maddest mirthful mood
> Strange pangs would flash along Childe Harold's brow
> As if the memory of some deadly feud
> Or disappointed passion lurked below,

though he protested that such identification was not intended. 'Instruct Mr Murray not to allow his shopman to call the work 'Child of Harrow's Pilgrimage'! ! ! ! as he has done to some of my astonished friends, who wrote to inquire after my *sanity* on the occasion, as well they might.'

Childe Harold was the first of the long line of Byronic Heroes. Byron's heroes met the requirements of a public brought up on the novels of the 'all-horrid' pens of Mrs

Radcliffe and her followers. They dominate his poems. The other characters are of importance only in so far as they affect them. The settings are carefully chosen to intensify the impression they will make. Byron standardized his heroes to such an extent that they lack individuality; and the unity of their conception is so complete that it is enough for one characteristic trait to be mentioned for the whole man to come immediately to mind. By making their monologues resemble his expressions of personal feeling in his lyric poetry, Byron was responsible for the fact that his readers always thought they saw him masquerading in his heroes' cloaks.

The settings of Byron's poems were entirely suited to the taste of the age. His descriptive writing is at its best in the fourth canto of 'Childe Harold', in which he writes of Italy, for in a few words he could make his page alight with its atmosphere: Venice, 'a fairy city of the heart, rising like water-columns from the sea'; Ferrara with its 'wide and grass-grown streets'; and the Capitol under 'the deep blue sky of Rome'.

The third and fourth cantos of 'Childe Harold' were written when Byron was already in exile from England. The four years which separated them from the first two cantos had been marked by his complicated love-affairs and his unhappy marriage. His feelings had found expression in the angry lines he wrote to Caroline Lamb ('Remember thee! Remember thee!'– p. 44) and in a series of very emotional poems to his sister.

Byron's poetic activity during these years, however, was not confined to pieces occasioned by his personal life. He had embarked in 1812 on the series of tales which acted like heady wine on his public. Of this group of poems 'The Giaour' and 'Mazeppa' are fully representative. All the characteristic ingredients of the genre are present. The Giaour's face bears the necessary imprint of past grief:

> Dark and unearthly is the scowl
> That glares beneath his dusky cowl.
> The flash of that dilating eye
> Reveals too much of times gone by . . .

while the ruined cloister he sweeps through and the distant sounds of chanting bring suitable Gothic associations. Both poems are written in the first person, which brings the reader into the closest possible touch with the heroes. In both the action is very dramatic.

In 1815 Byron had published another collection of lyrics, the *Hebrew Melodies*. The ease with which he wrote was not always to his advantage. Like Shelley, he tended to flow on – there seemed no reason to stop – so that far too often excellent lines were lost in the stream of mediocrity. But these short pieces gain by it. There is no straining after effect. The words move with ease to the measure.

In 1815 Byron also published his 'Ode to Napoleon Buonaparte'. History had presented him with a Hero ready made. There was in this a curious anomaly. Politically Byron could not but hate the tyranny of Napoleon's rule. All his life he spoke, wrote, and worked on behalf of the politically oppressed. His maiden speech in the House of Lords had been in support of the claims of Nottingham frameworkers; he celebrated Bonnivard's martyrdom with a thetorical trumpet-blast (p. 55); he worked with the Carbonari in Italy and in the cause of Greek independence. The direction of his political endeavours remained constant. But when he writes of Napoleon, one feels beneath the condemnation of the 'Pagod with the feet of clay', this 'Dark Spirit', the contrary pull of admiration,

> And Monarchs bowed the trembling limb,
> And thanked him for a throne!

This attitude to Napoleon, compounded as it was of contrary emotions, became one of the characteristic features of the Byronic movement in Europe.

In 1816 Byron had settled in Italy and was enjoying it. The emotional temperature of his letters, which had run very high at the time of leaving England, had dropped. They were now full of amusing gossip, lit by the carnival lanterns of an endless succession of masked balls, visits to the opera, and conversaziones. And always they were spiced by a light, mocking

11

irony – Byron laughing at himself, at the figure he was cutting :

> I am going out this evening in my *cloak* and *Gondola*–there are two nice Mrs Radcliffe words for you.

Byron captured the froth and frivolity of this atmosphere in 'Beppo', which was a curtain-raiser to his greatest poem, 'Don Juan'.

At this time Byron also tried his hand at poetic drama. His plays were written to be read not acted. This is a hybrid form of literature which, with a few notable exceptions, has always proved unsatisfactory. The very fact that the plays were not intended for the stage led him to neglect the essential conditions of good drama : the interplay of contrasted characters and the compelling forward movement of the plot. The Russian poet Pushkin put his finger on Byron's limitations as a dramatist :

> Byron created only one character [his own] and in his tragedies he handed out the different traits and peculiarities of that character to his *dramatis personae*, giving to one his pride, to another his hatred, to a third his melancholy, and so on. In this way, from one powerful, sombre, and energetic personality he created several insignificant ones.

Hazlitt went further :

> 'Lord Byron's tragedies . . . have neither action, character, nor interest, but are a sort of *gossamer* tragedies, spun out and glittering, and spreading a flimsy veil over the face of nature. Yet he spins them on.'

In 1818 Shelley visited Byron in Venice. He has left an impression of one of their rides together in his poem 'Julian and Maddalo', in which with the gentlest irony he drew Byron striking an attitude :

> The sense that he was greater than his kind
> Had struck, methinks, his eagle spirit blind
> By gazing on its own exceeding light.

Shelley and Byron understood each other well, and their friendship was firmly grounded in mutual affection. There was much to draw them together. They were both in exile from England. They had certain political ideals in common, though Byron's attitude to politics was far more practical and realistic than Shelley's. Also, unlike, for example, that of the Lake Poets and Keats, the focus of their interests was not primarily literary. They were both at the same time aristocrats and rebels against convention. Byron wrote to John Murray after Shelley's death:

Alas! poor Shelley! how he would have laughed had he lived, and how we used to laugh now and then, at various things, which are grave in the Suburbs!

You are mistaken about Shelley. You do not know how mild, how tolerant, how good he was in Society; and as perfect a Gentleman as ever crossed a drawing-room . . .

All his egalitarian principles did not prevent Byron from despising Keats's middle-class milieu. He failed to grasp the full measure of Keats's quality. He allowed himself to be side-tracked by secondary considerations – for instance, his anger at Keats's abuse of Pope – and was only too ready finally to dismiss him as having been 'snuffed out by an article'. Shelley's death, on the other hand, hit Byron very hard. '[He] was, without exception, the *best* and least selfish man I ever knew,' he wrote to Murray.

Shelley died in 1822, the year in which Byron published 'The Vision of Judgement'. In this poem Byron is at his most witty and lighthearted. It is a well-sustained political jest in a lightly blasphemous framework, sparkling in the manner of a mock-heroic. It deals with the arrival of George III at the gates of heaven, where

> The angels all were singing out of tune,
>     And hoarse with having little else to do,
> Excepting to wind up the sun and moon,
>     Or curb a runaway young star or two.

It soons becomes clear that the inmates of heaven are, if anything, even more ridiculous than George III, so that there is nothing incongruous in his seeking admission. Satan, however, appears, claiming him as his subject, and a lengthy debate is embarked on. This is interrupted by the arrival of Southey, who drives everyone to distraction by his monstrous speech. Meanwhile George III has slipped in unperceived, and is left, well installed, 'practising the hundredth psalm'. When he wrote 'The Vision of Judgement' Byron was already well away with 'Don Juan'.

All Byron's best qualities are contained in 'Don Juan': his magnificent, ironic detachment, his humour, his iconoclasm, his vitality, and his zest for life. When he writes of love he makes one aware of its physical immediacy, and there are few poets, apart from Chaucer and Donne, who can convey this sense so forcibly. When he writes of society it is clear that though he had joined in the dance himself, he remained sufficiently detached from the whirling throng to observe its petty preoccupations, its self-delusions, its peccadilloes. The balloon of pretension is puffed up and then, very neatly, pricked. For this Byron was well served by his mastery of bathos, which in his hands, as in Pope's, became a most effective instrument of satire. The book takes in the whole of European society. Byron leads his picaresque hero through a series of adventures, ranging from Spain to Turkey and from Russia to England. The scene shifts from a desert island to a harem, from a battlefield to the court of Catherine the Great, and Don Juan, the most adaptable and resilient hero in English literature, takes whatever comes his way cheerfully in his stride. In 1819 Byron had written to a friend:

As to 'Don Juan', confess, confess—you dog and be candid—that it is the sublime of *that there* sort of writing—it may be bawdy but is it not good English? It may be profligate but is it not *life*, is it not *the thing*? Could any man have written it who has not lived in the world?

The final cantos of 'Don Juan' were published in 1824; in the same year Byron died of fever at Missolonghi; and the European literary scene lost one of its giants.

Many years later Matthew Arnold wrote:

> When Byron's eyes were shut in death,
> We bow'd our head and held our breath.

He taught us little : but our soul
Had *felt* him like the thunder's roll.

In these lines there is an acknowledgement of greatness, but there is a reservation – 'he taught us little'. That is typical of the English attitude to Byron. There has always been reluctance for one reason or another to allow him a place on the highest levels of poetic fame. This is not because much of what he wrote is second-rate, for that is equally true of Wordsworth and Coleridge. Nor is it because even in his best works there is much that is slap-dash and unfinished (for Byron hated working over his poetry), for there is a great deal of equally loose writing in Shelley's work. It appears that the reason lies not in what Byron wrote but in what he failed to write. He never looked beyond this world. He never aspired to the heights of metaphysics or mysticism. His poetry was devoid of spirituality. This was his fatal flaw, and it was one which he shared with Pope – a circumstance from which he would have derived much comfort.

In Europe his reputation was immeasurably higher. He was judged among English poets to be second only to Shakespeare. The reasons for this are clear. He stood for all the aspirations of the European Romantic movement, both as a man and as a poet. He was cast in a large mould and surveyed the social scene with an ironical detachment comparable to that of Voltaire. The subject-matter of his poetry was of universal interest and application : and, as his language was almost devoid of imagery, his poetry lost comparatively little in translation.

After his death, Pushkin, speaking of some of his lost memoirs, remarked that he was glad they were lost. He felt that whereas in his poems Byron had revealed himself unconsciously, carried away by poetic enthusiasm, in cold-blooded prose he would have lied and posed and ranted against his enemies. That is true of Byron's best poetry: in it he dispensed with lies and pose and rant. 'Here at last,' wrote John Ruskin, and his words can serve as a final spur to reading Byron, 'I had found a man who spoke only of what he had seen and known; and spoke without exaggeration, without mystery, without enmity, and without mercy. "That is *so*; – make what you will of it!" '

The present selection has been made on the principle that, wherever possible, it is better to give fewer but longer extracts from poems themselves of considerable length, and thus to present a clearer impression of Byron's work than could be given by a series of snippets, which would often break off just as they had begun to capture the reader's interest.

'On a Distant View of Harrow' is taken from *Hours of Idleness* (1807); 'She walks in beauty', 'Oh! snatched away in beauty's bloom', 'The Vision of Belshazzar', and 'The Destruction of Sennacherib', from *Hebrew Melodies* (1815); 'Fare thee well' and 'Stanzas to Augusta' from *Domestic Pieces* (1816); the remainder of the shorter poems, except for the Sonnet on Chillon, from *Occasional Pieces* (1807–24).

The text followed has been in general that of Ernest Hartley Coleridge's edition in seven volumes (London, 1898–1904). The editor is grateful to Miss J. M. Morrell and Miss Tatiana Wolff for their help and advice in making his selection, particularly in the difficult task of choosing the most representative passages from 'Childe Harold' and 'Don Juan'.

A. S. B. GLOVER

# CHRONOLOGY OF
## BYRON'S LIFE AND WORKS

1788 Born, London, 22 January.

1798 Succeeded to the family title, and is made ward in Chancery.

1800 Sent to Harrow School.

1803 Proposed marriage to Mary Chaworth, who rejected him.

1805 Went to Trinity College, Cambridge.

1807 Published his juvenilia, *Hours of Idleness*, which was mauled in the *Edinburgh Review*.

1808 Lived at his family seat, Newstead Abbey, in pseudo-dissipation.

1809 Took his seat in the House of Lords.
'English Bards and Scotch Reviewers', his reply to the attack from the *Edinburgh Review*.
Left England with John Hobhouse for an extended tour through Europe, visiting Portugal, Spain, and Greece.

1810 In Greece and the Near East, where he visited the site of Troy, Constantinople, and swam the Hellespont in emulation of Leander.

1811 Residence in London.

1812 'Childe Harold', Cantos I and II.

1813 'The Giaour'; 'The Bride of Abydos'; 'The Corsair'.
Lady Caroline Lamb's infatuation for him at its height.

1814 Proposed a second time to Miss Milbanke, and was accepted.
'Ode to Napoleon Buonaparte'; 'Lara'.

1815 January, married Miss Milbanke. In December, birth of his daughter, Augusta Ada.

*Hebrew Melodies* (which includes 'The Vision of Belshazzar', 'The Destruction of Sennacherib', 'She walks in beauty').

1816 Lady Byron separated from him in January

He left England for good in April, travelling in Switzerland with the Shelleys, thence to Venice.

'Childe Harold', Canto III; 'The Prisoner of Chillon'.

1817 Birth of his daughter Allegra, child of Claire Clairmont, Mary Shelley's step-sister.

'The Lament of Tasso'; 'Manfred'.

1818 'Childe Harold', Canto IV; 'Beppo'. Began 'Don Juan'.

1819 Met Teresa, Countess Guiccioli, with whom he lived for a time in Venice.

'Mazeppa'; 'Don Juan', Cantos I and II, published anonymously.

1820 Living in Ravenna with Countess Guiccioli.

'The Prophecy of Dante'.

1821 'Don Juan', Cantos III, IV, V published, still anonymously; 'Marino Faliero'; 'Cain'; 'Sardanapalus'; 'The Two Foscari'.

1822 With Leigh Hunt produced a periodical, *The Liberal*, the first number containing 'The Vision of Judgment', the second, 'Heaven and Earth'.

Attended the cremation of Shelley's body.

1823 'Don Juan', Cantos VI–XIV; 'Werner'.

Sailed from Genoa to join the Greek insurgents.

1824 Died at Missolonghi, 19 April. Buried at Hucknall Torkard, near the family seat of Newstead.

1832–5 His *Life*, by Moore, and *Collected Works* published.

# ON A DISTANT VIEW
## OF THE VILLAGE AND SCHOOL OF
## HARROW ON THE HILL

*Oh! mihi praeteritos referat si Jupiter annos.* VIRGIL

YE scenes of my childhood, whose loved recollection
   Embitters the present, compared with the past;
Where science first dawned on the powers of reflection,
   And friendships were formed, too romantic to last;

Where fancy, yet, joys to trace the resemblance
   Of comrades, in friendship and mischief allied;
How welcome to me your ne'er fading remembrance,
   Which rests in the bosom, though hope is denied!

Again I revisit the hills where we sported,
   The streams where we swam, and the fields where we
      fought;
The school where, loud warned by the bell, we resorted,
   To pore o'er the precepts by pedagogues taught.

Again I behold where for hours I have pondered,
   As reclining, at eve, on yon tombstone I lay;
Or round the steep brow of the churchyard I wandered,
   To catch the last gleam of the sun's setting ray.

I once more view the room, with spectators surrounded,
   Where, as Zanga, I trod on Alonzo o'erthrown;
While, to swell my young pride, such applauses resounded,
   I fancied that Mossop himself was outshone:

Or, as Lear, I poured forth the deep imprecation,
  By my daughters, of kingdom and reason deprived;
Till, fired by loud plaudits and self-adulation,
  I regarded myself as a Garrick revivéd.

Ye dreams of my boyhood, how much I regret you!
  Unfaded your memory dwells in my breast;
Though sad and deserted, I ne'er can forget you:
  Your pleasures may still be in fancy possest.

To Ida full oft may remembrance restore me,
  While fate shall the shades of the future unroll!
Since darkness o'ershadows the prospect before me,
  More dear is the beam of the past to my soul.

But if, through the course of the years which await me,
  Some new scene of pleasure should open to view,
I will say, while with rapture the thought shall elate me,
  'Oh! such were the days which my infancy knew!'
                                        1806.

# SHE WALKS IN BEAUTY

She walks in beauty, like the night
   Of cloudless climes and starry skies;
And all that's best of dark and bright
   Meet in her aspect and her eyes:
Thus mellowed to that tender light
   Which heaven to gaudy day denies.

One shade the more, one ray the less,
   Had half impaired the nameless grace,
Which waves in every raven tress,
   Or softly lightens o'er her face;
Where thoughts serenely sweet express,
   How pure, how dear their dwelling-place.

And on that cheek, and o'er that brow,
   So soft, so calm, yet eloquent,
The smiles that win, the tints that glow,
   But tell of days in goodness spent,
A mind at peace with all below,
   A heart whose love is innocent!

# OH! SNATCHED AWAY IN
## BEAUTY'S BLOOM

Oh! snatched away in beauty's bloom,
On thee shall press no ponderous tomb;
   But on thy turf shall roses rear
   Their leaves, the earliest of the year;
And the wild cypress wave in tender gloom:

And oft by yon blue gushing stream
   Shall Sorrow lean her drooping head,
And feed deep thought with many a dream,
   And lingering pause and lightly tread;
   Fond wretch! as if her step disturbed the dead!

Away! we know that tears are vain,
   That death nor heeds nor hears distress:
Will this unteach us to complain?
   Or make one mourner weep the less?
And thou – who tell'st me to forget,
Thy looks are wan, thine eyes are wet.

# THE VISION OF BELSHAZZAR

THE King was on his throne,
　The Satraps thronged the hall:
A thousand bright lamps shone
　O er that high festival.
A thousand cups of gold,
　In Judah deemed divine –
Jehovah's vessels hold
　The godless Heathen's wine.

In that same hour and hall,
　The fingers of a hand
Came forth against the wall,
　And wrote as if on sand:
The fingers of a man; –
　A solitary hand
Along the letters ran,
　And traced them like a wand.

The monarch saw, and shook,
　And bade no more rejoice;
All bloodless waxed his look,
　And tremulous his voice.
'Let the men of lore appear,
　The wisest of the earth,
And expound the words of fear,
　Which mar our royal mirth.'

Chaldea's seers are good,
　But here they have no skill;
And the unknown letters stood
　Untold and awful still.

And Babel's men of age
  Are wise and deep in lore;
But now they were not sage,
  They saw – but knew no more.

A captive in the land,
  A stranger and a youth,
He heard the king's command,
  He saw that writing's truth.
The lamps around were bright,
  The prophecy in view;
He read it on that night –
  The morrow proved it true.

'Belshazzar's grave is made.
  His kingdom passed away,
He, in the balance weighed,
  Is light and worthless clay;
The shroud, his robe of state,
  His canopy the stone;
The Mede is at his gate!
  The Persian on his throne!'

# THE DESTRUCTION OF SENNACHERIB

THE Assyrian came down like the wolf on the fold,
And his cohorts were gleaming in purple and gold;
And the sheen of their spears was like stars on the sea,
When the blue wave rolls nightly on deep Galilee.

Like the leaves of the forest when summer is green,
That host with their banners at sunset were seen;
Like the leaves of the forest when autumn hath blown,
That host on the morrow lay withered and strown.

For the Angel of Death spread his wings on the blast,
And breathed in the face of the foe as he passed;
And the eyes of the sleepers waxed deadly and chill,
And their hearts but once heaved, and for ever grew still!

And there lay the steed with his nostril all wide,
But through it there rolled not the breath of his pride;
And the foam of his gasping lay white on the turf,
And cold as the spray of the rock-beating surf.

And there lay the rider distorted and pale,
With the dew on his brow, and the rust on his mail:
And the tents were all silent, the banners alone,
The lances unlifted, the trumpet unblown.

And the widows of Ashur are loud in their wail,
And the idols are broke in the temple of Baal;
And the might of the Gentile, unsmote by the sword,
Hath melted like snow in the glance of the Lord!

# FARE THEE WELL

*'Alas! they have been friends in youth;*
*But whispering tongues can poison truth:*
*And constancy lives in realms above;*
*And life is thorny; and youth is vain:*
*And to be wroth with one we love,*
*Doth work like madness in the brain;*

*

*But never either found another*
*To free the hollow heart from paining –*
*They stood aloof, the scars remaining,*
*Like cliffs, which had been rent asunder;*
*A dreary sea now flows between,*
*But neither heat, nor frost, nor thunder,*
*Shall wholly do away, I ween,*
*The marks of that which once hath been.'*

COLERIDGE'S *Christabel*


FARE thee well! and if for ever,
  Still for ever, fare thee well:
Even though unforgiving, never
  'Gainst thee shall my heart rebel.

Would that breast were bared before thee
  Where thy head so oft hath lain,
While that placid sleep came o'er thee
  Which thou ne'er canst know again:

Would that breast, by thee glanced over,
  Every inmost thought could show!
Then thou wouldst at last discover
  'Twas not well to spurn it so.

Though the world for this commend thee –
  Though it smile upon the blow,
Even its praises must offend thee,
  Founded on another's woe:

Though my many faults defaced me,
   Could no other arm be found,
Than the one which once embraced me,
   To inflict a cureless wound?

Yet, oh yet, thyself deceive not;
   Love may sink by slow decay,
But by sudden wrench, believe not
   Hearts can thus be torn away:

Still thine own its life retaineth –
   Still must mine, though bleeding, beat;
And the undying thought which paineth
   Is – that we no more may meet.

These are words of deeper sorrow
   Than the wail above the dead;
Both shall live, but every morrow
   Wake us from a widowed bed.

And when thou would solace gather,
   When our child's first accents flow,
Wilt thou teach her to say 'Father!'
   Though his care she must forego?

When her little hands shall press thee,
   When her lip to thine is pressed,
Think of him whose prayer shall bless thee,
   Think of him thy love *had* blessed!

Should her lineaments resemble
   Those thou never more may'st see,
Then thy heart will softly tremble
   With a pulse yet true to me.

All my faults perchance thou knowest,
    All my madness none can know;
All my hopes, where'er thou goest,
    Wither, yet with *thee* they go.

Every feeling hath been shaken;
    Pride, which not a world could bow,
Bows to thee – by thee forsaken,
    Even my soul forsakes me now:

But 'tis done – all words are idle –
    Words from me are vainer still;
But the thoughts we cannot bridle
    Force their way without the will.

Fare thee well! thus disunited,
    Torn from every nearer tie,
Seared in heart, and lone, and blighted,
    More than this I scarce can die.

                                        March 17, 1816.

# STANZAS TO AUGUSTA

THOUGH the day of my destiny's over,
　　And the star of my fate hath declined,
Thy soft heart refused to discover
　　The faults which so many could find;
Though thy soul with my grief was acquainted,
　　It shrunk not to share it with me,
And the love which my spirit hath painted
　　It never hath found but in *thee*.

Then when nature around me is smiling,
　　The last smile which answers to mine,
I do not believe it beguiling,
　　Because it reminds me of thine;
And when winds are at war with the ocean,
　　As the breasts I believed in with me,
If their billows excite an emotion,
　　It is that they bear me from *thee*.

Though the rock of my last hope is shivered,
　　And its fragments are sunk in the wave,
Though I feel that my soul is delivered
　　To pain – it shall not be its slave.
There is many a pang to pursue me:
　　They may crush, but they shall not contemn;
They may torture, but shall not subdue me –
　　'Tis of *thee* that I think – not of them.

Though human, thou didst not deceive me,
　　Though woman, thou didst not forsake,
Though loved, thou forborest to grieve me,
　　Though slandered, thou never couldst shake;

Though trusted, thou didst not disclaim me,
  Though parted, it was not to fly,
Though watchful, 'twas not to defame me,
  Nor, mute, that the world might belie.

Yet I blame not the world, nor despise it,
  Nor the war of the many with one;
If my soul was not fitted to prize it,
  'Twas folly not sooner to shun:
And if dearly that error hath cost me,
  And more than I once could foresee,
I have found that, whatever it lost me,
  It could not deprive me of *thee*.

From the wreck of the past, which hath perished,
  Thus much I at least may recall,
It hath taught me that what I most cherished
  Deserved to be dearest of all:
In the desert a fountain is springing,
  In the wide waste there still is a tree,
And a bird in the solitude singing,
  Which speaks to my spirit of *thee*.

                                        July 24, 1816.

# BRIGHT BE THE PLACE OF THY SOUL

BRIGHT be the place of thy soul!
  No lovelier spirit than thine
E'er burst from its mortal control,
  In the orbs of the blessed to shine.

On earth thou wert all but divine,
  As thy soul shall immortally be;
And our sorrow may cease to repine,
  When we know that thy God is with thee.

Light be the turf of thy tomb!
  May its verdure like emeralds be:
There should not be the shadow of gloom
  In aught that reminds us of thee.

Young flowers and an evergreen tree
  May spring from the spot of thy rest:
But nor cypress nor yew let us see;
  For why should we mourn for the blest?

                                        1808.

# WHEN WE TWO PARTED

When we two parted
  In silence and tears,
Half broken-hearted
  To sever for years,
Pale grew thy cheek and cold,
  Colder thy kiss;
Truly that hour foretold
  Sorrow to this.

The dew of the morning
  Sunk chill on my brow –
It felt like the warning
  Of what I feel now.
Thy vows are all broken,
  And light is thy fame;
I hear thy name spoken,
  And share in its shame.

They name thee before me,
  A knell to mine ear;
A shudder comes o'er me –
  Why wert thou so dear?
They know not I knew thee,
  Who knew thee too well: –
Long, long shall I rue thee,
  Too deeply to tell.

In secret we met –
  In silence I grieve,
That thy heart could forget,
  Thy spirit deceive.

If I should meet thee
   After long years,
How should I greet thee? –
   With silence and tears.

1808.

# LINES TO MR HODGSON

## WRITTEN ON BOARD THE LISBON PACKET

Huzza! Hodgson, we are going,
　　Our embargo's off at last;
Favourable breezes blowing
　　Bend the canvas o'er the mast.
From aloft the signal's streaming,
　　Hark! the farewell gun is fired;
Women screeching, tars blaspheming,
　　Tell us that our time's expired.
　　　　Here's a rascal
　　　　Come to task all,
　　Prying from the Custom-house;
　　　　Trunks unpacking
　　　　Cases cracking,
　　Not a corner for a mouse
'Scapes unsearched amid the racket,
Ere we sail on board the Packet.

Now our boatmen quit their mooring,
　　And all hands must ply the oar;
Baggage from the quay is lowering,
　　We're impatient, push from shore.
'Have a care! that case holds liquor –
　　Stop the boat – I'm sick – oh Lord!'
'Sick, ma'am, damme, you'll be sicker,
　　Ere you've been an hour on board.'
　　　　Thus are screaming
　　　　Men and women,
　　Gemmen, ladies, servants, Jacks;
　　　　Here entangling,
　　　　All are wrangling,
　　Stuck together close as wax. –

Such the general noise and racket,
Ere we reach the Lisbon Packet.

Now we've reached her, lo! the Captain,
    Gallant Kidd, commands the crew;
Passengers their berths are clapt in,
    Some to grumble, some to spew.
'Hey day! call you that a cabin?
    Why 'tis hardly three feet square;
Not enough to stow Queen Mab in –
    Who the deuce can harbour there?'
        'Who, sir? plenty –
        Nobles twenty
Did at once my vessel fill.' –
        'Did they? Jesus,
        How you squeeze us!
Would to God they did so still:
Then I'd scape the heat and racket
Of the good ship, Lisbon Packet.'

Fletcher! Murray! Bob! where are you?
    Stretched along the deck like logs –
Bear a hand, you jolly tar, you!
    Here's a rope's end for the dogs.
Hobhouse muttering fearful curses,
    As the hatchway down he rolls,
Now his breakfast, now his verses,
    Vomits forth – and damns our souls.
        'Here's a stanza
        On Braganza –
Help!' – 'A couplet?' – 'No, a cup
        Of warm water –'
        'What's the matter?'
'Zounds! my liver's coming up;

I shall not survive the racket
Of this brutal Lisbon Packet.'

Now at length we're off for Turkey,
 Lord knows when we shall come back!
Breezes foul and tempests murky
 May unship us in a crack,
But, since life at most a jest is,
 As philosophers allow,
Still to laugh by far the best is,
 Then laugh on – as I do now.
  Laugh at all things,
  Great and small things,
 Sick or well, at sea or shore;
  While we're quaffing,
  Let's have laughing –
 Who the devil cares for more? –
Some good wine! and who would lack it,
Ev'n on board the Lisbon Packet?'
    Falmouth Roads, June 30, 1809.

# WRITTEN AFTER SWIMMING
# FROM SESTOS TO ABYDOS

I F, in the month of dark December,
   Leander, who was nightly wont
( What maid will not the tale remember?)
   To cross thy stream, broad Hellespont!

If, when the wintry tempest roared,
   He sped to Hero, nothing loth,
And thus of old thy current poured,
   Fair Venus! how I pity both!

For *me*, degenerate modern wretch,
   Though in the genial month of May,
My dripping limbs I faintly stretch,
   And think I've done a feat today.

But since he crossed the rapid tide,
   According to the doubtful story,
To woo, – and – Lord knows what beside.
   And swam for Love, as I for Glory;

'Twere hard to say who fared the best:
   Sad mortals! thus the Gods still plague you!
He lost his labour, I my jest;
   For he was drowned, and I've the ague.

                 May 9, 1810.

# MAID OF ATHENS, ERE WE PART

Ζώη μοῦ, σάς ἀγαπῶ.

Maid of Athens, ere we part,
Give, oh, give back my heart!
Or, since that has left my breast,
Keep it now, and take the rest!
Hear my vow before I go,
Ζώη μοῦ, σάς ἀγαπῶ.

By those tresses unconfined,
Wooed by each Aegean wind;
By those lids whose jetty fringe
Kiss thy soft cheeks' blooming tinge;
By those wild eyes like the roe,
Ζώη μοῦ, σάς ἀγαπῶ.

By that lip I long to taste;
By that zone-encircled waist;
By all the token-flowers that tell
What words can never speak so well;
By love's alternate joy and woe,
Ζώη μοῦ, σάς ἀγαπῶ.

Maid of Athens! I am gone:
Think of me, sweet! when alone.
Though I fly to Istambol,
Athens holds my heart and soul:
Can I cease to love thee? No!
Ζώη μοῦ, σάς ἀγαπῶ.

Athens, 1810.

# ONE STRUGGLE MORE,
## AND I AM FREE

One struggle more, and I am free
  From pangs that rend my heart in twain;
One last long sigh to love and thee,
  Then back to busy life again.
It suits me well to mingle now
  With things that never pleased before:
Though every joy is fled below,
  What future grief can touch me more?

Then bring me wine, the banquet bring;
  Man was not formed to live alone:
I'll be that light, unmeaning thing,
  That smiles with all, and weeps with none.
It was not thus in days more dear,
  It never would have been, but thou
Hast fled, and left me lonely here;
  Thou'rt nothing, – all are nothing now.

In vain my lyre would lightly breathe!
  The smile that sorrow fain would wear
But mocks the woe that lurks beneath,
  Like roses o'er a sepulchre.
Though gay companions o'er the bowl
  Dispel awhile the sense of ill;
Though pleasure fires the maddening soul,
  The heart – the heart is lonely still!

On many a lone and lovely night
  It soothed to gaze upon the sky;
For then I deemed the heavenly light
  Shone sweetly on thy pensive eye:

And oft I thought at Cynthia's noon,
   When sailing o'er the Aegean wave,
'Now Thyrza gazes on that moon' –
   Alas, it gleamed upon her grave!

When stretched on fever's sleepless bed,
   And sickness shrunk my throbbing veins.
'"Tis comfort still,' I faintly said,
   'That Thyrza cannot know my pains:'
Like freedom to the time-worn slave –
   A boon 'tis idle then to give –
Relenting Nature vainly gave
   My life, when Thyrza ceased to live!

My Thyrza's pledge in better days,
   When love and life alike were new!
How different now thou meet'st my gaze!
   How tinged by time with sorrow's hue!
The heart that gave itself with thee
   Is silent – ah, were mine as still!
Though cold as e'en the dead can be,
   It feels, it sickens with the chill.

Thou bitter pledge! thou mournful token!
   Though painful, welcome to my breast!
Still, still, preserve that love unbroken,
   Or break the heart to which thou'rt pressed!
Time tempers love, but not removes,
   More hallowed when its hope is fled:
Oh! what are thousand living loves
   To that which cannot quit the dead?

# AND THOU ART DEAD,
## AS YOUNG AS FAIR

*'Heu, quanto minus est cum reliquis versari quam tui meminisse!'*

AND thou art dead, as young and fair,
    As aught of mortal birth;
And form so soft, and charms so rare,
    Too soon returned to Earth!
Though Earth received them in her bed,
And o'er the spot the crowd may tread
    In carelessness or mirth,
There is an eye which could not brook
A moment on that grave to look.

I will not ask where thou liest low,
    Nor gaze upon the spot;
There flowers or weeds at will may grow,
    So I behold them not:
It is enough for me to prove
That what I loved, and long must love,
    Like common earth can rot;
To me there needs no stone to tell,
'Tis Nothing that I loved so well.

Yet did I love thee to the last
    As fervently as thou,
Who didst not change through all the past,
    And canst not alter now.
The love where Death has set his seal,
Nor age can chill, nor rival steal,
    Nor falsehood disavow:
And, what were worse, thou canst not see
Or wrong, or change, or fault in me.

The better days of life were ours;
    The worst can be but mine:
The sun that cheers, the storm that lowers,
    Shall never more be thine.
The silence of that dreamless sleep
I envy now too much to weep;
    Nor need I to repine
That all those charms have passed away;
I might have watched through long decay.

The flower in ripened bloom unmatched
    Must fall the earliest prey;
Though by no hand untimely snatched,
    The leaves must drop away:
And yet it were a greater grief
To watch it withering, leaf by leaf,
    Than see it plucked today;
Since earthly eye but ill can bear
To trace the change to foul from fair.

I know not if I could have borne
    To see thy beauties fade;
The night that followed such a morn
    Had worn a deeper shade:
Thy day without a cloud hath passed,
And thou wert lovely to the last;
    Extinguished, not decayed;
As stars that shoot along the sky
Shine brightest as they fall from high.

As once I wept, if I could weep,
    My tears might well be shed,
To think I was not near to keep
    One vigil o'er thy bed;

To gaze, how fondly! on thy face,
To fold thee in a faint embrace,
   Uphold thy drooping head;
And show that love, however vain,
Nor thou nor I can feel again.

Yet how much less it were to gain,
   Though thou hast left me free,
The loveliest things that still remain,
   Than thus remember thee!
The all of thine that cannot die
Through dark and dread Eternity
   Returns again to me,
And more thy buried love endears
Than aught, except its living years.

February, 1812.

# REMEMBER THEE! REMEMBER THEE!

REMEMBER thee! remember thee!
　　Till Lethe quench life's burning stream
Remorse and Shame shall cling to thee,
　　And haunt thee like a feverish dream!

Remember thee! Aye, doubt it not.
　　Thy husband too shall think of thee:
By neither shalt thou be forgot,
　　Thou *false* to him, thou *fiend* to me!

# STANZAS FOR MUSIC

'*O Lachrymarum fons, tenero sacros*
*Ducentium ortus ex animo: quater*
*Felix! in imo qui scatentem*
*Pectore te, pia Nympha, sensit.*'

THERE'S not a joy the world can give like that it takes
away.
When the glow of early thought declines in feeling's dull
decay;
'Tis not on youth's smooth cheek the blush alone, which fades
so fast,
But the tender bloom of heart is gone, ere youth itself be past.

Then the few whose spirits float above the wreck of happiness
Are driven o'er the shoals of guilt or ocean of excess:
The magnet of their course is gone, or only points in vain
The shore to which their shivered sail shall never stretch
again.

Then the mortal coldness of the soul like death itself comes
down;
It cannot feel for others' woes, it dare not dream its own;
That heavy chill has frozen o'er the fountain of our tears,
And though the eye may sparkle still, 'tis where the ice
appears.

Though wit may flash from fluent lips, and mirth distract the
breast,
Through midnight hours that yield no more their former hope
of rest;
'Tis but as ivy-leaves around the ruined turret wreath,
All green and wildly fresh without, but worn and grey
beneath.

Oh could I feel as I have felt, – or be what I have been,
Or weep as I could once have wept, o'er many a vanished
    scene;
As springs in deserts found seem sweet, all brackish though
    they be,
So midst the withered waste of life, those tears would flow to
    me.

March, 1815.

# STANZAS FOR MUSIC

THERE be none of beauty's daughters
    With a magic like thee;
And like music on the waters
    Is thy sweet voice to me:
When, as if its sound were causing
The charmèd ocean's pausing,
The waves lie still and gleaming,
And the lulled winds seem dreaming:

And the midnight moon is weaving
    Her bright chain o'er the deep;
Whose breast is gently heaving,
    As an infant's asleep:
So the spirit bows before thee,
To listen and adore thee;
With a full but soft emotion,
Like the swell of summer's ocean.

# SONNET TO LAKE LEMAN

ROUSSEAU – Voltaire – our Gibbon – and De Staël –
  Leman! these names are worthy of thy shore,
  Thy shore of names like these! wert thou no more,
Their memory thy remembrance would recall:
To them thy banks were lovely as to all,
  But they have made them lovelier, for the lore
  Of mighty minds doth hallow in the core
Of human hearts the ruin of a wall
  Where dwelt the wise and wondrous; but by *thee*,
How much more, Lake of Beauty! do we feel,
  In sweetly gliding o'er thy crystal sea,
The wild glow of that not ungentle zeal,
  Which of the heirs of immortality
Is proud, and makes the breath of glory real!

Diodati, July, 1816.

# TO THOMAS MOORE

My boat is on the shore,
　　And my bark is on the sea;
But, before I go, Tom Moore,
　　Here's a double health to thee!

Here's a sigh to those who love me,
　　And a smile to those who hate;
And, whatever sky's above me,
　　Here's a heart for every fate.

Though the ocean roar around me,
　　Yet it still shall bear me on;
Though a desert should surround me,
　　It hath springs that may be won.

Were't the last drop in the well,
　　As I gasped upon the brink,
Ere my fainting spirit fell,
　　'Tis to thee that I would drink.

With that water, as this wine,
　　The libation I would pour
Should be – peace with thine and mine,
　　And a health to thee, Tom Moore.

July, 1817.

# SO WE'LL GO NO MORE A-ROVING

So we'll go no more a-roving
  So late into the night,
Though the heart be still as loving,
  And the moon be still as bright.

For the sword outwears its sheath,
  And the soul wears out the breast,
And the heart must pause to breathe,
  And love itself have rest.

Though the night was made for loving,
  And the day returns too soon,
Yet we'll go no more a-roving
  By the light of the moon.

1817.

# JOHN KEATS

Who killed John Keats?
  'I,' says the Quarterly,
So savage and Tartarly;
  ''Twas one of my feats.'

Who shot the arrow?
  'The poet-priest Milman
(So ready to kill man),
  Or Southey or Barrow.'

July, 1821.

# STANZAS

WRITTEN ON THE ROAD BETWEEN
FLORENCE AND PISA

Oh, talk not to me of a name great in story;
The days of your youth are the days of our glory;
And the myrtle and ivy of sweet two-and-twenty
Are worth all your laurels, though ever so plenty.

What are garlands and crowns to the brow that is
        wrinkled?
'Tis but as a dead-flower with May-dew besprinkled.
Then away with all such from the head that is hoary!
What care I for the wreaths that can *only* give glory?

Oh Fame! – if I e'er took delight in thy praises,
'Twas less for the sake of thy high-sounding phrases,
Than to see the bright eyes of the dear one discover
She thought that I was not unworthy to love her.

*There* chiefly I sought thee, *there* only I found thee;
Her glance was the best of the rays that surround thee;
When it sparkled o'er aught that was bright in my story,
I knew it was love, and I felt it was glory.

                                    November, 1821.

# ON THIS DAY I COMPLETE MY
# THIRTY-SIXTH YEAR

'Tis time this heart should be unmoved,
   Since others it hath ceased to move:
Yet, though I cannot be beloved,
      Still let me love!

My days are in the yellow leaf;
   The flowers and fruits of love are gone;
The worm, the canker, and the grief
      Are mine alone!

The fire that on my bosom preys
   Is lone as some volcanic isle;
No torch is kindled at its blaze –
      A funeral pile.

The hope, the fear, the jealous care,
   The exalted portion of the pain
And power of love, I cannot share,
      But wear the chain.

But 'tis not *thus* – and 'tis not *here* –
   Such thoughts should shake my soul, nor *now*,
Where glory decks the hero's bier,
      Or binds his brow.

The sword, the banner, and the field,
   Glory and Greece, around me see!
The Spartan, borne upon his shield,
      Was not more free.

Awake! (not Greece – she *is* awake!)
    Awake, my spirit! Think through *whom*
Thy life-blood tracks its parent lake,
        And then strike home!

Tread those reviving passions down,
    Unworthy manhood! – unto thee
Indifferent should the smile or frown
        Of beauty be.

If thou regret'st thy youth, *why live?*
    The land of honourable death
Is here: – up to the field, and give
        Away thy breath!

Seek out – less often sought than found –
    A soldier's grave, for thee the best;
Then look around, and choose thy ground,
        And take thy rest.

                    Missolonghi, Jan. 22, 1824.

# SONNET ON CHILLON

ETERNAL Spirit of the chainless Mind!
  Brightest in dungeons, Liberty! thou art;
  For there thy habitation is the heart –
The heart which love of thee alone can bind;
And when thy sons to fetters are consigned –
  To fetters, and the damp vault's dayless gloom,
  Their country conquers with their martyrdom,
And Freedom's fame finds wings on every wind.
Chillon! thy prison is a holy place,
  And thy sad floor an altar – for 'twas trod,
Until his very steps have left a trace
  Worn, as if thy cold pavement were a sod,
By Bonnivard!—May none those marks efface!
  For they appeal from tryanny to God.

June, 1816.

# ENGLISH BARDS AND SCOTCH REVIEWERS

## A SATIRE

*'I had rather be a kitten, and cry mew!*
*Than one of these same metre ballad-mongers.'*
SHAKSPEARE

... Time was, ere yet in these degenerate days
Ignoble themes obtained mistaken praise,
When sense and wit with poesy allied,
No fabled graces, flourished side by side;
From the same fount their inspiration drew,
And, reared by taste, bloomed fairer as they grew.
Then, in this happy isle, a Pope's pure strain
Sought the rapt soul to charm, nor sought in vain;
A polished nation's praise aspired to claim,
And raised the people's, as the poet's fame.
Like him great Dryden poured the tide of song,
In stream less smooth, indeed, yet doubly strong.
Then Congreve's scenes could cheer, or Otway's melt;
For Nature then an English audience felt –
But why these names, or greater still, retrace,
When all to feebler bards resign their place?
Yet to such times our lingering looks are cast,
When taste and reason with those times are past.
Now look around, and turn each trifling page,
Survey the precious works that please the age;
This truth at least let satire's self allow,
No dearth of bards can be complained of now.
The loaded press beneath her labour groans,
And printer's devils shake their weary bones;

While Southey's epics cram the creaking shelves,
And Little's lyrics shine in hot-pressed twelves.
Thus saith the Preacher: 'Nought beneath the sun
Is new;' yet still from change to change we run.
What varied wonders tempt us as they pass!
The cow-pox, tractors, galvanism, and gas,
In turns appear, to make the vulgar stare,
Till the swoln bubble bursts – and all is air!
Nor less new schools of poetry arise,
Where dull pretenders grapple for the prize:
O'er taste awhile these pseudo-bards prevail;
Each country book-club bows the knee to Baal,
And, hurling lawful genius from the throne,
Erects a shrine and idol of its own;
Some leaden calf – but whom it matters not,
From soaring Southey, down to grovelling Stott.


Behold! in various throngs the scribbling crew,
For notice eager, pass in long review:
Each spurs his jaded Pegasus apace,
And Rhyme and Blank maintain an equal race;
Sonnets on sonnets crowd, and ode on ode;
And Tales of Terror jostle on the road;
Immeasurable measures move along;
For simpering folly loves a varied song,
To strange, mysterious dulness still the friend,
Admires the strain she cannot comprehend.
Thus Lays of Minstrels – may they be the last! –
On half-strung harps whine mournful to the blast.
While mountain spirits prate to river sprites,
That dames may listen to the sound at nights;
And goblin brats, of Gilpin Horner's brood
Decoy young Border-nobles through the wood,

And skip at every step, Lord knows how high,
And frighten foolish babes, the Lord knows why;
While high-born ladies in their magic cell,
Forbidding knights to read who cannot spell,
Despatch a courier to a wizard's grave,
And fight with honest men to shield a knave.

Next view in state, proud prancing on his roan,
The golden-crested haughty Marmion,
Now forging scrolls, now foremost in the fight,
Not quite a felon, yet but half a knight,
The gibbet or the field prepared to grace;
A mighty mixture of the great and base.
And think'st thou, Scott! by vain conceit perchance,
On public taste to foist thy stale romance,
Though Murray with his Miller may combine
To yield thy muse just half-a-crown per line?
No! when the sons of song descend to trade,
Their bays are sear, their former laurels fade.
Let such forego the poet's sacred name,
Who rack their brains for lucre, not for fame:
Still for stern Mammon may they toil in vain!
And sadly gaze on gold they cannot gain!
Such be their meed, such still the just reward
Of prostituted muse and hireling bard!
For this we spurn Apollo's venal son,
And bid a long 'good night to Marmion.'

These are the themes that claim our plaudits now;
These are the bards to whom the muse must bow;
While Milton, Dryden, Pope, alike forgot,
Resign their hallowed bays to Walter Scott ...

. . . .

Next comes the dull disciple of thy school,
That mild apostate from poetic rule,

The simple Wordsworth, framer of a lay
As soft as evening in his favourite May,
Who warns his friend 'to shake off toil and trouble,
And quit his books, for fear of growing double;'
Who, both by precept and example, shows
That prose is verse, and verse is merely prose;
Convincing all, by demonstration plain,
Poetic souls delight in prose insane;
And Christmas stories tortured into rhyme
Contain the essence of the true sublime.
Thus, when he tells the tale of Betty Foy,
The idiot mother of 'an idiot boy;'
A moon-struck, silly lad, who lost his way,
And, like his bard, confounded night with day;
So close on each pathetic part he dwells,
And each adventure so sublimely tells,
That all who view the 'idiot in his glory'
Conceive the Bard the hero of the story.

Shall gentle Coleridge pass unnoticed here,
To turgid ode and tumid stanza dear?
Though themes of innocence amuse him best,
Yet still obscurity's a welcome guest.
If Inspiration should her aid refuse
To him who takes a pixy for a muse,
Yet none in lofty numbers can surpass
The bard who soars to elegize an ass:
So well the subject suits his noble mind,
He brays, the laureate of the long-eared kind. . . .

# THE GIAOUR

### A FRAGMENT OF A TURKISH TALE

## *Advertisement*

THE tale which these disjointed fragments present, is founded upon circumstances now less common in the East than formerly; either because the ladies are more circumspect than in the 'olden time', or because the Christians have better fortune, or less enterprise. The story, when entire, contained the adventures of a female slave, who was thrown, in the Mussulman manner, into the sea for infidelity, and avenged by a young Venetian, her lover, at the time the Seven Islands were possessed by the Republic of Venice, and soon after the Arnauts were beaten back from the Morea, which they had ravaged for some time subsequent to the Russian invasion. The desertion of the Mainotes, on being refused the plunder of Misitra, led to the abandonment of that enterprise, and to the desolation of the Morea, during which the cruelty exercised on all sides was unparalleled even in the annals of the faithful.

> ... Who thundering comes on blackest steed,
> With slackened bit and hoof of speed?
> Beneath the clattering iron's sound
> The caverned echoes wake around
> In lash for lash, and bound for bound;
> The foam that streaks the courser's side
> Seems gathered from the ocean-tide:
> Though weary waves are sunk to rest,
> There's none within his rider's breast;
> And though tomorrow's tempest lower,
> 'Tis calmer than thy heart, young Giaour!

I know thee not, I loathe thy race,
But in thy lineaments I trace
What time shall strengthen, not efface:
Though young and pale, that sallow front
Is scathed by fiery passion's brunt;
Though bent on earth thine evil eye,
As meteor-like thou glidest by,
Right well I view and deem thee one
Whom Othman's sons should slay or shun.

On – on he hastened, and he drew
My gaze of wonder as he flew:
Though like a demon of the night
He passed, and vanished from my sight,
His aspect and his air impressed
A troubled memory on my breast,
And long upon my startled ear
Rung his dark courser's hoofs of fear.
He spurs his steed; he nears the steep,
That, jutting, shadows o'er the deep;
He winds around; he hurries by;
The rock relieves him from mine eye;
For, well I ween, unwelcome he
Whose glance is fixed on those that flee;
And not a star but shines too bright
On him who takes such timeless flight.
He wound along; but ere he passed
One glance he snatched, as if his last,
A moment checked his wheeling steed,
A moment breathed him from his speed,
A moment on his stirrup stood –
Why looks he o'er the olive wood?
The crescent glimmers on the hill,
The Mosque's high lamps are quivering still

Though too remote for sound to wake
In echoes of the far tophaike,
The flashes of each joyous peal
Are seen to prove the Moslem's zeal,
Tonight, set Rhamazani's sun;
Tonight, the Bairam feast's begun;
Tonight – but who and what art thou
Of foreign garb and fearful brow?
And what are these to thine or thee,
That thou should'st either pause or flee?

He stood – some dread was on his face,
Soon hatred settled in its place:
It rose not with the reddening flush
Of transient anger's hasty blush,
But pale as marble o'er the tomb,
Whose ghastly whiteness aids its gloom.
His brow was bent, his eye was glazed;
He raised his arm, and fiercely raised,
And sternly shook his hand on high,
As doubting to return or fly;
Impatient of his flight delayed,
Here loud his raven charger neighed –
Down glanced that hand, and grasped his blade;
That sound had burst his waking dream,
As slumber starts at owlet's scream.
The spur hath lanced his courser's sides;
Away, away, for life he rides:
Swift as the hurled on high jerreed
Springs to the touch his startled steed;
The rock is doubled, and the shore
Shakes with the clattering tramp no more;
The crag is won, no more is seen
His Christian crest and haughty mien.

'Twas but an instant he restrained
That fiery barb so sternly reined;
'Twas but a moment that he stood,
Then sped as if by death pursued;
But in that instant o'er his soul
Winters of memory seemed to roll,
And gather in that drop of time
A life of pain, an age of crime.
O'er him who loves, or hates, or fears,
Such moment pours the grief of years:
What felt *he* then, at once opprest
By all that most distracts the breast?
That pause, which pondered o'er his fate,
Oh, who its dreary length shall date!
Though in time's record nearly nought,
It was eternity to thought!
For infinite as boundless space
The thought that conscience must embrace,
Which in itself can comprehend
Woe without name, or hope, or end.

    The hour is past, the Giaour is gone;
And did he fly or fall alone?
Woe to that hour he came or went!
The curse for Hassan's sin was sent
To turn a palace to a tomb:
He came, he went, like the Simoom,
That harbinger of fate and gloom,
Beneath whose widely-wasting breath
The very cypress droops to death —
Dark tree, still sad when others' grief is fled,
The only constant mourner o'er the dead!

The steed is vanished from the stall;
No serf is seen in Hassan's hall;
The lonely spider's thin grey pall
Waves slowly widening o'er the wall;
The bat builds in his harem bower,
And in the fortress of his power
The owl usurps the beacon-tower;
The wild-dog howls o'er the fountain's brim,
With baffled thirst, and famine, grim;
For the stream has shrunk from its marble bed,
Where the weeds and the desolate dust are spread.
'Twas sweet of yore to see it play
And chase the sultriness of day,
As springing high the silver dew
In whirls fantastically flew,
And flung luxurious coolness round
The air, and verdure o'er the ground.
'Twas sweet, when cloudless stars were bright,
To view the wave of watery light,
And hear its melody by night.
And oft had Hassan's childhood played
Around the verge of that cascade;
And oft upon his mother's breast
That sound had harmonized his rest;
And oft had Hassan's youth along
Its bank been soothed by beauty's song;
And softer seem'd each melting tone
Of music mingled with its own.
But ne'er shall Hassan's age repose
Along the brink at twilight's close:
The stream that filled that font is fled —
The blood that warmed his heart is shed!
And here no more shall human voice
Be heard to rage, regret, rejoice.

The last sad note that swelled the gale
Was woman's wildest funeral wail:
*That* quenched in silence, all is still,
But the lattice that flaps when the wind is shrill:
Though raves the gust, and floods the rain,
No hand shall close its clasp again.
On desert sands 'twere joy to scan
The rudest steps of fellow man,
So here the very voice of grief
Might wake an echo like relief –
At least 'twould say, 'All are not gone;
There lingers life, though but in one' –
For many a gilded chamber's there,
Which solitude might well forbear;
Within that dome as yet decay
Hath slowly worked her cankering way –
But gloom is gathered o'er the gate,
Nor there the fakir's self will wait;
Nor there will wandering dervise stay,
For bounty cheers not his delay;
Nor there will weary stranger halt
To bless the sacred 'bread and salt'.
Alike must wealth and poverty
Pass heedless and unheeded by,
For courtesy and pity died
With Hassan on the mountain side.
His roof, that refuge unto men,
Is desolation's hungry den.
The guest flies the hall, and the vassal from labour,
Since his turban was cleft by the infidel's sabre!

    .     .     .

  I hear the sound of coming feet,
But not a voice mine ear to greet;

More near – each turban I can scan,
And silver-sheathed ataghan;
The foremost of the band is seen
An Emir by his garb of green:
'Ho! who art thou?' – 'This low salam
Replies of Moslem faith I am.'
'The burthen ye so gently bear,
Seems one that claims your utmost care,
And, doubtless, holds some precious freight,
My humble bark would gladly wait.'

'Thou speakest sooth; thy skiff unmoor,
And waft us from the silent shore;
Nay, leave the sail still furled, and ply
The nearest oar that's scattered by,
And midway to those rocks where sleep
The channeled waters dark and deep.
Rest from your task – so – bravely done,
Of course had been right swiftly run;
Yet 'tis the longest voyage, I trow,
That one of – .         .         .
         .         .         .

Sullen it plunged, and slowly sank,
The calm wave rippled to the bank;
I watched it as it sank, methought
Some motion from the current caught
Bestirred it more, – 'twas but the beam
That checkered o'er the living stream:
I gazed, till vanishing from view,
Like lessening pebble it withdrew;
Still less and less, a speck of white
That gemmed the tide, then mocked the sight;
And all its hidden secrets sleep,
Known but to Genii of the deep,

Which, trembling in their coral caves,
They dare not whisper to the waves.

. . . .

As rising on its purple wing
The insect-queen of eastern spring,
O'er emerald meadows of Kashmeer
Invites the young pursuer near,
And leads him on from flower to flower
A weary chase and wasted hour,
Then leaves him, as it soars on high,
With panting heart and tearful eye:
So beauty lures the full-grown child,
With hue as bright, and wing as wild:
A chase of idle hopes and fears,
Begun in folly, closed in tears.
If won, to equal ills betrayed,
Woe waits the insect and the maid;
A life of pain, the loss of peace,
From infant's play, and man's caprice:
The lovely toy so fiercely sought
Hath lost its charm by being caught,
For every touch that wooed its stay
Hath brushed its brightest hues away,
Till charm, and hue, and beauty gone,
'Tis left to fly or fall alone.
With wounded wing, or bleeding breast,
Ah! where shall either victim rest?
Can this with faded pinion soar
From rose to tulip as before?
Or beauty, blighted in an hour,
Find joy within her broken bower?
No: gayer insects fluttering by
Ne'er droop the wing o'er those that die,

And lovelier things have mercy shown
To every failing but their own,
And every woe a tear can claim
Except an erring sister's shame.

    .     .     .     .

The mind, that broods o'er guilty woes,
  Is like the scorpion girt by fire;
In circle narrowing as it glows,
The flames around their captive close,
Till inly searched by thousand throes,
  And maddening in her ire,
One sad and sole relief she knows,
The sting she nourished for her foes,
Whose venom never yet was vain,
Gives but one pang, and cures all pain,
And darts into her desperate brain:
So do the dark in soul expire,
Or live like scorpion girt by fire;
So writhes the mind remorse hath riven,
Unfit for earth, undoomed for heaven,
Darkness above, despair beneath,
Around it flame, within it death!

    .     .     .     .

Black Hassan from the harem flies,
Nor bends on woman's form his eyes;
The unwonted chase each hour employs,
Yet shares he not the hunter's joys.
Not thus was Hassan wont to fly
When Leila dwelt in his Serai.
Doth Leila there no longer dwell?
That tale can only Hassan tell:
Strange rumours in our city say
Upon that eve she fled away
When Rhamazan's last sun was set,
And flashing from each minaret

Millions of lamps proclaimed the feast
Of Bairam through the boundless East.
'Twas then she went as to the bath,
Which Hassan vainly searched in wrath;
For she was flown her master's rage
In likeness of a Georgian page,
And far beyond the Moslem's power
Had wronged him with the faithless Giaour.
Somewhat of this had Hassan deemed;
But still so fond, so fair she seemed,
Too well he trusted to the slave
Whose treachery deserved a grave:
And on that eve had gone to mosque,
And thence to feast in his kiosk.
Such is the tale his Nubians tell,
Who did not watch their charge too well;
But others say, that on that night,
By pale Phingari's trembling light,
The Giaour upon his jet-black steed
Was seen, but seen alone to speed
With bloody spur along the shore,
Nor maid nor page behind him bore.

.    .    .    .

Her eye's dark charm 'twere vain to tell,
But gaze on that of the gazelle,
It will assist thy fancy well;
As large, as languishingly dark,
But soul beamed forth in every spark
That darted from beneath the lid,
Bright as the jewel of Giamschid.
Yea, *Soul*, and should our prophet say
That form was nought but breathing clay,
By Allah! I would answer nay;

Though on Al-Sirat's arch I stood,
Which totters o'er the fiery flood,
With Paradise within my view,
And all his Houris beckoning through.
Oh! who young Leila's glance could read
And keep that portion of his creed,
Which saith that woman is but dust,
A soulless toy for tyrant's lust?
On her might Muftis gaze, and own
That through her eye the Immortal shone;
On her fair cheek's unfading hue
The young pomegranate's blossoms strew
Their bloom in blushes ever new;
Her hair in hyacinthine flow,
When left to roll its folds below,
As midst her handmaids in the hall
She stood superior to them all,
Hath swept the marble where her feet
Gleamed whiter than the mountain sleet
Ere from the cloud that gave it birth
It fell, and caught one stain of earth.
The cygnet nobly walks the water;
So moved on earth Circassia's daughter,
The loveliest bird of Franguestan!
As rears her crest the ruffled swan,
   And spurns the wave with wings of pride,
When pass the steps of stranger man
   Along the banks that bound her tide;
Thus rose fair Leila's whiter neck: –
Thus armed with beauty would she check
Intrusion's glance, till folly's gaze
Shrunk from the charms it meant to praise:
Thus high and graceful as her gait;
Her heart as tender to her mate;

Her mate – stern Hassan, who was he?
Alas! that name was not for thee!

    .      .      .      .

    Stern Hassan hath a journey ta'en
With twenty vassals in his train,
Each armed, as best becomes a man,
With arquebuss and ataghan;
The chief before, as decked for war,
Bears in his belt the scimitar
Stain'd with the best of Arnaut blood,
When in the pass the rebels stood,
And few returned to tell the tale
Of what befell in Parne's vale.
The pistols which his girdle bore
Were those that once a pasha wore,
Which still, though gemmed and bossed with gold,
Even robbers tremble to behold.
'Tis said he goes to woo a bride
More true than her who left his side;
The faithless slave that broke her bower,
And – worse than faithless – for a Giaour!

    .      .      .      .

    The sun's last rays are on the hill,
And sparkle in the fountain rill,
Whose welcome waters, cool and clear,
Draw blessings from the mountaineer:
Here may the loitering merchant Greek
Find that repose 'twere vain to seek
In cities lodged too near his lord,
And trembling for his secret hoard –
Here may he rest where none can see,
In crowds a slave, in deserts free;

And with forbidden wine may stain
The bowl a Moslem must not drain.

       .       .       .       .

  The foremost Tartar's in the gap,
Conspicuous by his yellow cap;
The rest in lengthening line the while
Wind slowly through the long defile:
Above, the mountain rears a peak,
Where vultures whet the thirsty beak,
And theirs may be a feast tonight,
Shall tempt them down ere morrow's light;
Beneath, a river's wintry stream
Has shrunk before the summer beam,
And left a channel bleak and bare,
Save shrubs that spring to perish there:
Each side the midway path there lay
Small broken crags of granite grey
By time, or mountain lightning, riven
From summits clad in mists of heaven;
For where is he that hath beheld
The peak of Liakura unveiled?

       .       .       .       .

  They reach the grove of pine at last:
'Bismillah! now the peril's past;
For yonder view the opening plain,
And there we'll prick our steeds amain:'
The Chiaus spake, and as he said,
A bullet whistled o'er his head;
The foremost Tartar bites the ground!
  Scarce had they time to check the rein,
Swift·from their steeds the riders bound;
  But three shall never mount again:
Unseen the foes that gave the wound,
  The dying ask revenge in vain.

With steel unsheathed, and carbine bent,
Some o'er their courser's harness leant,
    Half sheltered by the steed;
Some fly behind the nearest rock,
And there await the coming shock,
    Nor tamely stand to bleed
Beneath the shaft of foes unseen,
Who dare not quit their craggy screen.
Stern Hassan only from his horse
Disdains to light, and keeps his course,
Till fiery flashes in the van
Proclaim too sure the robber-clan
Have well secured the only way
Could now avail the promised prey;
Then curled his very beard with ire,
And glared his eye with fiercer fire:
'Though far and near the bullets hiss,
I've 'scaped a bloodier hour than this.'
And now the foe their covert quit,
And call his vassals to submit;
But Hassan's frown and furious word
Are dreaded more than hostile sword,
Nor of his little band a man
Resigned carbine or ataghan,
Nor raised the craven cry, Amaun!
In fuller sight, more near and near,
The lately ambushed foes appear,
And, issuing from the grove, advance
Some who on battle-charger prance.
Who leads them on with foreign brand,
Far flashing in his red right hand?
''Tis he! 'tis he! I know him now;
I know him by his pallid brow;

I know him by the evil eye
That aids his envious treachery;
I know him by his jet-black barb:
Though now arrayed in Arnaut garb,
Apostate from his own vile faith,
It shall not save him from the death:
'Tis he! well met in any hour,
Lost Leila's love, accursed Giaour!'


   As rolls the river into ocean,
In sable torrent wildly streaming;
   As the sea-tide's opposing motion,
In azure column proudly gleaming,
Beats back the current many a rood,
In curling foam and mingling flood,
While eddying whirl, and breaking wave,
Roused by the blast of winter, rave;
Through sparkling spray, in thundering clash,
The lightnings of the waters flash
In awful whiteness o'er the shore,
That shines and shakes beneath the roar;
Thus – as the stream and ocean greet,
With waves that madden as they meet –
Thus join the bands, whom mutual wrong,
And fate, and fury, drive along.
The bickering sabres' shivering jar;
   And pealing wide or ringing near
   Its echoes on the throbbing ear,
The deathshot hissing from afar;
The shock, the shout, the groan of war,
   Reverberate along that vale,
   More suited to the shepherd's tale:
Though few the numbers – theirs the strife,
That neither spares nor speaks for life!

Ah! fondly youthful hearts can press,
To seize and share the dear caress;
But love itself could never pant
For all that beauty sighs to grant
With half the fervour hate bestows
Upon the last embrace of foes,
When grappling in the fight they fold
Those arms that ne'er shall lose their hold:
Friends meet to part; love laughs at faith;
True foes, once met, are joined till death!

    .     .     .

With sabre shivered to the hilt,
Yet dripping with the blood he spilt;
Yet strained within the severed hand
Which quivers round that faithless brand;
His turban far behind him rolled,
And cleft in twain its firmest fold;
His flowing robe by falchion torn,
And crimson as those clouds of morn
That, streaked with dusky red, portend
The day shall have a stormy end;
A stain on every bush that bore
A fragment of his palampore
His breast with wounds unnumbered riven,
His back to earth, his face to heaven,
Fallen Hassan lies – his unclosed eye
Yet lowering on his enemy,
As if the hour that sealed his fate
Surviving left his quenchless hate;
And o'er him bends that foe with brow
As dark as his that bled below.

    .     .     .     .

  'Yes, Leila sleeps beneath the wave,
But his shall be a redder grave;

Her spirit pointed well the steel
Which taught that felon heart to feel.
He called the Prophet, but his power
Was vain against the vengeful Giaour:
He called on Allah – but the word
Arose unheeded or unheard.
Thou Paynim fool! could Leila's prayer
Be passed, and thine accorded there?
I watched my time, I leagued with these,
The traitor in his turn to seize;
My wrath is wreaked, the deed is done,
And now I go – but go alone.'

.    .    .    .

  The browsing camels' bells are tinkling:
His mother looked from her lattice high –
  She saw the dews of eve besprinkling
The pasture green beneath her eye,
  She saw the planets faintly twinkling:
''Tis twilight – sure his train is nigh.'
She could not rest in the garden-bower,
But gazed through the grate of his steepest tower:
'Why comes he not? his steeds are fleet,
Nor shrink they from the summer heat;
Why sends not the bridegroom his promised
    gift?
Is his heart more cold, or his barb less swift?
Oh, false reproach! yon Tartar now
Has gained our nearest mountain's brow,
And warily the steep descends,
And now within the valley bends;
And he bears the gift at his saddle bow –
How could I deem his courser slow?
Right well my largess shall repay
His welcome speed, and weary way.'

The Tartar lighted at the gate,
But scarce upheld his fainting weight!
His swarthy visage spake distress,
But this might be from weariness;
His garb with sanguine spots was dyed,
But these might be from his courser's side;
He drew the token from his vest –
Angel of Death! 'tis Hassan's cloven crest!
His calpac rent – his caftan red –
'Lady, a fearful bride thy son hath wed:
Me, not from mercy, did they spare,
But this empurpled pledge to bear.
Peace to the brave! whose blood is spilt:
Woe to the Giaour! for his the guilt.'

    .    .    .    .

A turban carved in coarsest stone,
A pillar with rank weeds o'ergrown,
Whereon can now be scarcely read
The Koran verse that mourns the dead,
Point out the spot where Hassan fell
A victim in that lonely dell.
There sleeps as true an Osmanlie
As e'er at Mecca bent the knee;
As ever scorned forbidden wine,
Or prayed with face towards the shrine,
In orisons resumed anew
At solemn sound of 'Allah Hu!'
Yet died he by a stranger's hand,
And stranger in his native land;
Yet died he as in arms he stood,
And unavenged, at least in blood.
But him the maids of Paradise
  Impatient to their halls invite,
And the dark Heaven of Houris' eyes
  On him shall glance for ever bright;

They come – their kerchiefs green they wave,
And welcome with a kiss the brave!
Who falls in battle 'gainst a Giaour
Is worthiest an immortal bower.

    &middot;    &middot;    &middot;    &middot;

  But thou, false Infidel! shalt writhe
Beneath avenging Monkir's scythe;
And from its torment 'scape alone
To wander round lost Eblis' throne;
And fire unquenched, unquenchable,
Around, within, thy heart shall dwell;
Nor ear can hear nor tongue can tell
The tortures of that inward hell!
But first, on earth as vampire sent,
Thy corse shall from its tomb be rent:
Then ghastly haunt thy native place,
And suck the blood of all thy race;
There from thy daughter, sister, wife,
At midnight drain the stream of life;
Yet loathe the banquet which perforce
Must feed thy livid living corse:
Thy victims ere they yet expire
Shall know the demon for their sire,
As cursing thee, thou cursing them,
Thy flowers are withered on the stem.
But one that for thy crime must fall,
The youngest, most beloved of all,
Shall bless thee with a *father's* name –
That word shall wrap thy heart in flame!
Yet must thou end thy task, and mark
Her cheek's last tinge, her eye's last spark,
And the last glassy glance must view
Which freezes o'er its lifeless blue;

Then with unhallowed hand shalt tear
The tresses of her yellow hair,
Of which in life a lock when shorn
Affection's fondest pledge was worn,
But now is borne away by thee,
Memorial of thine agony!
Wet with thine own best blood shall drip
Thy gnashing tooth and haggard lip;
Then stalking to thy sullen grave,
Go – and with Gouls and Afrits rave;
Till these in horror shrink away
From spectre more accursed than they!

   .     .     .     .

'How name ye yon lone Caloyer?
  His features I have scanned before
In mine own land: 'tis many a year,
  Since, dashing by the lonely shore,
I saw him urge as fleet a steed
As ever served a horseman's need.
But once I saw that face, yet then
It was so marked with inward pain,
I could not pass it by again;
It breathes the same dark spirit now,
As death were stamped upon his brow.

''Tis twice three years at summer tide
  Since first among our freres he came;
And here it soothes him to abide
  For some dark deed he will not name.
But never at our vesper prayer,
Nor e'er before confession chair
Kneels he, nor recks he when arise
Incense or anthem to the skies,

But broods within his cell alone,
His faith and race alike unknown.
The sea from Paynim land he crost,
And here ascended from the coast;
Yet seems he not of Othman race,
But only Christian in his face:
I'd judge him some stray renegade,
Repentant of the change he made,
Save that he shuns our holy shrine,
Nor tastes the sacred bread and wine.
Great largess to these walls he brought,
And thus our abbot's favour bought;
But were I prior, not a day
Should brook such stranger's further stay,
Or pent within our penance cell
Should doom him there for aye to dwell.
Much in his visions mutters he
Of maiden whelmed beneath the sea;
Of sabres clashing, foemen flying,
Wrongs avenged, and Moslem dying.
On cliff he hath been known to stand,
And rave as to some bloody hand
Fresh severed from its parent limb,
Invisible to all but him,
Which beckons onward to his grave,
And lures to leap into the wave.'

. . . .

Dark and unearthly is the scowl
That glares beneath his dusky cowl:
The flash of that dilating eye
Reveals too much of times gone by;
Though varying, indistinct its hue,
Oft will his glance the gazer rue,

For in it lurks that nameless spell,
Which speaks, itself unspeakable,
A spirit yet unquelled and high,
That claims and keeps ascendency;
And like the bird whose pinions quake,
But cannot fly the gazing snake,
Will others quail beneath his look,
Nor 'scape the glance they scarce can brook.
From him the half-affrighted friar
When met alone would fain retire,
As if that eye and bitter smile
Transferred to others fear and guile:
Not oft to smile descendeth he,
And when he doth 'tis sad to see
That he but mocks at misery.
How that pale lip will curl and quiver!
Then fix once more as if for ever;
As if his sorrow or disdain
Forbade him e'er to smile again.
Well were it so – such ghastly mirth
From joyaunce ne'er derived its birth.
But sadder still it were to trace
What once were feelings in that face:
Time hath not yet the features fixed,
But brighter traits with evil mixed;
And there are hues not always faded,
Which speak a mind not all degraded
Even by the crimes through which it waded:
The common crowd but see the gloom
Of wayward deeds, and fitting doom;
The close observer can espy
A noble soul, and lineage high:
Alas! though both bestowed in vain,
Which grief could change, and guilt could stain,

It was no vulgar tenement
To which such lofty gifts were lent,
And still with little less than dread
On such the sight is riveted.
The roofless cot, decayed and rent,
    Will scarce delay the passer-by;
The tower by war or tempest bent,
While yet may frown one battlement,
Demands and daunts the stranger's eye;
Each ivied arch, and pillar lone,
Pleads haughtily for glories gone!

'His floating robe around him folding,
    Slow sweeps he through the columned aisle;
With dread beheld, with gloom beholding
    The rites that sanctify the pile.
But when the anthem shakes the choir,
And kneel the monks, his steps retire;
By yonder lone and wavering torch
His aspect glares within the porch;
There will he pause till all is done –
And hear the prayer, but utter none.
See – by the half-illumined wall
His hood fly back, his dark hair fall,
That pale brow wildly wreathing round,
As if the Gorgon there had bound
The sablest of the serpent-braid
That o'er her fearful forehead strayed:
For he declines the convent oath
And leaves those locks unhallowed growth,
But wears our garb in all beside;
And, not from piety but pride,
Gives wealth to walls that never heard
Of his one holy vow nor word.

Lo! – mark ye, as the harmony
Peals louder praises to the sky,
That livid cheek, that stony air
Of mixed defiance and despair!
Saint Francis, keep him from the shrine!
Else may we dread the wrath divine
Made manifest by awful sign.
If ever evil angel bore
The form of mortal, such he wore:
By all my hope of sins forgiven,
Such looks are not of earth nor heaven!'

To love the softest hearts are prone,
But such can ne'er be all his own;
Too timid in his woes to share,
Too meek to meet, or brave despair;
And sterner hearts alone may feel
The wound that time can never heal.
The rugged metal of the mine,
Must burn before its surface shine,
But plunged within the furnace-flame,
It bends and melts – though still the same;
Then tempered to thy want, or will,
'Twill serve thee to defend or kill;
A breast-plate for thine hour of need,
Or blade to bid thy foeman bleed;
But if a dagger's form it bear,
Let those who shape its edge, beware!
Thus passion's fire, and woman's art,
Can turn and tame the sterner heart;
From these its form and tone are ta'en,
And what they make it, must remain,
But break – before it bend again.

If solitude succeed to grief,
Release from pain is slight relief;
The vacant bosom's wilderness
Might thank the pang that made it less.
We loathe what none are left to share:
Even bliss – 'twere woe alone to bear;
The heart once left thus desolate
Must fly at last for ease – to hate.
It is as if the dead could feel
The icy worm around them steal,
And shudder, as the reptiles creep
To revel o'er their rotting sleep,
Without the power to scare away
The cold consumers of their clay!
It is as if the desert-bird,
   Whose beak unlocks her bosom's stream
    To still her famished nestlings' scream,
Nor mourns a life to them transferred,
Should rend her rash devoted breast,
And find them flown her empty nest.
The keenest pangs the wretched find
   Are rapture to the dreary void,
The leafless desert of the mind,
   The waste of feelings unemployed.
Who would be doomed to gaze upon
A sky without a cloud or sun?
Less hideous far the tempest's roar
Than ne'er to brave the billows more –
Thrown, when the war of winds is o'er,
A lonely wreck on fortune's shore,
'Mid sullen calm, and silent bay,
Unseen to drop by dull decay; –
Better to sink beneath the shock
Than moulder piecemeal on the rock!

    .     .     .     .

'Father! thy days have passed in peace,
  'Mid counted beads, and countless prayer;
To bid the sins of others cease,
  Thyself without a crime or care,
Save transient ills that all must bear,
Has been thy lot from youth to age;
And thou wilt bless thee from the rage
Of passions fierce and uncontrolled,
Such as thy penitents unfold,
Whose secret sins and sorrows rest
Within thy pure and pitying breast.
My days, though few, have passed below
In much of joy, but more of woe;
Yet still in hours of love or strife,
I've 'scaped the weariness of life:
Now leagued with friends, now girt by foes,
I loathed the languor of repose.
Now nothing left to love or hate,
No more with hope or pride elate,
I'd rather be the thing that crawls
Most noxious o'er a dungeon's walls,
Than pass my dull, unvarying days,
Condemned to meditate and gaze.
Yet, lurks a wish within my breast
For rest – but not to feel 'tis rest.
Soon shall my fate that wish fulfil;
  And I shall sleep without the dream
Of what I was, and would be still,
  Dark as to thee my deeds may seem:
My memory now is but the tomb
Of joys long dead; my hope, their doom:
Though better to have died with those
Than bear a life of lingering woes.

My spirit shrunk not to sustain
The searching throes of ceaseless pain;
Nor sought the self-accorded grave
Of ancient fool and modern knave:
Yet death I have not feared to meet;
And the field it had been sweet,
Had danger wooed me on to move
The slave of glory, not of love.
I've braved it – not for honour's boast;
I smile at laurels won or lost;
To such let others carve their way,
For high renown, or hireling pay:
But place again before my eyes –
Aught that I deem a worthy prize –
The maid I love, the man I hate,
And I will hunt the steps of fate,
To save or slay, as these require,
Through rending steel, and rolling fire:
Nor needest thou doubt this speech from one
Who would but do – what he *hath* done.
Death is but what the haughty brave,
The weak must bear, the wretch must crave;
Then let life go to him who gave:
I have not quailed to danger's brow
When high and happy – need I *now*?

.        .        .

'I loved her, Friar! nay, adored –
   But these are words that all can use –
I proved it more in deed than word;
There's blood upon that dinted sword,
   A stain its steel can never lose:
'Twas shed for her, who died for me,
   It warmed the heart of one abhorred:
Nay, start not – no – nor bend thy knee,
   Nor midst my sins such act record;

Thou wilt absolve me from the deed,
For he was hostile to thy creed!
The very name of Nazarene
Was wormwood to his Paynim spleen.
Ungrateful fool! since but for brands
Well wielded in some hardy hands,
And wounds by Galileans given –
The surest pass to Turkish heaven –
For him his Houris still might wait
Impatient at the Prophet's gate.
I loved her – love will find its way
Through paths where wolves would fear to prey;
And if it dares enough, 'twere hard
If passion met not some reward –
No matter how, or where, or why,
I did not vainly seek, nor sigh:
Yet sometimes, with remorse, in vain
I wish she had not loved again.
She died – I dare not tell thee how;
But look – 'tis written on my brow!
There read of Cain the curse and crime,
In characters unworn by time:
Still, ere thou dost condemn me, pause;
Not mine the act, though I the cause.
Yet did he but what I had done
Had she been false to more than one.
Faithless to him, he gave the blow;
But true to me, I laid him low:
Howe'er deserved her doom might be,
Her treachery was truth to me;
To me she gave her heart, that all
Which tyranny can ne'er enthral;
And I, alas! too late to save!
Yet all I then could give, I gave,
'Twas some relief, our foe a grave.

His death sits lightly; but her fate
Has made me — what thou well mayest hate.
  His doom was sealed — he knew it well,
Warned by the voice of stern Taheer,
Deep in whose darkly boding ear
The deathshot pealed of murder near,
  As filed the troop to where they fell!
He died too in the battle broil,
A time that heeds nor pain nor toil;
One cry to Mahomet for aid,
One prayer to Allah all he made:
He knew and crossed me in the fray —
I gazed upon him where he lay,
And watched his spirit ebb away:
Though pierced like pard by hunters' steel,
He felt not half that now I feel.
I searched, but vainly searched, to find
The workings of a wounded mind;
Each feature of that sullen corse
Betrayed his rage, but no remorse.
Oh, what had vengeance given to trace
Despair upon his dying face!
The late repentance of that hour,
When penitence hath lost her power
To tear one terror from the grave,
And will not soothe, and cannot save.

·    ·    ·    ·

'The cold in clime are cold in blood,
  Their love can scarce deserve the name;
But mine was like a lava flood
  That boils in Etna's breast of flame.
I cannot prate in puling strain
Of ladye-love, and beauty's chain:

If changing cheek, and scorching vein,
Lips taught to writhe, but not complain,
If bursting heart, and maddening brain,
And daring deed, and vengeful steel,
And all that I have felt, and feel,
Betoken love — that love was mine,
And shown by many a bitter sign.
'Tis true, I could not whine nor sigh,
I knew but to obtain or die.
I die — but first I have possessed,
And come what may, I *have been* blessed.
Shall I the doom I sought upbraid?
No — reft of all, yet undismayed
But for the thought of Leila slain,
Give me the pleasure with the pain,
So would I live and love again.
I grieve, but not, my holy guide!
For him who dies, but her who died:
She sleeps beneath the wandering wave —
Ah! had she but an earthly grave,
This breaking heart and throbbing head
Should seek and share her narrow bed.
She was a form of life and light,
That, seen, became a part of sight;
And rose, where'er I turned mine eye,
The morning-star of memory!


'Yes, love indeed is light from heaven;
  A spark of that immortal fire
With angels shared, by Allah given,
  To lift from earth our low desire.
Devotion wafts the mind above,
But Heaven itself descends in love;
A feeling from the Godhead caught,
To wean from self each sordid thought;

A ray of him who formed the whole;
A glory circling round the soul!
I grant *my* love imperfect, all
That mortals by the name miscall;
Then deem it evil, what thou wilt;
But say, oh say, *hers* was not guilt!
She was my life's unerring light:
That quenched, what beam shall break my night?
Oh! would it shone to lead me still,
Although to death or deadliest ill!
Why marvel ye, if they who lose
   This present joy, this future hope,
   No more with sorrow meekly cope;
In phrensy then their fate accuse;
In madness do those fearful deeds
   That seem to add but guilt to woe?
Alas! the breast that inly bleeds
   Hath nought to dread from outward blow;
Who falls from all he knows of bliss,
Cares little into what abyss.
Fierce as the gloomy vulture's now
   To thee, old man, my deeds appear:
I read abhorrence on thy brow,
   And this too was I born to bear!
'Tis true, that, like that bird of prey,
With havock have I marked my way:
But this was taught me by the dove,
To die – and know no second love.
This lesson yet hath man to learn,
Taught by the thing he dares to spurn:
The bird that sings within the brake,
The swan that swims upon the lake,
One mate, and one alone, will take.
And let the fool still prone to range,
And sneer on all who cannot change,

Partake his jest with boasting boys;
I envy not his varied joys,
But deem such feeble, heartless man,
Less than yon solitary swan;
Far, far beneath the shallow maid
He left believing and betrayed.
Such shame at least was never mine –
Leila! each thought was only thine!
My good, my guilt, my weal, my woe,
My hope on high – my all below.
Earth holds no other like to thee,
Or, if it doth, in vain for me:
For worlds I dare not view the dame
Resembling thee, yet not the same.
The very crimes that mar my youth,
This bed of death – attest my truth!
'Tis all too late – thou wert, thou art
The cherished madness of my heart!


'And she was lost – and yet I breathed,
    But not the breath of human life:
A serpent round my heart was wreathed,
    And stung my every thought to strife.
Alike all time, abhorred all place,
Shuddering I shrunk from Nature's face,
Where every hue that charmed before
The blackness of my bosom wore.
The rest thou dost already know,
And all my sins, and half my woe.
But talk no more of penitence;
Thou see'st I soon shall part from hence:
And if thy holy tale were true,
The deed that's done canst *thou* undo?
Think me not thankless – but this grief
Looks not to priesthood for relief.

My soul's estate in secret guess:
But wouldst thou pity more, say less.
When thou canst bid my Leila live,
Then will I sue thee to forgive;
Then plead my cause in that high place
Where purchased masses proffer grace.
Go, when the hunter's hand hath wrung
From forest-cave her shrieking young,
And calm the lonely lioness:
But soothe not – mock not *my* distress!

'In earlier days, and calmer hours,
    When heart with heart delights to blend,
Where bloom my native valley's bowers
    I had – Ah! have I now? – a friend!
To him this pledge I charge thee send,
    Memorial of a youthful vow;
I would remind him of my end:
    Though souls absorbed like mine allow
Brief thought to distant friendship's claim,
Yet dear to him my blighted name.
'Tis strange – he prophesied my doom,
    And I have smiled – I then could smile –
When prudence would his voice assume,
    And warn – I recked not what – the while:
But now remembrance whispers o'er
Those accents scarcely marked before.
Say – that his bodings came to pass,
    And he will start to hear their truth,
    And wish his words had not been sooth:
Tell him, unheeding as I was,
    Through many a busy bitter scene
    Of all our golden youth had been,

In pain, my faltering tongue had tried
To bless his memory ere I died;
But Heaven in wrath would turn away,
If guilt should for the guiltless pray.
I do not ask him not to blame,
Too gentle he to wound my name;
And what have I to do with fame?
I do not ask him not to mourn,
Such cold request might sound like scorn;
And what than friendship's manly tear
May better grace a brother's bier?
But bear this ring, his own of old,
And tell him -- what thou dost behold!
The withered frame, the ruined mind,
The wrack by passion left behind,
A shrivelled scroll, a scattered leaf,
Seared by the autumn blast of grief!

    .    .    .    .

'Tell me no more of fancy's gleam,
No, father, no, 'twas not a dream;
Alas! the dreamer first must sleep,
I only watched, and wished to weep;
But could not, for my burning brow
Throbbed to the very brain as now:
I wished but for a single tear,
As something welcome, new, and dear;
I wished it then, I wish it still;
Despair is stronger than my will.
Waste not thine orison, despair
Is mightier than thy pious prayer:
I would not, if I might, be blest;
I want no paradise, but rest.

'Twas then, I tell thee, father! then
I saw her; yes, she lived again;
And shining in her white symar,
As through yon pale grey cloud the star
Which now I gaze on, as on her,
Who looked and looks far lovelier;
Dimly I view its trembling spark;
Tomorrow's night shall be more dark;
And I, before its rays appear,
That lifeless thing the living fear.
I wander, father! for my soul
Is fleeting towards the final goal.
I saw her, friar! and I rose
Forgetful of our former woes;
And rushing from my couch, I dart,
And clasp her to my desperate heart;
I clasp – what is it that I clasp?
No breathing form within my grasp,
No heart that beats reply to mine,
Yet, Leila! yet the form is thine!
And art thou, dearest, changed so much,
As meet my eye, yet mock my touch?
Ah! were thy beauties e'er so cold,
I care not; so my arms enfold
The all they ever wished to hold.
Alas! around a shadow prest,
They shrink upon my lonely breast;
Yet still 'tis there! In silence stands,
And beckons with beseeching hands!
With braided hair, and bright black eye –
I knew 'twas false – she could not die!
But he is dead! within the dell
I saw him buried where he fell;
He comes not, for he cannot break
From earth; why then art *thou* awake?

They told me wild waves rolled above
The face I view, the form I love;
They told me – 'twas a hideous tale!
I'd tell it, but my tongue would fail:
If true, and from thine ocean-cave
Thou com'st to claim a calmer grave;
Oh! pass thy dewy fingers o'er
This brow that then will burn no more;
Or place them on my hopeless heart:
But, shape or shade! whate'er thou art,
In mercy ne'er again depart!
Or farther with thee bear my soul
Than winds can waft or waters roll!

  .  .  .  .

'Such is my name, and such my tale.
 Confessor! to thy secret ear
I breathe the sorrows I bewail,
 And thank thee for the generous tear
This glazing eye could never shed.
Then lay me with the humblest dead,
And, save the cross above my head,
Be neither name nor emblem spread,
By prying stranger to be read,
Or stay the passing pilgrim's tread.'

 He passed – nor of his name and race
Hath left a token or a trace,
Save what the father must not say
Who shrived him on his dying day:
This broken tale was all we knew
Of her he loved, or him he slew.

# ODE TO NAPOLEON BUONAPARTE

'Tis done – but yesterday a King!
   And armed with kings to strive –
And now thou art a nameless thing:
   So abject – yet alive!
Is this the man of thousand thrones,
Who strewed our earth with hostile bones,
   And can he thus survive?
Since he, miscalled the Morning Star,
Nor man nor fiend hath fallen so far.

Ill-minded man! why scourge thy kind
   Who bowed so low the knee?
By gazing on thyself grown blind,
   Thou taughtest the rest to see.
With might unquestioned – power to save –
Thine only gift hath been the grave,
   To those that worshipped thee;
Nor till thy fall could mortals guess
Ambition's less than littleness!

Thanks for that lesson – it will teach
   To after-warriors more,
Than high philosophy can preach,
   And vainly preached before.
That spell upon the minds of men
Breaks never to unite again,
   That led them to adore
Those Pagod things of sabre-sway,
With fronts of brass, and feet of clay.

The triumph, and the vanity,
   The rapture of the strife –
The earthquake voice of victory,
   To thee the breath of life;
The sword, the sceptre, and that sway
Which man seemed made but to obey,
   Wherewith renown was rife –
All quelled! – Dark Spirit! what must be
The madness of thy memory!

The desolator desolate!
   The victor overthrown!
The arbiter of others' fate
   A suppliant for his own!
Is it some yet imperial hope,
That with such change can calmly cope?
   Or dread of death alone?
To die a prince – or live a slave –
Thy choice is most ignobly brave!

He who of old would rend the oak,
   Dreamed not of the rebound;
Chained by the trunk he vainly broke –
   Alone – how looked he round?
Thou, in the sternness of thy strength,
An equal deed hast done at length,
   And darker fate hast found:
He fell, the forest prowlers' prey;
But thou must eat thy heart away!

The Roman, when his burning heart
   Was slaked with blood of Rome,
Threw down the dagger – dared depart,
   In savage grandeur, home.

He dared depart in utter scorn
Of men that such a yoke had borne,
　Yet left him such a doom!
His only glory was that hour
Of self-upheld abandoned power.

The Spaniard, when the lust of sway
　Had lost its quickening spell,
Cast crowns for rosaries away,
　An empire for a cell;
A strict accountant of his beads,
A subtle disputant on creeds,
　His dotage trifled well:
Yet better had he neither known
A bigot's shrine, nor despot's throne.

But thou – from thy reluctant hand
　The thunderbolt is wrung –
Too late thou leavest the high command
　To which thy weakness clung;
All evil spirit as thou art,
It is enough to grieve the heart
　To see thine own unstrung;
To think that God's fair world hath been
The footstool of a thing so mean;

And earth hath spilt her blood for him,
　Who thus can hoard his own!
And monarchs bowed the trembling limb,
　And thanked him for a throne!
Fair freedom! we may hold thee dear,
When thus thy mightiest foes their fear
　In humblest guise have shown.
Oh! ne'er may tyrant leave behind
A bright name to lure mankind!

Thine evil deeds are writ in gore,
   Nor written thus in vain –
Thy triumphs tell of fame no more,
   Or deepen every stain:
If thou hadst died as honour dies,
Some new Napoleon might arise,
   To shame the world again –
But who would soar the solar height,
To set in such a starless night?

Weighed in the balance, hero dust
   Is vile as vulgar clay;
Thy scales, mortality! are just
   To all that pass away:
But yet methought the living great
Some higher sparks should animate,
   To dazzle and dismay:
Nor deemed contempt could thus make mirth
Of these, the conquerors of the earth.

And she, proud Austria's mournful flower,
   Thy still imperial bride;
How bears her breast the torturing hour?
   Still clings she to thy side?
Must she too bend, must she too share
Thy late repentance, long despair,
   Thou throneless homicide?
If still she loves thee, hoard that gem;
'Tis worth thy vanished diadem!

Then haste thee to thy sullen isle,
   And gaze upon the sea;
That element may meet thy smile –
   It ne'er was ruled by thee!

Or trace with thine all idle hand,
In loitering mood upon the sand,
   That earth is now as free!
That Corinth's pedagogue hath now
Transferred his by-word to thy brow.

Thou Timour! in his captive's cage
   What thoughts will there be thine,
While brooding in thy prisoned rage?
   But one – 'The world *was* mine!'
Unless, like he of Babylon,
All sense is with thy sceptre gone,
   Life will not long confine
That spirit poured so widely forth –
So long obeyed – so little worth!

Or, like the thief of fire from heaven,
   Wilt thou withstand the shock?
And share with him, the unforgiven,
   His vulture and his rock!
Foredoomed by God – by man accurst,
And that last act, though not thy worst,
   The very Fiend's arch mock;
He in his fall preserved his pride,
And, if a mortal, had as proudly died!

There was a day – there was an hour,
   While earth was Gaul's – Gaul thine –
When that immeasurable power
   Unsated to resign
Had been an act of purer fame
Than gathers round Marengo's name
   And gilded thy decline,
Through the long twilight of all time,
Despite some passing clouds of crime.

But thou forsooth must be a king
   And don the purple vest,
As if that foolish robe could wring
   Remembrance from thy breast.
Where is that faded garment? where
The gewgaws thou wert fond to wear,
   The star, the string, the crest?
Vain froward child of empire! say,
Are all thy playthings snatched away?

Where may the wearied eye repose,
   When gazing on the great;
Where neither guilty glory glows,
   Nor despicable state?
Yes – One – the first – the last – the best –
The Cincinnatus of the West,
   Whom envy dared not hate,
Bequeath the name of Washington,
To make man blush there was but One!

# MAZEPPA

## I

'Twas after dread Pultowa's day,
 When fortune left the royal Swede –
Around a slaughtered army lay,
 No more to combat and to bleed.
The power and glory of the war,
 Faithless as their vain votaries, men,
Had passed to the triumphant Czar,
 And Moscow's walls were safe again –
Until a day more dark and drear,
And a more memorable year,
Should give to slaughter and to shame
A mightier host and haughtier name;
A greater wreck, a deeper fall,
A shock to one – a thunderbolt to all.

## II

Such was the hazard of the die;
The wounded Charles was taught to fly
By day and night through field and flood,
Stained with his own and subjects' blood;
For thousands fell that flight to aid:
And not a voice was heard to upbraid
Ambition in his humbled hour,
When truth had nought to dread from power.
His horse was slain, and Gieta gave
His own – and died the Russians' slave.
This too sinks after many a league
Of well sustained, but vain fatigue;

And in the depth of forests darkling,
The watch-fires in the distance sparkling –
   The beacons of surrounding foes –
A king must lay his limbs at length.
   Are these the laurels and repose
For which the nations strain their strength?
They laid him by a savage tree,
In outworn nature's agony;
His wounds were stiff, his limbs were stark,
The heavy hour was chill and dark;
The fever in his blood forbade
A transient slumber's fitful aid:
And thus it was; but yet through all,
Kinglike the monarch bore his fall,
And made, in this extreme of ill,
His pangs the vassals of his will:
All silent and subdued were they,
As once the nations round him lay.


### III

A band of chiefs! – alas! how few,
   Since but the fleeting of a day
Had thinned it; but this wreck was true
   And chivalrous: upon the clay
Each sate him down, all sad and mute,
   Beside his monarch and his steed;
For danger levels man and brute,
   And all are fellows in their need.
Among the rest, Mazeppa made
His pillow in an old oak's shade –
Himself as rough, and scarce less old,
The Ukraine's hetman, calm and bold:
But first, outspent with this long course,
The Cossack prince rubbed down his horse,

And made for him a leafy bed,
  And smoothed his fetlocks and his mane,
  And slacked his girth, and stripped his rein,
And joyed to see how well he fed;
For until now he had the dread
His wearied courser might refuse
To browse beneath the midnight dews:
But he was hardy as his lord,
And little cared for bed and board;
But spirited and docile too,
Whate'er was to be done, would do.
Shaggy and swift, and strong of limb,
All Tartar-like he carried him;
Obeyed his voice, and came to call,
And knew him in the midst of all:
Though thousands were around, – and night,
Without a star, pursued her flight, –
That steed from sunset until dawn
His chief would follow like a fawn.


IV

  This done, Mazeppa spread his cloak,
And laid his lance beneath his oak,
Felt if his arms in order good
The long day's march had well withstood –
If still the powder filled the pan,
  And flints unloosened kept their lock –
His sabre's hilt and scabbard felt,
And whether they had chafed his belt;
And next the venerable man,
From out his haversack and can,
  Prepared and spread his slender stock
And to the monarch and his men
The whole or portion offered then

With far less of inquietude
Than courtiers at a banquet would.
And Charles of this his slender share
With smiles partook a moment there,
To force of cheer a greater show,
And seem above both wounds and woe; —
And then he said — 'Of all our band,
Though firm of heart and strong of hand,
In skirmish, march, or forage, none
Can less have said or more have done
Than thee, Mazeppa! On the earth
So fit a pair had never birth,
Since Alexander's days till now,
As thy Bucephalus and thou:
All Scythia's fame to thine should yield
For pricking on o'er flood and field.'
Mazeppa answered — 'Ill betide
The school wherein I learned to ride!'
Quoth Charles — 'Old Hetman, wherefore so,
Since thou hast learned the art so well?'
Mazeppa said — ''Twere long to tell;
And we have many a league to go,
With every now and then a blow,
And ten to one at least the foe,
Before our steeds may graze at ease,
Beyond the swift Borysthenes:
And, sire, your limbs have need of rest,
And I will be the sentinel
Of this your troop.' — 'But I request,'
Said Sweden's monarch, 'thou wilt tell
This tale of thine, and I may reap,
Perchance, from this the boon of sleep;
For at this moment from my eyes
The hope of present slumber flies.'

'Well, sire, with such a hope, I'll track
My seventy years of memory back:
I think 'twas in my twentieth spring, –
Ay, 'twas, – when Casimir was king –
John Casimir, – I was his page
Six summers, in my earlier age:
A learnéd monarch, faith! was he,
And most unlike your majesty:
He made no wars, and did not gain
New realms to lose them back again;
And (save debates in Warsaw's diet)
He reigned in most unseemly quiet;
Not that he had no cares to vex,
He loved the muses and the sex;
And sometimes these so froward are,
They made him wish himself at war;
But soon his wrath being o'er, he took
Another mistress – or new book;
And then he gave prodigious fêtes –
All Warsaw gathered round his gates
To gaze upon his splendid court,
And dames, and chiefs, of princely port.
He was the Polish Solomon,
So sung his poets, all but one,
Who, being unpensioned, made a satire,
And boasted that he could not flatter.
It was a court of jousts and mimes,
Where every courtier tried at rhymes;
Even I for once produced some verses,
And signed my odes "Despairing Thyrsis."
There was a certain Palatine,
    A Count of far and high descent,
Rich as a salt or silver mine;
And he was proud, ye may divine,
As if from heaven he had been sent:

He had such wealth in blood and ore
   As few could match beneath the throne;
And he would gaze upon his store,
And o'er his pedigree would pore,
Until by some confusion led,
Which almost looked like want of head,
   He thought their merits were his own.
His wife was not of his opinion;
   His junior she by thirty years;
Grew daily tired of his dominion;
   And, after wishes, hopes, and fears,
   To virtue a few farewell tears,
A restless dream or two, some glances
At Warsaw's youth, some songs, and dances,
Awaited but the usual chances,
Those happy accidents which render
The coldest dames so very tender,
To deck her Count with titles given,
'Tis said, as passports into heaven;
But, strange to say, they rarely boast
Of these, who have deserved them most.

### V

' I was a goodly stripling then;
   At seventy years I so may say,
That there were few, or boys or men,
   Who, in my dawning time of day,
Of vassal or of knight's degree,
Could vie in vanities with me;
For I had strength, youth, gaiety,
A port, not like to this ye see,
But smooth, as all is rugged now;
   For time, and care, and war, have ploughed
My very soul from out my brow;
   And thus I should be disavowed

By all my kind and kin, could they
Compare my day and yesterday;
This change was wrought, too, long ere age
Had ta'en my features for his page:
With years, ye know, have not declined
My strength, my courage, or my mind,
Or at this hour I should not be
Telling old tales beneath a tree,
With starless skies my canopy.
But let me on: Theresa's form –
Methinks it glides before me now,
Between me and yon chestnut's bough,
The memory is so quick and warm;
And yet I find no words to tell
The shape of her I loved so well:
She had the Asiatic eye,
   Such as our Turkish neighbourhood,
   Hath mingled with our Polish blood,
Dark as above us is the sky;
But through it stole a tender light,
Like the first moonrise of midnight;
Large, dark, and swimming in the stream,
Which seemed to melt to its own beam;
All love, half langour, and half fire,
Like saints that at the stake expire,
And lift their raptured looks on high,
As though it were a joy to die.
A brow like a midsummer lake,
   Transparent with the sun therein,
When waves no murmur dare to make,
   And heaven beholds her face within.
A cheek and lip – but why proceed?
   I loved her then – I love her still;
And such as I am, love indeed
   In fierce extremes – in good and ill.

But still we love even in our rage,
And haunted to our very age
With the vain shadow of the past,
As is Mazeppa to the last.

## VI

'We met – we gazed – I saw, and sighed,
She did not speak, and yet replied;
There are ten thousand tones and signs
We hear and see, but none defines –
Involuntary sparks of thought,
Which strike from out the heart o'erwrought,
And form a strange intelligence,
Alike mysterious and intense,
Which link the burning chain that binds,
Without their will, young hearts and minds
Conveying, as the electric wire,
We know not how, the absorbing fire.
I saw, and sighed – in silence wept,
And still reluctant distance kept,
Until I was made known to her,
And we might then and there confer
Without suspicion – then, even then,
  I longed, and was resolved to speak;
But on my lips they died again,
  The accents tremulous and weak,
Until one hour. – There is a game,
  A frivolous and foolish play,
  Wherewith we while away the day;
It is – I have forgot the name –
And we to this, it seems, were set,
By some strange chance, which I forget:

I reck'd not if I won or lost,
   It was enough for me to be
   So near to hear, and oh! to see
The being whom I loved the most. –
I watched her as a sentinel,
(May ours this dark night watch as well!)
   Until I saw, and thus it was,
That she was pensive, nor perceived
Her occupation, nor was grieved
Nor glad to lose or gain; but still
Played on for hours, as if her will
Yet bound her to the place, though not
That hers might be the winning lot.

   Then through my brain the thought did pass
Even as a flash of lightning there,
That there was something in her air
Which would not doom me to despair;
And on the thought my words broke forth,
   All incoherent as they were –
Their eloquence was little worth,
But yet she listened – 'tis enough –
   Who listens once will listen twice;
   Her heart, be sure, is not of ice,
And one refusal no rebuff.

### VII

'I loved, and was beloved again –
   They tell me, Sire, you never knew
   Those gentle frailties; if 'tis true,
I shorten all my joy or pain;
To you 'twould seem absurd as vain;
But all men are not born to reign,
Or o'er their passions, or as you
Thus o'er themselves and nations too.

I am – or rather *was* – a prince,
  A chief of thousands, and could lead
  Them on where each would foremost bleed;
But could not o'er myself evince
The like control – but to resume:
  I loved, and was beloved again;
In sooth, it is a happy doom,
  But yet where happiest ends in pain. –
We met in secret, and the hour
Which led me to that lady's bower
Was fiery expectation's dower.
My days and nights were nothing – all
Except that hour which doth recall
In the long lapse from youth to age
  No other like itself – I'd give
  The Ukraine back again to live
It o'er once more – and be a page,
The happy page, who was the lord
Of one soft heart, and his own sword,
And had no other gem nor wealth
Save nature's gift of youth and health.
We met in secret – doubly sweet,
Some say, they find it so to meet;
I know not that – I would have given
  My life but to have called her mine
In the full view of earth and heaven;
  For I did oft and long repine
That we could only meet by stealth.


VIII

'For lovers there are many eyes,
  And such there were on us; the devil
  On such occasions should be civil –

The devil! – I'm loth to do him wrong,
  It might be some untoward saint,
Who would not be at rest too long,
  But to his pious bile gave vent –
But one fair night, some lurking spies
Surprised and seized us both.
The Count was something more than wroth –
I was unarmed; but if in steel,
All cap-à-pie from head to heel,
What 'gainst their numbers could I do?
'Twas near his castle, far away
  From city or from succour near,
And almost on the break of day;
I did not think to see another,
  My moments seemed reduced to few;
And with one prayer to Mary Mother,
  And, it may be, a saint or two,
As I resigned me to my fate,
They led me to the castle gate:
  Theresa's doom I never knew,
Our lot was henceforth separate.
An angry man, ye may opine,
Was he, the proud Count Palatine;
And he had reason good to be,
  But he was most enraged lest such
  An accident should chance to touch
Upon his future pedigree;
Nor less amazed, that such a blot
His noble 'scutcheon should have got,
While he was highest of his line
  Because unto himself he seemed
  The first of men, nor less he deemed
In others' eyes, and most in mine.

'Sdeath! with a *page* – perchance a king
Had reconciled him to the thing;
But with a stripling of a page –
I felt – but cannot paint his rage.


### IX

'"Bring forth the horse!" – the horse was brought;
 In truth, he was a noble steed,
 A Tartar of the Ukraine breed,
Who looked as though the speed of thought
Were in his limbs; but he was wild,
 Wild as the wild deer, and untaught,
With spur and bridle undefiled –
 'Twas but a day he had been caught;
And snorting, with erected mane,
And struggling fiercely, but in vain,
In the full foam of wrath and dread
To me the desert-born was led:
They bound me on, that menial throng,
Upon his back with many a thong;
They loosed him with a sudden lash –
Away! – away! – and on we dash! –
Torrents less rapid and less rash.


### X

' Away! – away! – my breath was gone –
I saw not where he hurried on:
'Twas scarcely yet the break of day,
And on he foamed – away! – away! –
The last of human sounds which rose,
As I was darted from my foes,
Was the wild shout of savage laughter,
Which on the wind came roaring after

A moment from that rabble rout:
With sudden wrath I wrenched my head,
  And snapped the cord, which to the mane
  Had bound my neck in lieu of rein,
And, writhing half my form about,
Howled back my curse; but 'midst the tread,
The thunder of my courser's speed,
Perchance they did not hear nor heed:
It vexes me – for I would fain
Have paid their insult back again.
I paid it well in after days:
There is not of that castle gate,
Its drawbridge and portcullis' weight,
Stone, bar, moat, bridge, or barrier left;
Nor of its fields a blade of grass,
  Save what grows on a ridge of wall,
  Where stood the hearth-stone of the hall;
And many a time ye there might pass,
Nor dream that e'er the fortress was.
I saw its turrets in a blaze,
Their crackling battlements all cleft,
  And the hot lead pour down like rain
From off the scorched and blackening roof,
Whose thickness was not vengeance-proof.
  They little thought that day of pain,
When launched, as on the lightning's flash,
They bade me to destruction dash,
  That one day I should come again,
With twice five thousand horse, to thank
  The Count for his uncourteous ride.
They played me then a bitter prank,
When, with the wild horse for my guide,
They bound me to his foaming flank:
At length I played them one as frank –

For time at last sets all things even –
   And if we do but watch the hour,
   There never yet was human power
Which could evade, if unforgiven,
The patient search and vigil long
Of him who treasures up a wrong.


## XI

'Away, away, my steed and I,
   Upon the pinions of the wind.
   All human dwellings left behind,
We sped like meteors through the sky,
When with its crackling sound the night
Is chequered with the northern light:
Town – village – none were on our track,
   But a wild plain of far extent,
And bounded by a forest black;
   And, save the scarce seen battlement
On distant heights of some strong hold,
Against the Tartars built of old,
No trace of man. The year before
A Turkish army had marched o'er;
And where the Spahi's hoof hath trod,
The verdure flies the bloody sod: –
The sky was dull, and dim, and grey,
   And a low breeze crept moaning by –
   I could have answered with a sigh –
But fast we fled, away, away –
And I could neither sigh nor pray;
And my cold sweat-drops fell like rain
Upon the courser's bristling mane;
But, snorting still with rage and fear,
He flew upon his far career:
At times I almost thought, indeed,
He must have slackened in his speed;

But no – my bound and slender frame
  Was nothing to his angry might,
And merely like a spur became:
Each motion which I made to free
My swoln limbs from their agony
  Increased his fury and affright:
I tried my voice, – 'twas faint and low,
But yet he swerved as from a blow;
And, starting to each accent, sprang
As from a sudden trumpet's clang:
Meantime my cords were wet with gore,
Which, oozing through my limbs, ran o'er;
And in my tongue the thirst became
A something fierier far than flame.

### XII

' We neared the wild wood – 'twas so wide,
I saw no bounds on either side;
'Twas studded with old sturdy trees,
That bent not to the roughest breeze
Which howls down from Siberia's waste,
And strips the forest in its haste, –
But these were few and far between,
Set thick with shrubs more young and green,
Luxuriant with their annual leaves,
Ere strown by those autumnal eves
That nip the forest's foliage dead,
Discoloured with a lifeless red,
Which stands thereon like stiffened gore
Upon the slain when battle's o'er,
And some long winter's night hath shed
Its frost o'er every tombless head,
So cold and stark, the raven's beak
May peck unpierced each frozen cheek:

'Twas a wild waste of underwood,
And here and there a chestnut stood,
The strong oak, and the hardy pine;
   But far apart – and well it were,
Or else a different lot were mine –
   The boughs gave way, and did not tear
My limbs; and I found strength to bear
My wounds, already scarred with cold –
My bonds forbade to loose my hold.
We rustled through the leaves like wind,
Left shrubs, and trees, and wolves behind;
By night I heard them on the track,
Their troop came hard upon our back,
With their long gallop, which can tire
The hound's deep hate, and hunter's fire:
Where'er we flew they followed on,
Nor left us with the morning sun;
Behind I saw them, scarce a rood,
At day-break winding through the wood,
And through the night had heard their feet
Their stealing, rustling step repeat.
Oh! how I wished for spear or sword,
At least to die amidst the horde,
And perish – if it must be so –
At bay, destroying many a foe!
When first my courser's race begun,
I wished the goal already won;
But now I doubted strength and speed:
Vain doubt! his swift and savage breed
Had nerved him like the mountain-roe –
Nor faster falls the blinding snow
Which whelms the peasant near the door
Whose threshold he shall cross no more,

Bewildered with the dazzling blast,
Than through the forest-paths he passed –
Untired, untamed, and worse than wild;
All furious as a favoured child
Balked of its wish; or fiercer still –
A woman piqued – who has her will.

### XIII

'The wood was passed; 'twas more than noon,
But chill the air, although in June;
Or it might be my veins ran cold –
Prolonged endurance tames the bold;
And I was then not what I seem,
But headlong as a wintry stream,
And wore my feelings out before
I well could count their causes o'er:
And what with fury, fear, and wrath,
The tortures which beset my path,
Cold, hunger, sorrow, shame, distress,
Thus bound in nature's nakedness;
Sprung from a race whose rising blood
When stirred beyond its calmer mood,
And trodden hard upon, is like
The rattle-snake's, in act to strike –
What marvel if this worn-out trunk
Beneath its woes a moment sunk?
The earth gave way, the skies rolled round,
I seemed to sink upon the ground;
But erred, for I was fastly bound.
My heart turned sick, my brain grew sore,
And throbbed awhile, then beat no more:
The skies spun like a mighty wheel;
I saw the trees like drunkards reel,

And a slight flash sprang o'er my eyes,
Which saw no farther. He who dies
Can die no more than then I died;
O'ertortured by that ghastly ride.
I felt the blackness come and go,
    And strove to wake; but could not make
My senses climb up from below:
I felt as on a plank at sea,
When all the waves that dash o'er thee,
At the same time upheave and whelm,
And hurl thee towards a desert realm.
My undulating life was as
The fancied lights that flitting pass
Our shut eyes in deep midnight, when
Fever begins upon the brain;
But soon it passed, with little pain,
    But a confusion worse than such:
    I own that I should deem it much,
Dying, to feel the same again;
And yet I do suppose we must
Feel far more ere we turn to dust:
No matter; I have bared my brow
Full in Death's face – before – and now.

### XIV

'My thoughts came back; where was I? Cold,
    And numb, and giddy: pulse by pulse
Life reassumed its lingering hold,
And throb by throb – till grown a pang;
    Which for a moment would convulse,
    My blood reflowed, though thick and chill;
My ear with uncouth noises rang,
    My heart began once more to thrill;
My sight returned, though dim; alas!
And thickened, as it were, with glass.

Methought the dash of waves was nigh;
There was a gleam too of the sky,
Studded with stars; — it is no dream;
The wild horse swims the wilder stream!
The bright broad river's gushing tide
Sweeps, winding onward, far and wide,
And we are half-way, struggling o'er
To yon unknown and silent shore.
The waters broke my hollow trance,
And with a temporary strength
    My stiffened limbs were rebaptized.
My courser's broad breast proudly braves,
And dashes off the ascending waves,
And onward we advance!
We reach the slippery shore at length,
    A haven I but little prized,
For all behind was dark and drear
And all before was night and fear.
How many hours of night or day
In those suspended pangs I lay,
I could not tell; I scarcely knew
If this were human breath I drew.


XV

'With glossy skin, and dripping mane,
    And reeling limbs, and reeking flank,
The wild steed's sinewy nerves still strain
    Up the repelling bank.
We gain the top: a boundless plain
Spreads through the shadow of the night,
    And onward, onward, onward, seems,
    Like precipices in our dreams,
To stretch beyond the sight;

120

And here and there a speck of white,
  Or scattered spot of dusky green,
In masses broke into the light,
As rose the moon upon my right:
  But nought distinctly seen
In the dim waste would indicate
The omen of a cottage gate;
No twinkling taper from afar
Stood like a hospitable star;
Not even an ignis-fatuus rose
To make him merry with my woes:
  That very cheat had cheered me then!
Although detected, welcome still,
Reminding me, through every ill,
  Of the abodes of men.


XVI

'Onward we went – but slack and slow;
  His savage force at length o'erspent,
The drooping courser, faint and low,
  All feebly foaming went.
A sickly infant had had power
To guide him forward in that hour!
  But, useless all to me,
His new-born tameness nought availed –
My limbs were bound; my force had failed,
  Perchance, had they been free.
With feeble effort still I tried
To rend the bonds so starkly tied,
  But still it was in vain;
My limbs were only wrung the more,
And soon the idle strife gave o'er,
  Which but prolonged their pain:
The dizzy race seemed almost done,
Although no goal was nearly won:

Some streaks announced the coming sun –
   How slow, alas! he came!
Methought that mist of dawning grey
Would never dapple into day;
How heavily it rolled away –
   Before the eastern flame
Rose crimson, and deposed the stars,
And called the radiance from their cars,
And filled the earth, from his deep throne,
With lonely lustre, all his own.

## XVII

'Up rose the sun; the mists were curled
Back from the solitary world
Which lay around – behind – before;
What booted it to traverse o'er
Plain, forest, river? Man nor brute,
Nor dint of hoof, nor print of foot,
Lay in the wild luxuriant soil;
No sign of travel – none of toil;
The very air was mute:
And not an insect's shrill small horn,
Nor matin bird's new voice was borne
From herb nor thicket. Many a werst,
Panting as if his heart would burst,
The weary brute still staggered on;
And still we were – or seemed – alone:
At length, while reeling on our way,
Methought I heard a courser neigh,
From out yon tuft of blackening firs.
Is it the wind those branches stirs?
No, no! from out the forest prance
   A trampling troop; I see them come!
In one vast squadron they advance!
   I strove to cry – my lips were dumb.

The steeds rush on in plunging pride;
But where are they the reins to guide?
A thousand horse – and none to ride!
With flowing tail, and flying mane,
Wide nostrils never stretched by pain,
Mouths bloodless to the bit or rein,
And feet that iron never shod,
And flanks unscarred by spur or rod,
A thousand horse, the wild, the free,
Like waves that follow o'er the sea,
    Came thickly thundering on,
As if our faint approach to meet;
The sight re-nerved my courser's feet,
A moment staggering, feebly fleet,
A moment, with a faint low neigh,
    He answered, and then fell!
With gasps and glazing eyes he lay,
    And reeking limbs immoveable,
      His first and last career is done!
On came the troop – they saw him stoop,
    They saw me strangely bound along
    His back with many a bloody thong.
They stop – they start – they snuff the air,
Gallop a moment here and there,
Approach, retire, wheel round and round,
Then plunging back with sudden bound,
Headed by one black mighty steed,
Who seemed the patriarch of his breed,
    Without a single speck or hair
Of white upon his shaggy hide;
They snort -- they foam – neigh – swerve aside,
And backward to the forest fly,
By instinct, from a human eye.
    They left me there to my despair,

Linked to the dead and stiffening wretch,
Whose lifeless limbs beneath me stretch,
Relieved from that unwonted weight,
From whence I could not extricate
Nor him nor me – and there we lay
   The dying on the dead!
I little deemed another day
   Would see my houseless, helpless head.


'And there from morn till twilight bound,
I felt the heavy hours toil round,
With just enough of life to see
My last of suns go down on me,
In hopeless certainty of mind,
That makes us feel at length resigned
To that which our foreboding years
Presents the worst and last of fears
Inevitable – even a boon,
Nor more unkind for coming soon,
Yet shunned and dreaded with such care,
As if it only were a snare
   That prudence might escape:
At times both wished for and implored,
At times sought with self-pointed sword,
Yet still a dark and hideous close
To even intolerable woes,
   And welcome in no shape.
And, strange to say, the sons of pleasure,
They who have revelled beyond measure
In beauty, wassail, wine, and treasure,
Die calm, or calmer, oft than he
Whose heritage was misery.

For he who hath in turn run through
All that was beautiful and new,
   Hath nought to hope, and nought to leave;
And, save the future, (which is viewed
Not quite as men are base or good,
But as their nerves may be endued,)
   With nought perhaps to grieve:
The wretch still hopes his woes must end,
And death, whom he should deem his friend,
Appears, to his distempered eyes,
Arrived to rob him of his prize,
The tree of his new Paradise.
Tomorrow would have given him all,
Repaid his pangs, repaired his fall;
Tomorrow would have been the first
Of days no more deplored or curst,
But bright, and long, and beckoning years,
Seen dazzling through the mist of tears,
Guerdon of many a painful hour;
Tomorrow would have given him power
To rule, to shine, to smite, to save –
And must it dawn upon his grave?

## XVIII

'The sun was sinking – still I lay
   Chained to the chill and stiffening steed,
I thought to mingle there our clay;
   And my dim eyes of death had need,
   No hope arose of being freed.
I cast my last looks up the sky,
   And there between me and the sun
I saw the expecting raven fly,
Who scarce would wait till both should die,
   Ere his repast begun;

He flew, and perched, then flew once more,
And each time nearer than before;
I saw his wing through twilight flit,
And once so near me he alit
   I could have smote, but lacked the strength;
But the slight motion of my hand,
And feeble scratching of the sand,
The exerted throat's faint struggling noise,
Which scarcely could be called a voice,
   Together scared him off at length.
I know no more – my latest dream
   Is something of a lovely star
   Which fixed my dull eyes from afar,
And went and came with wandering beam,
And of the cold, dull, swimming, dense
Sensation of recurring sense,
   And then subsiding back to death,
   And then again a little breath,
A little thrill, a short suspense,
   An icy sickness curdling o'er
My heart, and sparks that crossed my brain –
A gasp, a throb, a start of pain,
   A sigh, and nothing more.

### XIX

'I woke – where was I? – Do I see
A human face look down on me?
And doth a roof above me close?
Do these limbs on a couch repose?
Is this a chamber where I lie?
And is it mortal yon bright eye,
That watches me with gentle glance?
   I closed my own again once more,
As doubtful that the former trance
   Could not as yet be o'er.

A slender girl, long-haired, and tall,
Sate watching by the cottage wall.
The sparkle of her eye I caught,
Even with my first return of thought;
For ever and anon she threw
  A prying, pitying glance on me
  With her black eyes so wild and free:
I gazed, and gazed, until I knew
  No vision it could be, –
But that I lived, and was released
From adding to the vulture's feast:
And when the Cossack maid beheld
My heavy eyes at length unsealed,
She smiled – and I essayed to speak,
But failed – and she approached, and made
  With lip and finger signs that said,
I must not strive as yet to break
The silence, till my strength should be
Enough to leave my accents free;
And then her hand on mine she laid,
And smoothed the pillow for my head,
And stole along on tiptoe tread,
  And gently oped the door, and spake
In whispers – ne'er was voice so sweet!
Even music followed her light feet.

  But those she called were not awake,
And she went forth; but, ere she passed,
Another look on me she cast,
  Another sign she made, to say,
That I had nought to fear, that all
Were near, at my command or call,
  And she would not delay
Her due return: – while she was gone,
Methought I felt too much alone.

'She came with mother and with sire –
What need of more? – I will not tire
With long recital of the rest,
Since I became the Cossack's guest.
They found me senseless on the plain.

  They bore me to the nearest hut,
They brought me into life again –
Me – one day o'er their realm to reign!
  Thus the vain fool who strove to glut
His rage, refining on my pain,
  Sent me forth to the wilderness,
Bound, naked, bleeding, and alone,
To pass the desert to a throne, –
  What mortal his own doom may guess?
  Let none despond, let none despair!
Tomorrow the Borysthenes
May see our coursers graze at ease
Upon his Turkish bank, – and never
Had I such welcome for a river
  As I shall yield when safely there.
Comrades, good night!' – The Hetman threw
  His length beneath the oak-tree shade,
  With leafy couch already made,
A bed nor comfortless nor new
To him, who took his rest whene'er
The hour arrived, no matter where:
  His eyes the hastening slumbers steep.
And if ye marvel Charles forgot
To thank his tale, *he* wondered not, –
  The king had been an hour asleep.

# THE VISION OF JUDGMENT

## I

Saint Peter sat by the celestial gate:
  His keys were rusty, and the lock was dull,
So little trouble had been given of late;
  Not that the place by any means was full,
But since the Gallic era 'eighty-eight'
  The devils had ta'en a longer, stronger pull,
And 'a pull altogether', as they say
At sea – which drew most souls another way.

## II

The angels all were singing out of tune,
  And hoarse with having little else to do,
Excepting to wind up the sun and moon,
  Or curb a runaway young star or two,
Or wild colt of a comet, which too soon
  Broke out of bounds o'er the ethereal blue,
Splitting some planet with its playful tail,
As boats are sometimes by a wanton whale.

## III

The guardian seraphs had retired on high,
  Finding their charges past all care below:
Terrestrial business filled nought in the sky
  Save the recording angel's black bureau:
Who found, indeed, the facts to multiply
  With such rapidity of vice and woe,
That he had stripped off both his wings in quills,
And yet was in arrear of human ills.

IV

His business so augmented of late years,
 That he was forced, against his will, no doubt,
(Just like those cherubs, earthly ministers,)
 For some resource to turn himself about,
And claim the help of his celestial peers,
 To aid him ere he should be quite worn out,
By the increased demand for his remarks:
Six angels and twelve saints were named his clerks.

V

This was a handsome board – at least for heaven;
 And yet they had even then enough to do,
So many conquerors' cars were daily driven,
 So many kingdoms fitted up anew;
Each day, too, slew its thousands six or seven,
 Till at the crowning carnage, Waterloo,
They threw their pens down in divine disgust –
The page was so besmeared with blood and dust.

VI

This by the way; 'tis not mine to record
 What angels shrink from: even the very devil
On this occasion his own work abhorred,
 So surfeited with the infernal revel:
Though he himself had sharpened every sword,
 It almost quenched his innate thirst of evil.
(Here Satan's sole good work deserves insertion –
'Tis, that he has both generals in reversion.)

VII

Let's skip a few short years of hollow peace,
 Which peopled earth no better, hell as wont,
And heaven none – they form the tyrant's lease,
 With nothing but new names subscribed upon't;

'Twill one day finish: meantime they increase,
    'With seven heads and ten horns,' and all in front,
Like Saint John's foretold beast; but ours are born
    Less formidable in the head than horn.

### VIII

In the first year of freedom's second dawn
    Died George the Third; although no tyrant, one
Who shielded tyrants, till each sense withdrawn
    Left him nor mental nor external sun:
A better farmer ne'er brushed dew from lawn,
    A worse king never left a realm undone!
    He died – but left his subjects still behind,
One half as mad – and 'tother no less blind.

### IX

He died! – his death made no great stir on earth;
    His burial made some pomp; there was profusion
Of velvet, gilding, brass, and no great dearth
    Of aught but tears – save those shed by collusion
For these things may be bought at their true worth;
    Of elegy there was the due infusion –
Bought also; and the torches, cloaks and banners,
Heralds, and relics of old Gothic manners,

### X

Formed a sepulchral melodrame. Of all
    The fools who flocked to swell or see the show,
Who cared about the corpse? The funeral
    Made the attraction, and the black the woe.
There throbbed not there a thought which pierced the pall;
    And when the gorgeous coffin was laid low,
It seemed the mockery of hell to fold
The rottenness of eighty years in gold.

### XI

So mix his body with the dust! It might
  Return to what it *must* far sooner, were
The natural compound left alone to fight
  Its way back into earth, and fire, and air;
But the unnatural balsams merely blight
  What nature made him at his birth, as bare
As the mere million's base unmummied clay –
Yet all his spices but prolong decay.

### XII

He's dead – and upper earth with him has done;
  He's buried; save the undertaker's bill,
Or lapidary scrawl, the world is gone
  For him, unless he left a German will;
But where's the proctor who will ask his son?
  In whom his qualities are reigning still,
Except that household virtue, most uncommon,
Of constancy to a bad, ugly woman.

### XIII

'God save the king!' It is a large economy
  In God to save the like; but if he will
Be saving, all the better; for not one am I
  Of those who think damnation better still:
I hardly know too if not quite alone am I
  In this small hope of bettering future ill
By circumscribing, with some slight restriction,
The eternity of hell's hot jurisdiction.

### XIV

I know this is unpopular; I know
  'Tis blasphemous; I know one may be damned
For hoping no one else may e'er be so;
  I know my catechism; I know we are crammed

With the best doctrines till we quite o'erflow;
  I know that all save England's church have shammed,
And that the other twice two hundred churches
And synagogues have made a *damned* bad purchase.

### XV

God help us all! God help me too! I am,
  God knows, as helpless as the devil can wish,
And not a whit more difficult to damn,
  Than is to bring to land a late-hooked fish,
Or to the butcher to purvey the lamb;
  Not that I'm fit for such a noble dish,
As one day will be that immortal fry
Of almost every body born to die.

### XVI

Saint Peter sat by the celestial gate,
  And nodded o'er his keys; when, lo! there came
A wondrous noise he had not heard of late –
  A rushing sound of wind, and stream, and flame;
In short, a roar of things extremely great,
  Which would have made aught save a saint exclaim;
But he, with first a start and then a wink,
Said, 'There's another star gone out, I think!'

### XVII

But ere he could return to his repose,
  A cherub flapped his right wing o'er his eyes –
At which Saint Peter yawned, and rubbed his nose:
  'Saint porter,' said the angel, 'prithee rise!'
Waving a goodly wing, which glowed, as glows
  An earthly peacock's tail, with heavenly dyes;
To which the saint replied, 'Well, what's the matter?
Is Lucifer come back with all this clatter?'

### XVIII

'No,' quoth the cherub; 'George the Third is dead.'
  'And who *is* George the Third?' replied the apostle:
'*What George! What Third!*' 'The king of England,' said
  The angel. 'Well! he won't find kings to jostle
Him on his way; but does he wear his head?
  Because the last we saw here had a tussle,
And ne'er would have got into heaven's good graces,
Had he not flung his head in all our faces.

### XIX

'He was, if I remember, king of France;
  That head of his, which could not keep a crown
On earth, yet ventured in my face to advance
  A claim to those of martyrs – like my own:
If I had had my sword, as I had once
  When I cut ears off, I had cut him down;
But having but my *keys*, and not my brand,
I only knocked his head from out his hand.

### XX

'And then he set up such a headless howl,
  That all the saints came out and took him in;
And there he sits by St Paul, cheek by jowl;
  That fellow Paul – the parvenu! The skin
Of Saint Bartholomew, which makes his cowl
  In heaven, and upon earth redeemed his sin,
So as to make a martyr, never sped
Better than did this weak and wooden head.

### XXI

'But had it come up here upon its shoulders,
  There would have been a different tale to tell:
The fellow-feeling in the saints beholders
  Seems to have acted on them like a spell;

And so this very foolish head heaven solders
   Back on its trunk: it may be very well,
And seems the custom here to overthrow
Whatever has been wisely done below.'

### XXII

The angel answered, 'Peter! do not pout:
   The king who comes has head and all entire,
And never knew much what it was about –
   He did as doth the puppet – by its wire,
And will be judged like all the rest, no doubt:
   My business and your own is not to inquire
Into such matters, but to mind our cue –
Which is to act as we are bid to do.'

### XXIII

While thus they spake, the angelic caravan,
   Arriving like a rush of mighty wind,
Cleaving the fields of space, as doth the swan
   Some silver stream (say Ganges, Nile, or Inde,
Or Thames, or Tweed), and 'midst them an old man
   With an old soul, and both extremely blind,
Halted before the gate, and in his shroud
Seated their fellow-traveller on a cloud.

### XXIV

But bringing up the rear of this bright host
   A Spirit of a different aspect waved
His wings, like thunder-clouds above some coast
   Whose barren beach with frequent wrecks is paved;
His brow was like the deep when tempest-tossed;
   Fierce and unfathomable thoughts engraved
Eternal wrath on his immortal face,
And *where* he gazed a gloom pervaded space.

### XXV

As he drew near, he gazed upon the gate
  Ne'er to be entered more by him or Sin,
With such a glance of supernatural hate,
  As made Saint Peter wish himself within;
He pottered with his keys at a great rate,
  And sweated through his apostolic skin:
Of course his perspiration was but ichor,
Or some such other spiritual liquor.

### XXVI

The very cherubs huddled all together,
  Like birds when soars the falcon; and they felt
A tingling to the tip of every feather,
  And formed a circle like Orion's belt
Around their poor old charge; who scarce knew whither
  His guards had led him, though they gently dealt
With royal manes (for by many stories,
And true, we learn the angels all are Tories).

### XXVII

As things were in this posture, the gate flew
  Asunder, and the flashing of its hinges
Flung over space an universal hue
  Of many-coloured flame, until its tinges
Reached even our speck of earth, and made a new
  Aurora borealis spread its fringes
O'er the North Pole; the same seen, when ice-bound,
By Captain Parry's crew, in 'Melville's Sound.'

### XXVIII

And from the gate thrown open issued beaming
  A beautiful and mighty Thing of Light,
Radiant with glory, like a banner streaming
  Victorious from some world-o'erthrowing fight:

My poor comparisons must needs be teeming
　　With earthly likenesses, for here the night
Of clay obscures our best conceptions, saving
Johanna Southcote, or Bob Southey raving.

### XXIX

'Twas the archangel Michael: all men know
　　The make of angels and archangels, since
There's scarce a scribbler has not one to show,
　　From the fiends' leader to the angels' prince.
There also are some altar-pieces, though
　　I really can't say that they much evince
One's inner notions of immortal spirits;
But let the connoisseurs explain *their* merits.

### XXX

Michael flew forth in glory and in good;
　　A goodly work of him from whom all glory
And good arise; the portal past – he stood;
　　Before him the young cherubs and saints hoary –
(I say *young*, begging to be understood
　　By looks, not years; and should be very sorry
To state, they were not older than St Peter,
But merely that they seemed a little sweeter).

### XXXI

The cherubs and the saints bowed down before
　　That arch-angelic hierarch, the first
Of essences angelical who wore
　　The aspect of a god; but this ne'er nursed
Pride in his heavenly bosom, in whose core
　　No thought, save for his Maker's service, durst
Intrude, however glorified and high;
He knew him but the viceroy of the sky.

XXXII

He and the sombre, silent Spirit met —
   They knew each other both for good and ill;
Such was their power, that neither could forget
   His former friend and future foe; but still
There was a high, immortal, proud regret
   In either's eye, as if 'twere less their will
Than destiny to make the eternal years
Their date of war, and their 'champ clos' the spheres.

XXXIII

But here they were in neutral space: we know
   From Job, that Satan hath the power to pay
A heavenly visit thrice a — year or so;
   And that 'the sons of God', like those of clay,
Must keep him company; and we might show
   From the same book, in how polite a way
The dialogue is held between the Powers
Of Good and Evil — but 'twould take up hours.

XXXIV

And this is not a theologic tract,
   To prove with Hebrew and with Arabic,
If Job be allegory or a fact,
   But a true narrative; and thus I pick
From out the whole but such and such an act
   As sets aside the slightest thought of trick.
'Tis every tittle true, beyond suspicion,
And accurate as any other vision.

XXXV

The spirits were in neutral space, before
   The gate of heaven; like eastern thresholds is
The place where Death's grand cause is argued o'er,
   And souls despatched to that world or to this;

And therefore Michael and the other wore
  A civil aspect: though they did not kiss,
Yet still between his Darkness and his Brightness
There passed a mutual glance of great politeness.

### XXXVI

The Archangel bowed, not like a modern beau,
  But with a graceful oriental bend,
Pressing one radiant arm just where below
  The heart in good men is supposed to tend.
He turned as to an equal, not too low,
  But kindly; Satan met his ancient friend
With more hauteur, as might an old Castilian
Poor noble meet a mushroom rich civilian.

### XXXVII

He merely bent his diabolic brow
  An instant; and then raising it, he stood
In act to assert his right or wrong, and show
  Cause why King George by no means could or should
Make out a case to be exempt from woe
  Eternal, more than other kings, endued
With better sense and hearts, whom history mentions,
Who long have 'paved hell with their good intentions.'

### XXXVIII

Michael began: 'What wouldst thou with this man,
  Now dead, and brought before the Lord? What ill
Hath he wrought since his mortal race began,
  That thou canst claim him? Speak! and do thy will,
If it be just: if in this earthly span
  He hath been greatly failing to fulfil
His duties as a king and mortal, say,
And he is thine; if not, let him have way.'

### XXXIX

'Michael!' replied the Prince of Air, 'even here,
  Before the gate of him thou servest, must
I claim my subject: and will make appear
  That as he was my worshipper in dust,
So shall he be in spirit, although dear
  To thee and thine, because nor wine nor lust
Were of his weaknesses; yet on the throne
He reigned o'er millions to serve me alone.

### XL

'Look to *our* earth, or rather *mine*; it was,
  *Once, more* thy master's: but I triumph not
In this poor planet's conquest; nor, alas!
  Need he thou servest envy me my lot:
With all the myriads of bright worlds which pass
  In worship round him, he may have forgot
Yon weak creation of such paltry things:
I think few worth damnation save their kings, –

### XLI

'And these but as a kind of quit-rent, to
  Assert my right as lord; and even had
I such an inclination, 'twere (as you
  Well know) superfluous; they are grown so bad,
That hell has nothing better left to do
  Than leave them to themselves: so much more mad
And evil by their own internal curse,
Heaven cannot make them better, nor I worse.

### XLII

'Look to the earth, I said, and say again:
  When this old, blind, mad, helpless, weak, poor worm
Began in youth's first bloom and flush to reign,
  The world and he both wore a different form,

And much of earth and all the watery plain
  Of ocean called him king: through many a storm
His isles had floated on the abyss of time;
For the rough virtues chose them for their clime.

### XLIII

'He came to his sceptre young; he leaves it old:
  Look to the state in which he found his realm,
And left it; and his annals too behold,
  How to a minion first he gave the helm;
How grew upon his heart a thirst for gold,
  The beggar's vice, which can but overwhelm
The meanest hearts; and for the rest, but glance
Thine eye along America and France.

### XLIV

''Tis true, he was a tool from first to last
  (I have the workmen safe); but as a tool
So let him be consumed. From out the past
  Of ages, since mankind have known the rule
Of monarchs – from the bloody rolls amassed
  Of sin and slaughter – from the Caesars' school,
Take the worst pupil; and produce a reign
More drenched with gore, more cumbered with the slain

### XLV

'He ever warred with freedom and the free:
  Nations as men, home subjects, foreign foes,
So that they uttered the word "Liberty!"
  Found George the Third their first opponent. Whose
History was ever stained as his will be
  With national and individual woes?
I grant his household abstinence; I grant
His neutral virtues, which most monarchs want;

### XLVI

'I know he was a constant consort; own
  He was a decent sire, and middling lord.
All this is much, and most upon a throne;
  As temperance, if at Apicius' board,
Is more than at an anchorite's supper shown.
  I grant him all the kindest can accord;
And this was well for him, but not for those
Millions who found him what oppression chose.

### XLVII

'The New World shook him off; the Old yet groans
  Beneath what he and his prepared, if not
Completed: he leaves heirs on many thrones
  To all his vices, without what begot
Compassion for him – his tame virtues; drones
  Who sleep, or despots who have now forgot
A lesson which shall be re-taught them, wake
Upon the thrones of earth; but let them quake!

### XLVIII

'Five millions of the primitive, who hold
  The faith which makes ye great on earth, implored
A *part* of that vast *all* they held of old, –
  Freedom to worship – not alone your Lord,
Michael, but you, and you, Saint Peter! Cold
  Must be your souls, if you have not abhorred
The foe to Catholic participation
In all the license of a Christian nation.

### XLIX

'True! he allowed them to pray God: but as
  A consequence of prayer, refused the law
Which would have placed them upon the same base
  With those who did not hold the saints in awe.'

But here Saint Peter started from his place,
    And cried, 'You may the prisoner withdraw:
Ere heaven shall ope her portals to this Guelph,
While I am guard, may I be damned myself!

L

'Sooner will I with Cerberus exchange
    My office (and *his* is no sinecure)
Than see this royal Bedlam — bigot range
    The azure fields of heaven, of that be sure!'
'Saint!' replied Satan, 'you do well to avenge
    The wrongs he made your satellites endure;
And if to this exchange you should be given,
I'll try to coax *our* Cerberus up to heaven.'

LI

Here Michael interposed: 'Good saint! and devil!
    Pray, not so fast; you both outrun discretion.
Saint Peter! you were wont to be more civil:
    Satan! excuse this warmth of his expression,
And condescension to the vulgar's level:
    Even saints sometimes forget themselves in session.
Have you got more to say?' — 'No.' — 'If you please,
I'll trouble you to call your witnesses.'

LII

Then Satan turned and waved his swarthy hand,
    Which stirred with its electric qualities
Clouds farther off than we can understand,
    Although we find him sometimes in our skies;
Infernal thunder shook both sea and land
    In all the planets, and hell's batteries
Let off the artillery, which Milton mentions
As one of Satan's most sublime inventions.

### LIII

This was a signal unto such damned souls
  As have the privilege of their damnation
Extended far beyond the mere controls
  Of worlds past, present, or to come; no station
Is theirs particularly in the rolls
  Of hell assigned; but where their inclination
Or business carries them in search of game,
They may range freely – being damned the same.

### LIV

They are proud of this – as very well they may,
  It being a sort of knighthood, or gilt key
Stuck in their loins; or like to an 'entrée'
  Up the back stairs, or such free-masonry.
I borrow my comparisons from clay,
  Being clay myself. Let not those spirits be
Offended with such base low likenesses;
We know their posts are nobler far than these.

### LV

When the great signal ran from heaven to hell –
  About ten million times the distance reckoned
From our sun to its earth, as we can tell
  How much time it takes up, even to a second,
For every ray that travels to dispel
  The fogs of London, through which, dimly beaconed,
The weathercocks are gilt some thrice a year,
If that the *summer* is not too severe:

### LVI

I say that I can tell – 'twas half a minute:
  I know the solar beams take up more time
Ere, packed up for their journey, they begin it;
  But then their telegraph is less sublime,

And if they ran a race, they would not win it
  'Gainst Satan's couriers bound for their own clime.
The sun takes up some years for every ray
To reach its goal – the devil not half a day

### LVII

Upon the verge of space, about the size
  Of half-a-crown, a little speck appeared
(I've seen a something like it in the skies
  In the Aegean, ere a squall); it neared,
And, growing bigger, took another guise;
  Like an aërial ship it tacked, and steered,
Or *was* steered (I am doubtful of the grammar
Of the last phrase, which makes the stanza stammer;

### LVIII

But take your choice); and then it grew a cloud;
  And so it was – a cloud of witnesses.
But such a cloud! No land e'er saw a crowd
  Of locusts numerous as the heavens saw these;
They shadowed with their myriads space; their loud
  And varied cries were like those of wild geese
(If nations may be likened to a goose),
And realized the phrase of 'hell broke loose'.

### LIX

Here crashed a sturdy oath of stout John Bull,
  Who damned away his eyes as heretofore:
There Paddy brogued 'By Jasus!' – 'What's your wull?'
  The temperate Scot exclaimed: the French ghost swore
In certain terms I sha'n't translate in full,
  As the first coachman will; and 'midst the war,
The voice of Jonathan was heard to express,
'*Our* president is going to war, I guess.'

LX

Besides there were the Spaniard, Dutch, and Dane;
   In short, an universal shoal of shades,
From Otaheite's isle to Salisbury Plain,
   Of all climes and professions, years and trades,
Ready to swear against the good king's reign,
   Bitter as clubs in cards are against spades:
All summoned by this grand 'subpoena', to
Try if kings mayn't be damned like me or you.

LXI

When Michael saw this host, he first grew pale,
   As angels can; next, like Italian twilight,
He turned all colours — as a peacock's tail,
   Or sunset streaming through a Gothic skylight
In some old abbey, or a trout not stale,
   Or distant lightning on the horizon *by* night,
Or a fresh rainbow, or a grand review
Of thirty regiments in red, green, and blue.

LXII

Then he addressed himself to Satan: 'Why —
   My good old friend, for such I deem you, though
Our different parties make us fight so shy,
   I ne'er mistake you for a *personal* foe;
Our difference is *political*, and I
   Trust that, whatever may occur below,
You know my great respect for you: and this
Makes me regret whate'er you do amiss —

LXIII

'Why, my dear Lucifer, would you abuse
   My call for witnesses? I did not mean
That you should half of earth and hell produce;
   'Tis even superfluous, since two honest, clean,

True testimonies are enough: we lose
    Our time, nay, our eternity, between
The accusation and defence: if we
    Hear both, 'twill stretch our immortality.'

### LXIV

Satan replied, 'To me the matter is
    Indifferent, in a personal point of view:
I can have fifty better souls than this
    With far less trouble than we have gone through
Already; and I merely argued his
    Late majesty of Britain's case with you
Upon a point of form: you may dispose
Of him; I've kings enough below, God knows!'

### LXV

Thus spoke the Demon (late called 'multifaced'
    By multo-scribbling Southey). 'Then we'll call
One or two persons of the myriads placed
    Around our congress, and dispense with all
The rest,' quoth Michael. 'Who may be so graced
    As to speak first? There's choice enough – who shall
It be?' Then Satan answered, 'There are many;
But you may choose Jack Wilkes as well as any.'

### LXVI

A merry, cock-eyed, curious-looking sprite
    Upon the instant started from the throng,
Dressed in a fashion now forgotten quite;
    For all the fashions of the flesh stick long
By people in the next world; where unite
    All the costumes since Adam's, right or wrong,
From Eve's fig-leaf down to the petticoat,
Almost as scanty, of days less remote.

### LXVII

The spirit looked around upon the crowds
  Assembled, and exclaimed, 'My friends of all
The spheres, we shall catch cold amongst these clouds;
  So let's to business: why this general call?
If those are freeholders I see in shrouds,
  And 'tis for an election that they bawl,
Behold a candidate with unturned coat!
Saint Peter, may I count upon your vote?'

### LXVIII

'Sir,' replied Michael, 'you mistake; these things
  Are of a former life, and what we do
Above is more august; to judge of kings
  Is the tribunal met: so now you know.'
'Then I presume those gentlemen with wings,'
  Said Wilkes, 'are cherubs; and that soul below
Looks much like George the Third, but to my mind
A good deal older – Bless me! is he blind?'

### LXIX

'He is what you behold him, and his doom
  Depends upon his deeds,' the Angel said: .
'If you have aught to arraign in him, the tomb
  Gives license to the humblest beggar's head
To lift itself against the loftiest.' – 'Some,'
  Said Wilkes, 'don't wait to see them laid in lead,
For such a liberty – and I, for one,
Have told them what I thought beneath the sun.'

### LXX

'*Above* the sun repeat, then, what thou hast
  To urge against him,' said the Archangel. 'Why,'
Replied the spirit, 'since old scores are past,
  Must I turn evidence? In faith, not I.

Besides, I beat him hollow at the last,
　　With all his Lords and Commons: in the sky
I don't like ripping up old stories, since
His conduct was but natural in a prince.

### LXXI

'Foolish, no doubt, and wicked, to oppress
　　A poor unlucky devil without a shilling;
But then I blame the man himself much less
　　Than Bute and Grafton, and shall be unwilling
To see him punished here for their excess,
　　Since they were both damned long ago, and still in
Their place below: for me, I have forgiven,
And vote his "*habeas corpus*" into heaven.'

### LXXII

'Wilkes,' said the Devil, 'I understand all this;
　　You turned to half a courtier ere you died,
And seem to think it would not be amiss
　　To grow a whole one on the other side
Of Charon's ferry; you forget that *his*
　　Reign is concluded; whatsoe'er betide,
He won't be sovereign more: you've lost your labour,
For at the best he will but be your neighbour.

### LXXIII

'However, I knew what to think of it,
　　When I beheld you in your jesting way,
Flitting and whispering round about the spit
　　Where Belial, upon duty for the day,
With Fox's lard was basting William Pitt
　　His pupil; I knew what to think, I say:
That fellow even in hell breeds farther ills;
I'll have him *gagged* – 'twas one of his own bills.

### LXXIV

'Call Junius!' From the crowd a shadow stalked,
  And at the name there was a general squeeze,
So that the very ghosts no longer walked
  In comfort, at their own aërial ease,
But were all rammed, and jammed (but to be balked,
  As we shall see), and jostled hands and knees,
Like wind compressed and pent within a bladder.
Or like a human colic, which is sadder.

### LXXV

The shadow came – a tall, thin, grey-haired figure,
  That looked as it had been a shade on earth;
Quick in its motions, with an air of vigour,
  But nought to mark its breeding or its birth:
Now it waxed little, then again grew bigger,
  With now an air of gloom, or savage mirth;
But as you gazed upon its features, they
Changed every instant – to *what*, none could say.

### LXXVI

The more intently the ghosts gazed, the less
  Could they distinguish whose the features were;
The Devil himself seemed puzzled even to guess;
  They varied like a dream – now here, now there;
And several people swore from out the press,
  They knew him perfectly; and one could swear
He was his father: upon which another
Was sure he was his mother's cousin's brother:

### LXXVII

Another, that he was a duke, or knight,
  An orator, a lawyer, or a priest,
A nabob, a man-midwife: but the wight
  Mysterious changed his countenance at least

As oft as they their minds: though in full sight
   He stood, the puzzle only was increased;
The man was a phantasmagoria in
Himself – he was so volatile and thin.

### LXXVIII

The moment that you had pronounced him *one*,
   Presto! his face changed, and he was another;
And when that change was hardly well put on,
   It varied, till I don't think his own mother
(If that he had a mother) would her son
   Have known, he shifted so from one to t'other;
Till guessing from a pleasure grew a task,
At this epistolary 'Iron Mask'.

### LXXIX

For sometimes he like Cerberus would seem –
   'Three gentlemen, at once' (as sagely says
Good Mrs Malaprop); then you might deem
   That he was not even *one*; now many rays
Were flashing round him; and now a thick steam
   Hid him from sight – like fogs on London days:
Now Burke, now Tooke, he grew to people's fancies,
And certes often like Sir Philip Francis.

### LXXX

I've an hypothesis – 'tis quite my own;
   I never let it out till now, for fear
Of doing people harm about the throne,
   And injuring some minister or peer,
On whom the stigma might perhaps be blown:
   It is – my gentle public, lend thine ear!
'Tis that what Junius we are wont to call
Was *really*, *truly*, nobody at all.

### LXXXI

I don't see wherefore letters should not be
 Written without hands, since we daily view
Them written without heads; and books, we see,
 Are filled as well without the latter too:
And really till we fix on somebody
 For certain sure to claim them as his due,
Their author, like the Niger's mouth, will bother
The world to say if *there* be mouth or author.

### LXXXII

'And who and what art thou?' the Archangel said.
 'For *that* you may consult my title-page,'
Replied this mighty shadow of a shade:
 'If I have kept my secret half an age,
I scarce shall tell it now.' – 'Canst thou upbraid,'
 Continued Michael, 'George Rex, or allege
Aught further?' Junius answered, 'You had better
First ask him for *his* answer to my letter:

### LXXXIII

'My charges upon record will outlast
 The brass of both his epitaph and tomb.'
'Repent'st thou not,' said Michael, 'of some past
 Exaggeration? something which may doom
Thyself if false, as him if true? Thou wast
 Too bitter – is it not so? – in thy gloom
Of passion?' – 'Passion!' cried the phantom dim,
'I loved my country, and I hated him.

### LXXXIV

'What I have written, I have written: let
 The rest be on his head or mine!' So spoke
Old 'Nominis Umbra'; and while speaking yet,
 Away he melted in celestial smoke.

Then Satan said to Michael, 'Don't forget
   To call George Washington and John Horne Tooke,
And Franklin'; – but at this time there was heard
A cry for room, though not a phantom stirred.

### LXXXV

At length with jostling, elbowing, and the aid
   Of cherubim appointed to that post,
The devil Asmodeus to the circle made
   His way, and looked as if his journey cost
Some trouble. When his burden down he laid,
   'What's this?' cried Michael; 'why, 'tis not a ghost?
'I know it,' quoth the incubus; 'but he
Shall be one, if you leave the affair to me.

### LXXXVI

'Confound the renegado! I have sprained
   My left wing, he's so heavy; one would think
Some of his works about his neck were chained.
   But to the point; hovering o'er the brink
Of Skiddaw (where as usual it still rained),
   I saw a taper, far below me, wink,
And stooping, caught this fellow at a libel –
No less on history than the Holy Bible.

### LXXXVII

'The former is the devil's scripture, and
   The latter yours, good Michael; so the affair
Belongs to all of us, you understand.
   I snatched him up just as you see him there,
And brought him off for sentence out of hand:
   I've scarcely been ten minutes in the air –
At least a quarter it can hardly be:
I dare say that his wife is still at tea.'

### LXXXVIII

Here Satan said, 'I know this man of old,
   And have expected him for some time here;
A sillier fellow you will scarce behold,
   Or more conceited in his petty sphere:
But surely it was not worth while to fold
   Such trash below your wing, Asmodeus dear:
We had the poor wretch safe (without being bored
With carriage) coming of his own accord.

### LXXXIX

'But since he's here, let's see what he has done.'
   'Done!' cried Asmodeus, 'he anticipates
The very business you are now upon,
   And scribbles as if head clerk to the Fates.
Who knows to what his ribaldry may run,
   When such an ass as this, like Balaam's, prates?'
'Let's hear,' quoth Michael, 'what he has to say:
You know we're bound to that in every way.'

### XC

Now the bard, glad to get an audience, which
   By no means often was his case below,
Began to cough, and hawk, and hem, and pitch
   His voice into that awful note of woe
To all unhappy hearers within reach
   Of poets when the tide of rhyme's in flow;
But stuck fast with his first hexameter,
Not one of all whose gouty feet would stir.

### XCI

But ere the spavined dactyls could be spurred
   Into recitative, in great dismay,
Both cherubim and seraphim were heard
   To murmur loudly through their long array;

And Michael rose ere he could get a word
   Of all his foundered verses under way,
And cried, 'For God's sake, stop, my friend! 'twere best –
*Non Di, non homines* – you know the rest.'

#### XCII

A general bustle spread throughout the throng,
   Which seemed to hold all verse in detestation;
The angels had of course enough of song
   When upon service; and the generation
Of ghosts had heard too much in life, not long
   Before, to profit by a new occasion;
The monarch, mute till then, exclaimed, 'What! what!
   *Pye* come again? No more – no more of that!'

#### XCIII

The tumult grew; an universal cough
   Convulsed the skies, as during a debate,
When Castlereagh has been up long enough
   (Before he was first minister of state,
I mean – the *slaves hear now*); some cried 'Off, off!'
   As at a farce; till, grown quite desperate,
The Bard Saint Peter prayed to interpose
(Himself an author) only for his prose.

#### XCIV

The varlet was not an ill-favoured knave;
   A good deal like a vulture in the face,
With a hook nose and a hawk's eye, which gave
   A smart and sharper-looking sort of grace
To his whole aspect, which, though rather grave,
   Was by no means so ugly as his case;
But that indeed was hopeless as can be,
Quite a poetic felony '*de se*'.

### XCV

Then Michael blew his trump, and stilled the noise
   With one still greater, as is yet the mode
On earth besides; except some grumbling voice,
   Which now and then will make a slight inroad
Upon decorous silence, few will twice
   Lift up their lungs when fairly overcrowded;
And now the bard could plead his own bad cause,
With all the attitudes of self-applause.

### XCVI

He said – (I only give the heads) – he said,
   He meant no harm in scribbling; 'twas his way
Upon all topics; 'twas, besides, his bread,
   Of which he buttered both sides; 'twould delay
Too long the assembly.(he was pleased to dread),
   And take up rather more time than a day,
To name his works – he would but cite a few –
'Wat Tyler' – 'Rhymes on Blenheim' – 'Waterloo'.

### XCVII

He had written praises of a regicide;
   He had written praises of all kings whatever;
He had written for republics far and wide,
   And then against them bitterer than ever;
For pantisocracy he once had cried
   Aloud, a scheme less moral than 'twas clever;
Then grew a hearty anti-jacobin –
Had turned his coat – and would have turned his skin.

### XCVIII

He had sung against all battles, and again
   In their high praise and glory; he had called
Reviewing 'the ungentle craft', and then
   Become as base a critic as e'er crawled –

Fed, paid, and pampered by the very men
   By whom his muse and morals had been mauled:
He had written much blank verse, and blanker prose,
And more of both than any body knows.

### XCIX

He had written Wesley's life: – here turning round
   To Satan, 'Sir, I'm ready to write yours,
In two octavo volumes, nicely bound,
   With notes and preface, all that most allures
The pious purchaser; and there's no ground
   For fear, for I can choose my own reviewers:
So let me have the proper documents
That I may add you to my other saints.'

### C

Satan bowed, and was silent. 'Well, if you,
   With amiable modesty, decline
My offer, what says Michael? There are few
   Whose memoirs could be rendered more divine.
Mine is a pen of all work; not so new
   As it was once, but I would make you shine
Like your own trumpet. By the way, my own
Has more of brass in it, and is as well blown.

### CI

'But talking about trumpets, here's my "Vision"!
   Now you shall judge, all people; yes, you shall
Judge with my judgment, and by my decision
   Be guided who shall enter heaven or fall.
I settle all these things by intuition,
   Times present, past, to come, heaven, hell, and all,
Like king Alfonso. When I thus see double,
I save the Deity some words of trouble.'

CII

He ceased, and drew forth an MS.; and no
   Persuasion on the part of devils, or saints,
Or angels, now could stop the torrent; so
   He read the first three lines of the contents;
But at the fourth, the whole spiritual show
   Had vanished, with variety of scents,
Ambrosial and sulphureous, as they sprang,
Like lightning, off from his 'melodious twang'.

CIII

Those grand heroics acted as a spell;
   The angels stopped their ears and plied their pinions;
The devils ran howling, deafened, down to hell;
   The ghosts fled, gibbering, for their own dominions –
(For 'tis not yet decided where they dwell,
   And I leave every man to his opinions);
Michael took refuge in his trump – but, lo!
His teeth were set on edge, he could not blow!

CIV

Saint Peter, who has hitherto been known
   For an impetuous saint, upraised his keys,
And at the fifth line knocked the poet down;
   Who fell like Phaeton, but more at ease,
Into his lake, for there he did not drown;
   A different web being by the Destinies
Woven for the Laureate's final wreath, whene'er
Reform shall happen either here or there.

CV

He first sank to the bottom – like his works,
   But soon rose to the surface – like himself;
For all corrupted things are buoyed like corks,
   By their own rottenness, light as an elf,

Or wisp that flits o'er a morass: he lurks,
   It may be, still, like dull books on a shelf,
In his own den, to scrawl some 'Life' or 'Vision',
As Welborn says – 'the devil turned precisian'.

### CVI

As for the rest, to come to the conclusion
   Of this true dream, the telescope is gone
Which kept my optics free from all delusion,
   And showed me what I in my turn have shown;
All I saw farther, in the last confusion,
   Was, that King George slipped into heaven for one;
And when the tumult dwindled to a calm,
I left him practising the hundredth psalm.

# CHILDE HAROLD'S PILGRIMAGE

## A ROMAUNT

### *From Canto I*

#### I

Oh, thou! in Hellas deemed of heavenly birth,
Muse! formed or fabled at the minstrel's will!
Since shamed full oft by later lyres on earth,
Mine dares not call thee from thy sacred hill:
Yet there I've wandered by thy vaunted rill;
Yes! sighed o'er Delphi's long deserted shrine,
Where, save that feeble fountain, all is still;
Nor mote my shell awake the weary Nine
To grace so plain a tale – this lowly lay of mine.

#### II

Whilome in Albion's isle there dwelt a youth,
Who ne in virtue's ways did take delight;
But spent his days in riot most uncouth,
And vexed with mirth the drowsy ear of night.
Ah, me! in sooth he was a shameless wight,
Sore given to revel and ungodly glee;
Few earthly things found favour in his sight
Save concubines and carnal companie,
And flaunting wassailers of high and low degree.

#### III

Childe Harold was he hight: – but whence his name
And lineage long, it suits me not say;
Suffice it, that perchance they were of fame,
And had been glorious in another day:

But one sad losel soils a name for aye,
However mighty in the olden time;
Nor all that heralds rake from coffined clay,
Nor florid prose, nor honied lies of rhyme,
Can blazon evil deeds, or consecrate a crime.

IV

Childe Harolde basked him in the noontide sun,
Disporting there like any other fly;
Nor deemed before his little day was done
One blast might chill him into misery.
But long ere scarce a third of his passed by,
Worse than adversity the Childe befell;
He felt the fulness of satiety:
Then loathed he in his native land to dwell,
Which seemed to him more lone than Eremite's sad cell.

V

For he through Sin's long labyrinth had run,
Nor made atonement when he did amiss,
Had sighed to many though he loved but one,
And that loved one, alas! could ne'er be his.
Ah, happy she! to 'scape from him whose kiss
Had been pollution unto aught so chaste;
Who soon had left her charms for vulgar bliss,
And spoiled her goodly lands to gild his waste,
Nor calm domestic peace had ever deigned to taste.

VI

And now Childe Harold was sore sick at heart,
And from his fellow bacchanals would flee;
'Tis said, at times the sullen tear would start,
But pride congealed the drop within his ee:

Apart he stalked in joyless reverie,
And from his native land resolved to go,
And visit scorching climes beyond the sea;
With pleasure drugged, he almost longed for woe,
And e'en for change of scene would seek the shades
   below.

### VII

The Childe departed from his father's hall:
It was a vast and venerable pile;
So old, it seeméd only not to fall,
Yet strength was pillared in each massy aisle.
Monastic dome! condemned to uses vile!
Where superstition once had made her den
Now Paphian girls were known to sing and smile;
And monks might deem their time was come agen,
If ancient tales say true, nor wrong these holy men.

### VIII

Yet oft-times in his maddest mirthful mood
Strange pangs would flash along Childe Harold's brow,
As if the memory of some deadly feud
Or disappointed passion lurked below:
But this none knew, nor haply cared to know;
For his was not that open, artless soul
That feels relief by bidding sorrow flow,
Nor sought he friend to counsel or condole,
Whate'er this grief mote be, which he could not control.

### IX

And none did love him! — though to hall and bower
He gathered revellers from far and near,
He knew them flatterers of the festal hour;
The heartless parasites of present cheer.

Yea! none did love him – not his lemans dear –
But pomp and power alone are woman's care,
And where these are light Eros finds a feere;
Maidens, like moths, are ever caught by glare,
And Mammon wins his way where Seraphs might
    despair.

X

Childe Harold had a mother – not forgot,
Though parting from that mother he did shun;
A sister whom he loved, but saw her not
Before his weary pilgrimage begun:
If friends he had, he bade adieu to none.
Yet deem not thence his breast a breast of steel:
Ye, who have known what 'tis to dote upon
A few dear objects, will in sadness feel
Such partings break the heart they fondly hope to heal.

XI

His house, his home, his heritage, his lands,
The laughing dames in whom he did delight,
Whose large blue eyes, fair locks, and snowy hands,
Might shake the saintship of an anchorite,
And long had fed his youthful appetite;
His goblets brimmed with every costly wine,
And all that mote to luxury invite,
Without a sigh, he left to cross the brine,
And traverse Paynim shores, and pass Earth's central
    line.

XII

The sails were filled, and fair the light winds blew,
As glad to waft him from his native home;
And fast the white rocks faded from his view,
And soon were lost in circumambient foam:

And then, it may be, of his wish to roam
Repented he, but in his bosom slept
The silent thought, nor from his lips did come
One word of wail, whilst others sate and wept,
And to the reckless gales unmanly moaning kept.

### XIII

But when the sun was sinking in the sea
He seized his harp, which he at times could string,
And strike, albeit with untaught melody,
When deemed he no strange ear was listening:
And now his fingers o'er it he did fling,
And tuned his farewell in the dim twilight.
While flew the vessel on her snowy wing,
And fleeting shores receded from his sight,
Thus to the elements he poured his last 'Good Night'.

'ADIEU, adieu! my native shore
    Fades o'er the waters blue;
The night-winds sigh, the breakers roar,
    And shrieks the wild sea-mew.
Yon sun that sets upon the sea
    We follow in his flight;
Farewell awhile to him and thee,
    My native land – Good Night!

' A few short hours and he will rise
    To give the morrow birth;
And I shall hail the main and skies,
    But not my mother earth.
Deserted is my own good hall,
    Its hearth is desolate;
Wild weeds are gathering on the wall;
    My dog howls at the gate.

'Come hither, hither, my little page!
  Why dost thou weep and wail?
Or dost thou dread the billows' rage,
  Or tremble at the gale?
But dash the tear-drop from thine eye;
  Our ship is swift and strong:
Our fleetest falcon scarce can fly
  More merrily along.'

'Let winds be shrill, let waves roll high,
  I fear not wave nor wind:
Yet marvel not, Sir Childe, that I
  Am sorrowful in mind;
For I have from my father gone,
  A mother whom I love,
And have no friend, save these alone,
  But thee – and One above.

'My father blessed me fervently,
  Yet did not much complain;
But sorely will my mother sigh
  Till I come back again.' –
'Enough, enough, my little lad!
  Such tears become thine eye;
If I thy guileless bosom had,
  Mine own would not be dry.

'Come hither, hither, my staunch yeoman,
  Why dost thou look so pale?
Or dost thou dread a French foeman?
  Or shiver at the gale?' –
'Deemest thou I tremble for my life?
  Sir Childe, I'm not so weak;
But thinking on an absent wife
  Will blanch a faithful cheek.

'My spouse and boys dwell near thy hall,
    Along the bordering lake,
And when they on their father call,
    What answer shall she make?' –
'Enough, enough, my yeoman good,
    Thy grief let none gainsay;
But I, who am of lighter mood,
    Will laugh to flee away.

'For who would trust the seeming sighs
    Of wife or paramour?
Fresh feres will dry the bright blue eyes
    We late saw streaming o'er.
For pleasures past I do not grieve,
    Nor perils gathering near;
My greatest grief is that I leave
    No thing that claims a tear.

'And now I'm in the world alone,
    Upon the wide, wide sea:
But why should I for others groan,
    When none will sigh for me?
Perchance my dog will whine in vain,
    Till fed by stranger hands;
But long ere I come back again
    He'd tear me where he stands.

'With thee, my bark, I'll swiftly go
    Athwart the foaming brine;
Nor care what land thou bear'st me to,
    So not again to mine.
Welcome, welcome, ye dark-blue waves!
    And when you fail my sight,
Welcome, ye deserts, and ye caves!
    My native land – Good Night!' ...

## From Canto III

### XXI

There was a sound of revelry by night,
And Belgium's capital had gathered then
Her Beauty and her Chivalry – and bright
The lamps shone o'er fair women and brave men;
A thousand hearts beat happily; and when
Music arose with its voluptuous swell,
Soft eyes looked love to eyes which spake again,
And all went merry as a marriage bell;
But hush! hark! a deep sound strikes like a rising knell!

### XXII

Did ye not hear it? – No; 'twas but the wind,
Or the car rattling o'er the stony street;
On with the dance! let joy be unconfined;
No sleep till morn, when youth and pleasure meet
To chase the glowing hours with flying feet –
But, hark! – that heavy sound breaks in once more,
As if the clouds its echo would repeat;
And nearer, clearer, deadlier than before!
Arm! arm! it is – it is – the cannon's opening roar!

### XXIII

Within a windowed niche of that high hall
Sate Brunswick's fated chieftain; he did hear
That sound the first amidst the festival,
And caught its tone with death's prophetic ear;
And when they smiled because he deemed it near,

His heart more truly knew that peal too well
Which stretched his father on a bloody bier,
And roused the vengeance blood alone could quell:
He rushed into the field, and, foremost fighting, fell.


### XXIV

Ah! then and there was hurrying to and fro,
And gathering tears, and tremblings of distress,
And cheeks all pale, which but an hour ago
Blushed at the praise of their own loveliness;
And there were sudden partings, such as press
The life from out young hearts, and choking sighs
Which ne'er might be repeated; who could guess
If ever more should meet those mutual eyes,
Since upon night so sweet such awful morn could rise!


### XXV

And there was mounting in hot haste – the steed,
The mustering squadron, and the clattering car,
Went pouring forward with impetuous speed,
And swiftly forming in the ranks of war;
And the deep thunder peal on peal afar;
And near, the beat of the alarming drum
Roused up the soldier ere the morning star;
While thronged the citizens with terror dumb,
Or whispering with white lips – 'The foe! They come!
    they come!'


### XXVI

And wild and high the 'Cameron's gathering' rose!
The war-note of Lochiel, which Albyn's hills
Have heard, and heard, too, have her Saxon foes: –
How in the noon of night that pibroch thrills,

Savage and shrill! But with the breath which fills
Their mountain-pipe, so fill the mountaineers
With the fierce native daring which instils
The stirring memory of a thousand years,
And Evan's, Donald's fame rings in each clansman's ears!

### XXVII

And Ardennes waves above them her green leaves,
Dewy with nature's tear-drops, as they pass,
Grieving, if aught inanimate e'er grieves,
Over the unreturning brave, – alas!
Ere evening to be trodden like the grass
Which now beneath them, but above shall grow
In its next verdure, when this fiery mass
Of living valour, rolling on the foe,
And burning with high hope, shall moulder cold and low.

### XXVIII

Last noon beheld them full of lusty life,
Last eve in beauty's circle proudly gay,
The midnight brought the signal-sound of strife,
The morn the marshalling in arms, – the day
Battle's magnificently-stern array!
The thunder-clouds close o'er it, which when rent
The earth is covered thick with other clay,
Which her own clay shall cover, heaped and pent,
Rider and horse, – friend, foe, – in one red burial blent!...

### CXIII

I have not loved the world, nor the world me;
I have not flattered its rank breath, nor bowed
To its idolatries a patient knee,
Nor coined my cheek to smiles, – nor cried aloud

In worship of an echo; in the crowd
They could not deem me one of such – I stood
Among them, but not of them – in a shroud
Of thoughts which were not their thoughts, and still could,
Had I not filed my mind, which thus itself subdued.

### CXIV

I have not loved the world, nor the world me, –
But let us part fair foes; I do believe,
Though I have found them not, that there may be
Words which are things, – hopes which will not deceive,
And virtues which are merciful, nor weave
Snares for the failing: I would also deem
O'er others' griefs that some sincerely grieve;
That two, or one, are almost what they seem, –
That goodness is no name, and happiness no dream. ...

## *From Canto IV*

### I

I STOOD in Venice, on the Bridge of Sighs;
A palace and a prison on each hand:
I saw from out the wave her structures rise
As from the stroke of the enchanter's wand:
A thousand years their cloudy wings expand
Around me, and a dying glory smiles
O'er the far times, when many a subject land
Looked to the wingéd Lion's marble piles,
Where Venice sate in state, throned on her hundred isles!

### II

She looks a sea Cybele, fresh from ocean,
Rising with her tiara of proud towers
At airy distance, with majestic motion,
A ruler of the waters and their powers:

And such she was; – her daughters had their dowers
From spoils of nations, and the exhaustless East
Poured in her lap all gems in sparkling showers.
In purple was she robed, and of her feast
Monarchs partook, and deemed their dignity increased

### III

In Venice Tasso's echoes are no more.
And silent rows the songless gondolier·
Her palaces are crumbling to the shore,
And music meets not always now the ear·
Those days are gone – the beauty still is here.
States fall, arts fade – but nature doth not die,
Nor yet forget how Venice once was dear,
The pleasant place of all festivity,
The revel of the earth – the masque of Italy!

### IV

But unto us she hath a spell beyond
Her name in story, and her long array
Of mighty shadows, whose dim forms despond
Above the Dogeless city's vanished sway;
Ours is a trophy which will not decay
With the Rialto; Shylock and the Moor,
And Pierre, can not be swept or worn away –
The keystones of the arch! though all were o'er,
For us repeopled were the solitary shore....

### XI

The spouseless Adriatic mourns her lord,
And annual marriage now no more renewed,
The Bucentaur lies rotting unrestored,
Neglected garment of her widowhood!

St Mark yet sees his Lion where he stood
Stand, but in mockery of his withered power,
Over the proud place where an Emperor sued,
And monarchs gazed and envied in the hour
When Venice was a queen with an unequalled dower.

### XII

The Suabian sued, and now the Austrian reigns –
An Emperor tramples where an Emperor knelt;
Kingdoms are shrunk to provinces, and chains
Clank over sceptred cities; nations melt
From power's high pinnacle, when they have felt
The sunshine for a while, and downward go
Like lauwine loosened from the mountain's belt;
Oh for one hour of blind old Dandolo!
Th' octogenarian chief, Byzantium's conquering foe.

### XIII

Before St Mark still glow his steeds of brass,
Their gilded collars glittering in the sun;
But is not Doria's menace come to pass?
Are they not bridled? – Venice, lost and won,
Her thirteen hundred years of freedom done,
Sinks, like a sea-weed, unto whence she rose!
Better be whelmed beneath the waves, and shun,
Even in destruction's depth, her foreign foes,
From whom submission wrings an infamous repose.

### XIV

In youth she was all glory – a new Tyre –
Her very by-word sprung from victory,
The 'Planter of the Lion', which through fire
And blood she bore o'er subject earth and sea;

Though making many slaves, herself still free,
And Europe's bulwark 'gainst the Ottomite;
Witness Troy's rival, Candia! Vouch it, ye
Immortal waves that saw Lepanto's fight!
For ye are names no time nor tyranny can blight.

### XV

Statues of glass – all shivered – the long file
Of her dead Doges are declined to dust;
But where they dwelt, the vast and sumptuous pile
Bespeaks the pageant of their splendid trust;
Their sceptre broken, and their sword in rust,
Have yielded to the stranger: empty halls,
Thin streets, and foreign aspects, such as must
Too oft remind her who and what enthrals,
Have flung a desolate cloud o'er Venice' lovely walls.

### XVI

When Athens' armies fell at Syracuse,
And fettered thousands bore the yoke of war,
Redemption rose up in the Attic Muse,
Her voice their only ransom from afar:
See! as they chant the tragic hymn, the car
Of the o'ermastered victor stops, the reins
Fall from his hands – his idle scimitar
Starts from its belt – he rends his captive's chains,
And bids him thank the bard for freedom and his strains.

### XVII

Thus, Venice! if no stronger claim were thine,
Were all thy proud historic deeds forgot –
Thy choral memory of the Bard divine,
Thy love of Tasso, should have cut the knot

Which ties thee to thy tyrants; and thy lot
Is shameful to the nations – most of all,
Albion! to thee: the Ocean queen should not
Abandon Ocean's children; in the fall
Of Venice think of thine, despite thy watery wall.


### XVIII

I loved her from my boyhood – she to me
Was as a fairy city of the heart,
Rising like water-columns from the sea –
Of joy the sojourn, and of wealth the mart;
And Otway, Radcliffe, Schiller, Shakespeare's art,
Had stamped her image in me, and even so,
Although I found her thus, we did not part;
Perchance even dearer in her day of woe,
Than when she was a boast, a marvel, and a show. . . .


### XXVI

The commonwealth of kings – the men of Rome!
And even since, and now, fair Italy!
Thou art the garden of the world, the home
Of all art yields, and nature can decree;
Even in thy desert, what is like to thee?
Thy very weeds are beautiful – thy waste
More rich than other climes fertility;
Thy wreck a glory, and thy ruin graced
With an immaculate charm which cannot be defaced.


### XXVII

The moon is up, and yet it is not night –
Sunset divides the sky with her – a sea
Of glory streams along the Alpine height
Of blue Friuli's mountains; Heaven is free

From clouds, but of all colours seems to be
Melted to one vast Iris of the west,
Where the day joins the past eternity;
While, on the other hand, meek Dian's crest
Floats through the azure air – an island of the blest!


### XXVIII

A single star is at her side, and reigns
With her o'er half the lovely heaven; but still
Yon sunny sea heaves brightly, and remains
Rolled o'er the peak of the far Rhaetian hill,
As day and night contending were, until
Nature reclaimed her order: – gently flows
The deep-dyed Brenta, where their hues instil
The odorous purple of a new-born rose,
Which streams upon her stream, and glassed within it
    glows,

### XXIX

Filled with the face of heaven, which, from afar,
Comes down upon the waters! all its hues,
From the rich sunset to the rising star,
Their magical variety diffuse:
And now they change – a paler shadow strews
Its mantle o'er the mountains; parting day
Dies like the dolphin, whom each pang imbues
With a new colour as it gasps away,
The last still loveliest, till – 'tis gone – and all is grey.


### XXX

There is a tomb in Arqua; – reared in air,
Pillared in their sarcophagus, repose
The bones of Laura's lover: here repair
Many familiar with his well-sung woes,

The pilgrims of his genius. He arose
To raise a language, and his land reclaim
From the dull yoke of her barbaric foes:
Watering the tree which bears his lady's name
With his melodious tears, he gave himself to fame.

### XXXI

They keep his dust in Arqua, where he died –
The mountain-village where his latter days
Went down the vale of years; and 'tis their pride –
An honest pride – and let it be their praise,
To offer to the passing stranger's gaze
His mansion and his sepulchre – both plain
And venerably simple – such as raise
A feeling more accordant with his strain
Than if a pyramid formed his monumental fane.

### XXXII

And the soft quiet hamlet where he dwelt
Is one of that complexion which seems made
For those who their mortality have felt,
And sought a refuge from their hopes decayed
In the deep umbrage of a green hill's shade,
Which shows a distant prospect far away
Of busy cities, now in vain displayed,
For they can lure no further; and the ray
Of a bright sun can make sufficient holiday,

### XXXIII

Developing the mountains, leaves, and flowers,
And shining in the brawling brook, where-by,
Clear as its current, glide the sauntering hours
With a calm languor, which, though to the eye

Idlesse it seem, hath its morality –
If from society we learn to live,
'Tis solitude should teach us how to die;
It hath no flatterers; vanity can give
No hollow aid; alone – man with his God must strive:

### XXXIV

Or, it may be, with demons, who impair
The strength of better thoughts, and seek their prey
In melancholy bosoms – such as were
Of moody texture from their earliest day,
And loved to dwell in darkness and dismay
Deeming themselves predestined to a doom
Which is not of the pangs that pass away;
Making the sun like blood, the earth a tomb,
The tomb a hell, and hell itself a murkier gloom.

### XXXV

Ferrara! in thy wide and grass-grown streets,
Whose symmetry was not for solitude,
There seems as 'twere a curse upon the seats
Of former sovereigns, and the antique brood
Of Este, which for many an age made good
Its strength within thy walls, and was of yore
Patron or Tyrant, as the changing mood
Of petty power impelled, of those who wore
The wreath which Dante's brow alone had worn before....

### XLII

Italia! oh Italia! thou who hast
The fatal gift of beauty, which became
A funeral dower of present woes and past –
On thy sweet brow is sorrow ploughed by shame,

And annals graved in characters of flame.
Oh, God! that thou wert in thy nakedness
Less lovely or more powerful, and couldst claim
Thy right, and awe the robbers back, who press
To shed thy blood, and drink the tears of thy distress;

### XLIII

Then might'st thou more appal – or, less desired,
Be homely and be peaceful, undeplored
For thy destructive charms; then, still untired,
Would not be seen the arméd torrents poured
Down the deep Alps; nor would the hostile horde
Of many-nationed spoilers from the Po
Quaff blood and water; nor the stranger's sword
Be thy sad weapon of defence – and so,
Victor or vanquished, thou the slave of friend or foe.

### XLIV

Wandering in youth, I traced the path of him,
The Roman friend of Rome's least-mortal mind,
The friend of Tully: as my bark did skim
The bright blue waters with a fanning wind,
Came Megara before me, and behind
Aegina lay, Piraeus on the right,
And Corinth on the left; I lay reclined
Along the prow, and saw all these unite
In ruin, even as he had seen the desolate sight;

### XLV

For Time hath not rebuilt them, but upreared
Barbaric dwellings on their shattered site,
Which only make more mourned and more endeared
The few last rays of their far-scattered light,

178

And the crushed relics of their vanished might.
The Roman saw these tombs in his own age,
These sepulchres of cities, which excite
Sad wonder, and his yet surviving page
The moral lesson bears, drawn from such pilgrimage.

### XLVI

That page is now before me, and on mine
*His* country's ruin added to the mass
Of perished states he mourned in their decline,
And I in desolation: all that *was*
Of then destruction *is*; and now, alas!
Rome – Rome imperial, bows her to the storm,
In the same dust and blackness, and we pass
The skeleton of her Titanic form,
Wrecks of another world, whose ashes still are warm.

### XLVII

Yet, Italy! through every other land
Thy wrongs should ring, and shall, from side to side;
Mother of Arts! as once of Arms! thy hand
Was then our guardian, and is still our guide;
Parent of our religion! whom the wide
Nations have knelt to for the keys of Heaven!
Europe, repentant of her parricide,
Shall yet redeem thee, and, all backward driven,
Roll the barbarian tide, and sue to be forgiven....

### LXXVIII

Oh Rome! my country! city of the soul!
The orphans of the heart must turn to thee,
Lone mother of dead empires! and control
In their shut breasts their petty misery.

What are our woes and sufferance? Come and see
The cypress, hear the owl, and plod your way
O'er steps of broken thrones and temples, ye!
Whose agonies are evils of a day —
A world is at our feet as fragile as our clay.

### LXXIX

The Niobe of nations! there she stands,
Childless and crownless, in her voiceless woe;
An empty urn within her withered hands,
Whose holy dust was scattered long ago;
The Scipios' tomb contains no ashes now;
The very sepulchres lie tenantless
Of their heroic dwellers: dost thou flow,
Old Tiber! through a marble wilderness?
Rise, with thy yellow waves, and mantle her distress.

### LXXX

The Goth, the Christian, time, war, flood, and fire,
Have dealt upon the seven-hilled city's pride;
She saw her glories star by star expire,
And up the steep barbarian monarchs ride,
Where the car climbed the Capitol; far and wide
Temple and tower went down, nor left a site:
Chaos of ruins! who shall trace the void,
O'er the dim fragments cast a lunar light,
And say, 'here was, or is,' where all is doubly night?

### LXXXI

The double night of ages, and of her,
Night's daughter, Ignorance, hath wrapt and wrap
All round us; we but feel our way to err:
The ocean hath his chart, the stars their map,

And Knowledge spreads them on her ample lap;
But Rome is as the desert, where we steer
Stumbling o'er recollections; now we clap
Our hands, and cry 'Eureka!' it is clear –
When but some false mirage of ruin rises near.

### LXXXII

Alas! the lofty city! and alas!
The trebly hundred triumphs! and the day
When Brutus made the dagger's edge surpass
The conqueror's sword in bearing fame away!
Alas, for Tully's voice, and Virgil's lay,
And Livy's pictured page! – but these shall be
Her resurrection; all beside – decay.
Alas, for earth, for never shall we see
That brightness in her eye she bore when Rome was free!...

### XCVI

Can tyrants but by tyrants conquered be,
And Freedom find no champion and no child
Such as Columbia saw arise when she
Sprung forth a Pallas, armed and undefiled?
Or must such minds be nourished in the wild,
Deep in the unpruned forest, 'midst the roar
Of cataracts, where nursing Nature smiled
On infant Washington? Has earth no more
Such seeds within her breast, or Europe no such shore?

### XCVII

But France got drunk with blood to vomit crime,
And fatal have her Saturnalia been
To Freedom's cause, in every age and clime;
Because the deadly days which we have seen,

And vile Ambition, that built up between
Man and his hopes an adamantine wall,
And the base pageant last upon the scene,
Are grown the pretext for the eternal thrall
Which nips life's tree, and dooms man's worst – his second
    fall.

### XCVIII

Yet, Freedom! yet thy banner, torn, but flying,
Streams like the thunder-storm *against* the wind;
Thy trumpet voice, though broken now and dying,
The loudest still the tempest leaves behind;
Thy tree hath lost its blossoms, and the rind,
Chopped by the axe, looks rough and little worth,
But the sap lasts, – and still the seed we find
Sown deep, even in the bosom of the North;
So shall a better spring less bitter fruit bring forth....

### CVII

Cypress and ivy, weed and wallflower grown
Matted and massed together, hillocks heaped
On what were chambers, arch crushed, column strown
In fragments, choked up vaults, and frescoes steeped
In subterranean damps, where the owl peeped,
Deeming it midnight: – temples, baths, or halls?
Pronounce who can; for all that Learning reaped
From her research hath been, that these are walls –
Behold the Imperial Mount! 'tis thus the mighty falls.

### CVIII

There is the moral of all human tales;
'Tis but the same rehearsal of the past,
First Freedom, and then Glory – when that fails,
Wealth, vice, corruption, – barbarism at last.

And History, with all her volumes vast,
Hath but *one* page, — 'tis better written here,
Where gorgeous Tyranny hath thus amassed
All treasures, all delights, that eye or ear,
Heart, soul could seek, tongue ask — away with words!
    draw near,

### CIX

Admire, exult — despise — laugh, weep, — for here
There is such matter for all feeling: — Man!
Thou pendulum betwixt a smile and tear,
Ages and realms are crowded in this span,
This mountain, whose obliterated plan
The pyramid of empires pinnacled,
Of Glory's gewgaws shining in the van
Till the sun's rays with added flame were filled!
Where are its golden roofs? Where those who dared to
    build?

### CX

Tully was not so eloquent as thou,
Thou nameless column with the buried base!
What are the laurels of the Caesar's brow?
Crown me with ivy from his dwelling-place.
Whose arch or pillar meets me in the face,
Titus or Trajan's? No — 'tis that of Time:
Triumph, arch, pillar, all he doth displace
Scoffing; and apostolic statues climb
To crush the imperial urn, whose ashes slept sublime,

### CXI

Buried in air, the deep blue sky of Rome,
And looking to the stars: they had contained
A spirit which with these would find a home,
The last of those who o'er the whole earth reigned,

The Roman globe, for after, none sustained,
But yielded back his conquests: — he was more
Than a mere Alexander, and, unstained
With household blood and wine, serenely wore
His sovereign virtues – still we Trajan's name adore....

### CXXVIII

Arches on arches! as it were that Rome,
Collecting the chief trophies of her line,
Would build up all her triumphs in one dome,
Her Coliseum stands; the moonbeams shine
As 'twere its natural torches, for divine
Should be the light which streams here, to illume
This long-explored but still exhaustless mine
Of contemplation; and the azure gloom
Of an Italian night, where the deep skies assume

### CXXIX

Hues which have words, and speak to ye of heaven,
Floats o'er this vast and wondrous monument,
And shadows forth its glory. There is given
Unto the things of earth, which Time hath bent,
A spirit's feeling, and where he hath leant
His hand, but broke his scythe, there is a power
And magic in the ruined battlement,
For which the palace of the present hour
Must yield its pomp, and wait till ages are its dower....

### CXXXIX

And here the buzz of eager nations ran,
In murmured pity, or load-roared applause,
As man was slaughtered by his fellow man.
And wherefore slaughtered? wherefore, but because

Such were the bloody Circus' genial laws,
And the imperial pleasure. – Wherefore not?
What matters where we fall to fill the maws
Of worms – on battle-plains or listed spot?
Both are but theatres where the chief actors rot.

CXL

I see before me the Gladiator lie:
He leans upon his hand – his manly brow
Consents to death, but conquers agony,
And his drooped head sinks gradually low –
And through his side the last drops, ebbing slow
From the red gash, fall heavy, one by one,
Like the first of a thunder-shower; and now
The arena swims around him – he is gone,
Ere ceased the inhuman shout which hailed the wretch who
    won.

CXLI

He heard it, but he heeded not – his eyes
Were with his heart, and that was far away;
He recked not of the life he lost nor prize,
But where his rude hut by the Danube lay,
*There* were his young barbarians all at play,
*There* was their Dacian mother – he, their sire,
Butchered to make a Roman holiday –
All this rushed with his blood – Shall he expire
And unavenged? – Arise! ye Goths, and glut your ire!

CXLII

But here, where murder breathed her bloody steam;
And here, where buzzing nations choked the ways,
And roared or murmured like a mountain stream
Dashing or winding as its torrent strays;

Here, where the Roman million's blame or praise
Was death or life, the playthings of a crowd;
My voice sounds much — and fall the stars' faint rays
On the arena void — seats crushed — walls bowed —
And galleries, where my steps seem echoes strangely loud.


### CXLIII

A ruin — yet what ruin! from its mass
Walls, palaces, half-cities, have been reared;
Yet oft the enormous skeleton ye pass,
And marvel where the spoil could have appeared.
Hath it indeed been plundered, or but cleared?
Alas! developed, opens the decay,
When the colossal fabric's form is neared:
It will not bear the brightness of the day,
Which streams too much on all years, man, have reft away.


### CXLIV

But when the rising moon begins to climb
Its topmost arch, and gently pauses there;
When the stars twinkle through the loops of time,
And the low night-breeze waves along the air
The garland-forest, which the grey walls wear,
Like laurels on the bald first Caesar's head;
When the light shines serene but doth not glare,
Then in this magic circle raise the dead:
Heroes have trod this spot — 'tis on their dust ye tread.


### CXLV

'While stands the Coliseum, Rome shall stand;
'When falls the Coliseum, Rome shall fall;
'And when Rome falls — the World.' From our own land
Thus spake the pilgrims o'er this mighty wall

In Saxon times, which we are wont to call
Ancient; and these three mortal things are still
On their foundations, and unaltered all;
Rome and her ruin past redemption's skill,
The World, the same wide den – of thieves, or what
    ye will....

### CLXXV

But I forget. – My Pilgrim's shrine is won,
And he and I must part – so let it be –
His task and mine alike are nearly done;
Yet once more let us look upon the sea;
The midland ocean breaks on him and me,
And from the Alban Mount we now behold
Our friend of youth, that ocean, which when we
Beheld it last by Calpe's rock unfold
Those waves, we followed on till the dark Euxine rolled

### CLXXVI

Upon the blue Symplegades; long years –
Long, though not very many, since have done
Their work on both; some suffering and some tears
Have left us nearly where we had begun:
Yet not in vain our mortal race hath run,
We have had our reward – and it is here;
That we can yet feel gladdened by the sun,
And reap from earth, sea, joy almost as dear
As if there were no man to trouble what is clear.

### CLXXVII

Oh! that the desert were my dwelling-place,
With one fair spirit for my minister,
That I might all forget the human race,
And, hating no one, love but only her!

Ye elements! – in whose ennobling stir
I feel myself exalted – can ye not
Accord me such a being? Do I err
In deeming such inhabit many a spot?
Though with them to converse can rarely be our lot.

### CLXXVIII

There is a pleasure in the pathless woods,
There is a rapture on the lonely shore,
There is society, where none intrudes,
By the deep sea, and music in its roar:
I love not Man the less, but Nature more,
From these our interviews, in which I steal
From all I may be, or have been before,
To mingle with the universe, and feel
What I can ne'er express, yet can not all conceal.

### CLXXIX

Roll on, thou deep and dark blue ocean – roll!
Ten thousand fleets sweep over thee in vain;
Man marks the earth with ruin – his control
Stops with the shore; – upon the watery plain
The wrecks are all thy deed, nor doth remain
A shadow of man's ravage, save his own,
When, for a moment, like a drop of rain,
He sinks into thy depths with bubbling groan,
Without a grave, unknelled, uncoffined, and unknown.

### CLXXX

His steps are not upon thy paths, – thy fields
Are not a spoil for him, – thou dost arise
And shake him from thee; the vile strength he wields
For earth's destruction thou dost all despise,

Spurning him from thy bosom to the skies,
And sendest him, shivering in thy playful spray
And howling, to his Gods, where haply lies
His petty hope in some near port or bay,
And dashest him again to earth: – there let him lay....

CLXXXIV

And I have loved thee, Ocean! and my joy
Of youthful sports was on thy breast to be
Borne, like thy bubbles, onward: from a boy
I wantoned with thy breakers – they to me
Were a delight; and if the freshening sea
Made them a terror – 'twas a pleasing fear,
For I was as it were a child of thee,
And trusted to thy billows far and near,
And laid my hand upon thy mane – as I do here.

CLXXXV

My task is done – my song hath ceased – my theme
Has died into an echo; it is fit
The spell should break of this protracted dream.
The torch shall be extinguished which hath lit
My midnight lamp – and what is writ, is writ, –
Would it were worthier! but I am not now
That which I have been – and my visions flit
Less palpably before me – and the glow
Which in my spirit dwelt is fluttering, faint, and low.

CLXXXVI

Farewell! a word that must be, and hath been –
A sound which makes us linger; – yet – farewell!
Ye! who have traced the Pilgrim to the scene
Which is his last, if in your memories dwell

189

A thought which once was his, if on ye swell
A single recollection, not in vain
He wore his sandal-shoon, and scallop-shell;
Farewell! with *him* alone may rest the pain,
If such there were – with *you*, the moral of his strain!

# DON JUAN

## FROM THE DEDICATION

*"Dost thou think, because thou art virtuous, there shall be no more Cakes and Ale? — Yes, by Saint Anne and Ginger shall be hot i' the mouth, too!"*

SHAKSPEARE, *Twelfth Night, or What You Will*

### I

Bob Southey! You're a poet — Poet-laureate,
    And representative of all the race,
Although 'tis true that you turned out a Tory at
    Last, — yours has lately been a common case, —
And now, my Epic Renegade! what are ye at?
    With all the Lakers, in and out of place?
A nest of tuneful persons, to my eye
    Like 'four and twenty blackbirds in a pye;

### II

'Which pye being opened they began to sing,'
    (This old song and new simile holds good),
'A dainty dish to set before the King,'
    Or Regent, who admires such kind of food; —
And Coleridge, too, has lately taken wing,
    But like a hawk encumbered with his hood,
Explaining metaphysics to the nation —
I wish he would explain his Explanation.

### III

You, Boy! are rather insolent, you know,
    At being disappointed in your wish
To supersede all warblers here below,
    And be the only blackbird in the dish;

And then you overstrain yourself, or so,
    And tumble downward like the flying fish
Gasping on deck, because you soar too high, Bob,
And fall, for lack of moisture quite a-dry, Bob!

IV

And Wordsworth, in a rather long 'Excursion',
    (I think the quarto holds five hundred pages),
Has given a sample from the vasty version
    Of his new system to perplex the sages;
'Tis poetry – at least by his assertion,
    And may appear so when the dog-star rages –
And he who understands it would be able
To add a story to the Tower of Babel.

V

You – Gentlemen! by dint of long seclusion
    From better company, have kept your own
At Keswick, and, through still continued fusion
    Of one another's minds, at last have grown
To deem as a most logical conclusion,
    That Poesy has wreaths for you alone:
There is a narrowness in such a notion,
Which makes me wish you'd change your lakes for ocean.

VI

I would not imitate the petty thought,
    Nor coin my self-love to so base a vice,
For all the glory your conversion brought,
    Since gold alone should not have been its price.
You have your salary; wasn't for that you wrought?
    And Wordsworth has his place in the Excise.
You're shabby fellows – true – but poets still,
And duly seated on the Immortal Hill.

### VII

Your bays may hide the baldness of your brows –
　　Perhaps some virtuous blushes; – let them go –
To you I envy neither fruit nor boughs –
　　And for the fame you would engross below,
The field is universal, and allows
　　Scope to all such as feel the inherent glow:
Scott, Rogers, Campbell, Moore, and Crabbe, will try
'Gainst you the question with posterity.

### VIII

For me, who, wandering with pedestrian Muses,
　　Contend not with you on the wingéd steed,
I wish your fate may yield ye, when she chooses,
　　The fame you envy, and the skill you need;
And, recollect, a poet nothing loses
　　In giving to his brethren their full meed
Of merit, and complaint of present days
Is not the certain path to future praise....

## From Canto I

### I

I WANT a hero: an uncommon want,
　　When every year and month sends forth a new one,
Till, after cloying the gazettes with cant,
　　The age discovers he is not the true one;
Of such as these I should not care to vaunt,
　　I'll therefore take our ancient friend Don Juan –
We all have seen him, in the pantomime,
Sent to the devil somewhat ere his time.

II

Vernon, the butcher Cumberland, Wolfe, Hawke,
　　Prince Ferdinand, Granby, Burgoyne, Keppel, Howe,
Evil and good, have had their tithe of talk,
　　And filled their sign-posts then, like Wellesley now;
Each in their turn like Banquo's monarchs stalk,
　　Followers of fame, 'nine farrow' of that sow:
France, too, had Buonaparté and Dumourier
Recorded in the Moniteur and Courier.

III

Barnave, Brissot, Condorcet, Mirabeau,
　　Petion, Clootz, Danton, Marat, La Fayette,
Were French, and famous people, as we know;
　　And there were others, scarce forgotten yet,
Joubert, Hoche, Marceau, Lannes, Desaix, Moreau,
　　With many of the military set,
Exceedingly remarkable at times,
But not at all adapted to my rhymes.

IV

Nelson was once Britannia's god of war,
　　And still should be so, but the tide is turned;
There's no more to be said of Trafalgar,
　　'Tis with our hero quietly inurned;
Because the army's grown more popular,
　　At which the naval people are concerned;
Besides, the prince is all for the land-service,
Forgetting Duncan, Nelson, Howe, and Jervis.

V

Brave men were living before Agamemnon
　　And since, exceeding valorous and sage,
A good deal like him too, though quite the same none;
　　But then they shone not on the poet's page,

And so have been forgotten: – I condemn none,
    But can't find any in the present age
Fit for my poem (that is, for my new one);
So, as I said, I'll take my friend Don Juan.

### VI

Most epic poets plunge *in medias res*
    (Horace makes this the heroic turnpike road),
And then your hero tells, whene'er you please,
    What went before – by way of episode,
While seated after dinner at his ease,
    Beside his mistress in some soft abode,
Palace, or garden, paradise, or cavern,
Which serves the happy couple for a tavern.

### VII

That is the usual method, but not mine –
    My way is to begin with the beginning;
The regularity of my design
    Forbids all wandering as the worst of sinning,
And therefore I shall open with a line
    (Although it cost me half an hour in spinning),
Narrating somewhat of Don Juan's father,
And also of his mother, if you'd rather.

### VIII

In Seville was he born, a pleasant city,
    Famous for oranges and women – he
Who has not seen it will be much to pity,
    So says the proverb – and I quite agree;
Of all the Spanish towns is none more pretty,
    Cadiz perhaps – but that you soon may see; –
Don Juan's parents lived beside the river,
A noble stream, and called the Guadalquivir.

IX

His father's name was José – *Don*, of course,
  A true Hidalgo, free from every stain
Of Moor or Hebrew blood, he traced his source
  Through the most Gothic gentlemen of Spain;
A better cavalier ne'er mounted horse,
  Or, being mounted, e'er got down again,
Than José, who begot our hero, who
Begot – but that's to come — Well, to renew:

X

His mother was a learnéd lady, famed
  For every branch of every science known –
In every Christian language ever named,
  With virtues equalled by her wit alone
She made the cleverest people quite ashamed,
  And even the good with inward envy groan,
Finding themselves so very much exceeded,
In their own way by all the things that she did.

XI

Her memory was a mine: she knew by heart
  All Calderon and greater part of Lopez,
So that if any actor missed his part
  She could have served him for the prompter's copy;
For her Feinagle's were an useless art,
  And he himself obliged to shut up shop – he
Could never make a memory so fine as
That which adorned the brain of Donna Inez.

XII

Her favourite science was the mathematical,
  Her noblest virtue was her magnanimity,
Her wit (she sometimes tried at wit) was Attic all,
  Her serious sayings darkened to sublimity;

In short, in all things she was fairly what I call
    A prodigy – her morning dress was dimity,
Her evening silk, or, in the summer, muslin,
And other stuffs, with which I won't stay puzzling.

### XIII

She knew the Latin – that is, 'the Lord's prayer',
    And Greek – the alphabet – I'm nearly sure;
She read some French romances here and there,
    Although her mode of speaking was not pure;
For native Spanish she had no great care,
    At least her conversation was obscure;
Her thoughts were theorems, her words a problem,
As if she deemed that mystery would ennoble 'em.

### XIV

She liked the English and the Hebrew tongue,
    And said there was analogy between 'em;
She proved it somehow out of sacred song,
    But I must leave the proofs to those who've seen 'em;
But this I heard her say, and can't be wrong,
    And all may think which way their judgments lean 'em;
'"Tis strange – the Hebrew noun which means "I am",
The English always use to govern d—n.'

### XV

Some women use their tongues – she *looked* a lecture,
    Each eye a sermon, and her brow a homily,
And all-in-all sufficient self-director,
    Like the lamented late Sir Samuel Romilly,
The Law's expounder, and the State's corrector,
    Whose suicide was almost an anomaly –
One sad example more, that 'All is vanity', –
(The jury brought their verdict in 'Insanity'.)

XVI

In short, she was a walking calculation,
    Miss Edgeworth's novels stepping from their covers,
Or Mrs Trimmer's books on education,
    Or 'Coelebs' Wife' set out in quest of lovers,
Morality's prim personification,
    In which not Envy's self a flaw discovers;
To others' share let 'female errors fall',
For she had not even one — the worst of all.

XVII

Oh! she was perfect past all parallel —
    Of any modern female saint's comparison;
So far above the cunning powers of hell,
    Her guardian angel had given up his garrison;
Even her minutest motions went as well
    As those of the best time-piece made by Harrison:
In virtues nothing earthly could surpass her,
Save thine 'incomparable oil', Macassar!

XVIII

Perfect she was, but as perfection is
    Insipid in this naughty world of ours,
Where our first parents never learned to kiss
    Till they were exiled from their earlier bowers,
Where all was peace, and innocence, and bliss,
    (I wonder how they got through the twelve hours),
Don José, like a lineal son of Eve,
Went plucking various fruit without her leave.

XIX

He was a mortal of the careless kind,
    With no great love for learning, or the learned,
Who chose to go where'er he had a mind,
    And never dreamed his lady was concerned;

The world, as usual, wickedly inclined
    To see a kingdom or a house o'erturned,
Whispered he had a mistress, some said *two*.
But for domestic quarrels *one* will do.


### XX

Now Donna Inez had, with all her merit,
    A great opinion of her own good qualities;
Neglect, indeed, requires a saint to bear it,
    And such, indeed, she was in her moralities;
But then she had a devil of a spirit,
    And sometimes mixed up fancies with realities,
And let few opportunities escape
Of getting her liege lord into a scrape.


### XXI

This was an easy matter with a man
    Oft in the wrong, and never on his guard;
And even the wisest, do the best they can,
    Have moments, hours, and days, so unprepared,
That you might 'brain them with their lady's fan';
    And sometimes ladies hit exceeding hard,
And fans turn into falchions in fair hands,
And why and wherefore no one understands.


### XXII

'Tis pity learnéd virgins ever wed
    With persons of no sort of education,
Or gentlemen, who, though well born and bred,
    Grow tired of scientific conversation:
I don't choose to say much upon this head,
    I'm a plain man, and in a single station,
But – Oh! ye lords of ladies intellectual,
Inform us truly, have they not hen-pecked you all?

### XXIII

Don José and his lady quarrelled – *why*,
  Not any of the many could divine,
Though several thousand people chose to try,
  'Twas surely no concern of theirs nor mine;
I loathe that low vice – curiosity;
  But if there's any thing in which I shine,
'Tis in arranging all my friends' affairs,
Not having, of my own, domestic cares.

### XXIV

And so I interfered, and with the best
  Intentions, but their treatment was not kind;
I think the foolish people were possessed,
  For neither of them could I ever find,
Although their porter afterwards confessed –
  But that's no matter, and the worst's behind,
For little Juan o'er me threw, down stairs,
A pail of housemaid's water unawares.

### XXV

A little curly-headed, good-for-nothing,
  And mischief-making monkey from his birth;
His parents ne'er agreed except in doting
  Upon the most unquiet imp on earth;
Instead of quarrelling, had they been but both in
  Their senses, they'd have sent young master forth
To school, or had him soundly whipped at home,
To teach him manners for the time to come.

### XXVI

Don José and the Donna Inez led
  For some time an unhappy sort of life,
Wishing each other, not divorced, but dead;
  They lived respectably as man and wife,

Their conduct was exceedingly well-bred,
 And gave no outward signs of inward strife,
Until at length the smothered fire broke out,
And put the business past all kind of doubt.


### XXVII

For Inez called some druggists, and physicians,
 And tried to prove her loving lord was *mad*,
But as he had some lucid intermissions,
 She next decided he was only *bad*;
Yet when they asked her for her depositions,
 No sort of explanation could be had,
Save that her duty both to man and God
Required this conduct – which seemed very odd.


### XXVIII

She kept a journal, where his faults were noted,
 And opened certain trunks of books and letters,
All which might, if occasion served, be quoted;
 And then she had all Seville for abettors,
Besides her good old grandmother (who doted);
 The hearers of her case became repeaters,
Then advocates, inquisitors, and judges,
Some for amusement, others for old grudges.


### XXIX

And then this best and meekest woman bore
 With such serenity her husband's woes,
Just as the Spartan ladies did of yore,
 Who saw their spouses killed, and nobly chose
Never to say a word about them more –
 Calmly she heard each calumny that rose,
And saw *his* agonies with such sublimity,
That all the world exclaimed, 'What magnanimity!'

XXX

No doubt this patience, when the world is damning us,
  Is philosophic in our former friends;
'Tis also pleasant to be deemed magnanimous,
  The more so in obtaining our own ends;
And what the lawyers called a *malus animus*
  Conduct like this by no means comprehends:
.Revenge in person's certainly no virtue,
But then 'tis not *my* fault, if *others* hurt you.

XXXI

And if our quarrels should rip up old stories,
  And help them with a lie or two additional,
*I*'m not to blame, as you well know — no more is
  Any one else — they were become traditional;
Besides, their resurrection aids our glories
  By contrast,. which is what we just were wishing all:
And science profits by this resurrection —
Dead scandals form good subjects for dissection.

XXXII

Their friends had tried at reconciliation,
  Then their relations, who made matters worse.
('Twere hard to tell upon a like occasion
  To whom it may be best to have recourse —
I can't say much for friend or yet relation):
  The lawyers did their utmost for divorce,
But scarce a fee was paid on either side
Before, unluckily, Don José died.

XXXIII

He died: and most unluckily, because,
  According to all hints I could collect
From counsel learnéd in those kinds of laws,
  (Although their talk's obscure and circumspect)

His death contrived to spoil a charming cause;
   A thousand pities also with respect
To public feeling, which on this occasion
Was manifested in a great sensation.

### XXXIV

But ah! he died; and buried with him lay
   The public feeling and the lawyers' fees:
His house was sold, his servants sent away,
   A Jew took one of his two mistresses,
A priest the other – at least so they say:
   I asked the doctors after his disease –
He died of the slow fever called the tertian,
And left his widow to her own aversion.

### XXXV

Yet José was an honourable man,
   That I must say, who knew him very well;
Therefore his frailties I'll no further scan,
   Indeed there were not many more to tell:
And if his passions now and then outran
   Discretion, and were not so peaceable
As Numa's (who was also named Pompilius),
He had been ill brought up, and was born bilious.

### XXXVI

Whate'er might be his worthlessness or worth,
   Poor fellow! he had many things to wound him.
Let's own – since it can do no good on earth –
   It was a trying moment that which found him
Standing alone beside his desolate hearth,
   Where all his household gods lay shivered round him.
No choice was left his feelings or his pride,
Save Death or Doctors' Commons – so he died.

XXXVII

Dying intestate, Juan was sole heir
　To a chancery suit, and messuages, and lands,
Which, with a long minority and care,
　Promised to turn out well in proper hands:
Inez became sole guardian, which was fair,
　And answered but to nature's just demands;
An only son left with an only mother
Is brought up much moie wisely than another.

XXXVIII

Sagest of women, even of widows, she
　Resolved that Juan should be quite a paragon,
And worthy of the noblest pedigree:
　(His sire was of Castile, his dam from Aragon):
Then for accomplishments of chivalry,
　In case our lord the king should go to war again,
He learned the arts of riding, fencing, gunnery,
And how to scale a fortress — or a nunnery.

XXXIX

But that which Donna Inez most desired,
　And saw into herself each day before all
The learnéd tutors whom for him she hired,
　Was, that his breeding should be strictly moral:
Much into all his studies she inquired,
　And so they were submitted first to her, all,
Arts, sciences, no branch was made a mystery
To Juan's eyes, excepting natural history.

XL

The languages, especially the dead,
　The sciences, and most of all the abstruse,
The arts, at least all such as could be said
　To be the most remote from common use,

In all these he was much and deeply read;
　　But not a page of any thing that's loose,
Or hints continuation of the species,
Was ever suffered, lest, he should grow vicious.

### XLI

His classic studies made a little puzzle,
　　Because of filthy loves of gods and goddesses,
Who in the earlier ages raised a bustle,
　　But never put on pantaloons or bodices;
His reverend tutors had at times a tussle,
　　And for their Aeneids, Iliads, and Odysseys,
Were forced to make an odd sort of apology.
For Donna Inez dreaded the mythology.

### XLII

Ovid's a rake, as half his verses show him,
　　Anacreon's morals are a still worse sample,
Catullus scarcely has a decent poem,
　　I don't think Sappho's Ode a good example,
Although Longinus tells us there is no hymn
　　Where the sublime soars forth on wings more ample;
But Virgil's songs are pure, except that horrid one
Beginning with 'Formosum Pastor Corydon.'

### XLIII

Lucretius' irreligion is too strong
　　For early stomachs, to prove wholesome food;
I can't help thinking Juvenal was wrong,
　　Although no doubt his real intent was good,
For speaking out so plainly in his song,
　　So much indeed as to be downright rude;
And then what proper person can be partial
To all those nauseous epigrams of Martial?

### XLIV

Juan was taught from out the best edition,
  Expurgated by learnéd men, who place,
Judiciously, from out the schoolboy's vision,
  The grosser parts; but, fearful to deface
Too much their modest bard by this omission,
  And pitying sore his mutilated case,
They only add them all in an appendix,
Which saves, in fact, the trouble of an index;

### XLV

For there we have them all 'at one fell swoop',
  Instead of being scattered through the pages;
They stand forth marshalled in a handsome troop,
  To meet the ingenuous youth of future ages,
Till some less rigid editor shall stoop
  To call them back into their separate cages,
Instead of standing staring altogether,
Like garden gods – and not so decent either.

### XLVI

The Missal too (it was the family Missal)
  Was ornamented in a sort of way
Which ancient mass-books often are, and this all
  Kinds of grotesques illumined; and how they,
Who saw those figures on the margin kiss all,
  Could turn their optics to the text and pray,
Is more than I know – but Don Juan's mother
Kept this herself, and gave her son another.

### XLVII

Sermons he read, and lectures he endured,
  And homilies, and lives of all the saints;
To Jerome and to Chrysostom inured,
  He did not take such studies for restraints;

But how faith is acquired, and then ensured,
  So well not one of the aforesaid paints
As Saint Augustine in his fine Confessions,
Which make the reader envy his transgressions.

### XLVIII

This, too, was a sealed book to little Juan –
  I can't but say that his mamma was right,
If such an education was the true one.
  She scarcely trusted him from out her sight;
Her maids were old, and if she took a new one,
  You might be sure she was a perfect fright;
She did this during even her husband's life –
I recommend as much to every wife.

### XLIX

Young Juan waxed in goodliness and grace;
  At six a charming child, and at eleven
With all the promise of as fine a face
  As e'er to man's maturer growth was given:
He studied steadily, and grew apace,
  And seemed, at least, in the right road to heaven,
For half his days were passed at church, the other
Between his tutors, confessor, and mother.

### L

At six, I said, he was a charming child,
  At twelve he was a fine, but quiet boy;
Although in infancy a little wild,
  They tamed him down amongst them: to destroy
His natural spirit not in vain they toiled.
  At least it seemed so; and his mother's joy
Was to declare how sage, and still, and steady,
Her young philosopher was grown already....

*Don Juan develops a youthful passion for Donna Julia –
'married, charming, chaste, and twenty-three' – grows pensive
and thinks 'unutterable thoughts'. She responds to his love, but
their idyll is rudely shattered by the return home of Donna Julia's
husband, Don Alfonso. Inexplicably suspicious, he searches every
nook and cranny of her bedroom, except under the bed-clothes where
Juan, forewarned by the maid, lies suffocating. Alfonso, however,
eventually spots a tell-tale pair of shoes and, set on revenge, rushes
out of the room brandishing a sword. There is nothing now for
Juan to do but fly out and away by the back stairs....*

### CXCIX

This was Don Juan's earliest scrape; but whether
   I shall proceed with his adventures is
Dependent on the public altogether;
   We'll see, however, what they say to this;
Their favour in an author's cap's a feather,
   And no great mischief's done by their caprice;
And if their approbation we experience,
Perhaps they'll have some more about a year hence.

### CC

My poem's epic, and is meant to be
   Divided in twelve books; each book containing,
With love, and war, a heavy gale at sea,
   A list of ships, and captains, and kings reigning,
New characters; the episodes are three:
   A panoramic view of hell's in training,
After the style of Virgil and of Homer,
So that my name of epic's no misnomer.

### CCI

All these things will be specified in time,
   With strict regard to Aristotle's rules,
The *Vade Mecum* of the true sublime,
   Which makes so many poets, and some fools:

Prose poets like blank verse, I'm fond of rhyme,
   Good workmen never quarrel with their tools;
I've got new mythological machinery,
And very handsome supernatural scenery.

### CCII

There's only one slight difference between
   Me and my epic brethren gone before,
And here the advantage is my own, I ween;
   (Not that I have not several merits more,
But this will more peculiarly be seen);
   They so embellish, that 'tis quite a bore
Their labyrinth of fables to thread through,
Whereas this story's actually true.

### CCIII

If any person doubt it, I appeal
   To history, tradition, and to facts,
To newspapers, whose truth all know and feel,
   To plays in five, and operas in three acts;
All these confirm my statement a good deal,
   But that which more completely faith exacts
Is, that myself, and several now in Seville,
*Saw* Juan's last elopement with the devil.

### CCIV

If ever I should condescend to prose,
   I'll write poetical commandments, which
Shall supersede beyond all doubt all those
   That went before; in these I shall enrich
My text with many things that no one knows,
   And carry precept to the highest pitch:
I'll call the work 'Longinus o'er a Bottle,
Or, Every Poet his *own* Aristotle.'...

### CCXXII

'Go, little book, from this my solitude!
　　I cast thee on the waters – go thy ways!
And if, as I believe, thy vein be good,
　　The world will find thee after many days.'
When Southey's read, and Wordsworth understood,
　　I can't help putting in my claim to praise –
The four first rhymes are Southey's every line:
For God's sake, reader! take them not for mine.


## From Canto II

### VIII

But to our tale: the Donna Inez sent
　　Her son to Cadiz only to embark;
To stay there had not answered her intent,
　　But why? – we leave the reader in the dark –
'Twas for a voyage that the young man was meant,
　　As if a Spanish ship were Noah's ark,
To wean him from the wickedness of earth,
And send him like a dove of promise forth.


### IX

Don Juan bade his valet pack his things
　　According to direction, then received
A lecture and some money: for four springs
　　He was to travel; and though Inez grieved
(As every kind of parting has its stings),
　　She hoped he would improve – perhaps believed:
A letter, too, she gave (he never read it)
Of good advice – and two or three of credit.

X

In the mean time, to pass her hours away,
    Brave Inez now set up a Sunday school
For naughty children, who would rather play
    (Like truant rogues) the devil, or the fool;
Infants of three years old were taught that day,
    Dunces were whipt, or set upon a stool:
The great success of Juan's education,
Spurred her to teach another generation.

XI

Juan embarked – the ship got under way,
    The wind was fair, the water passing rough;
A devil of a sea rolls in that bay,
    As I, who've crossed it oft, know well enough;
And standing on the deck, the dashing spray
    Flies in one's face, and makes it weather-tough:
And there he stood to take, and take again,
His first – perhaps his last – farewell of Spain.

XII

I can't but say it is an awkward sight
    To see one's native land receding through
The growing waters; it unmans one quite,
    Especially when life is rather new:
I recollect Great Britain's coast looks white,
    But almost every other country's blue,
When gazing on them, mystified by distance,
We enter on our nautical existence.

XIII

So Juan stood, bewildered on the deck:
    The wind sung, cordage strained, and sailors swore,
And the ship creaked, the town became a speck,
    From which away so fair and fast they bore.

The best of remedies is a beef-steak
    Against sea-sickness: try it, sir, before
You sneer, and I assure you this is true,
For I have found it answer – so may you.

### XIV

Don Juan stood, and, gazing from the stern,
    Beheld his native Spain receding far:
First partings form a lesson hard to learn,
    Even nations feel this when they go to war;
There is a sort of unexprest concern,
    A kind of shock that sets one's heart ajar,
At leaving even the most unpleasant people
And places, one keeps looking at the steeple.

### XV

But Juan had got many things to leave,
    His mother, and a mistress, and no wife,
So that he had much better cause to grieve,
    Than many persons more advanced in life:
And if we now and then a sigh must heave
    At quitting even those we quit in strife,
No doubt we weep for those the heart endears –
That is, till deeper griefs congeal our tears.

### XVI

So Juan wept, as wept the captive Jews
    By Babel's waters, still remembering Sion:
I'd weep, – but mine is not a weeping Muse,
    And such light griefs are not a thing to die on;
Young men should travel, if but to amuse
    Themselves; amd the next time their servants tie on
Behind their carriages their new portmanteau,
Perhaps it may be lined with this my canto.

### XVII

And Juan wept, and much he sighed and thought,
  While his salt tears dropped into the salt sea,
'Sweets to the sweet;' (I like so much to quote;
  You must excuse this extract, — 'tis where she,
The Queen of Denmark, for Ophelia brought
  Flowers to the grave;) and, sobbing often, he
Reflected on his present situation,
And seriously resolved on reformation.

### XVIII

'Farewell, my Spain! a long farewell!' he cried,
  'Perhaps I may revisit thee no more,
But die, as many an exiled heart hath died,
  Of its own thirst to see again thy shore:
Farewell, where Guadalquivir's waters glide!
  Farewell, my mother! and, since all is o'er,
Farewell, too, dearest Julia! — (here he drew
Her letter out again, and read it through.)

### XIX

'And oh! if e'er I should forget, I swear —
  But that's impossible, and cannot be —
Sooner shall this blue ocean melt to air,
  Sooner shall earth resolve itself to sea,
Than I resign thine image, oh, my fair!
  Or think of any thing, excepting thee;
A mind diseased no remedy can physic —
(Here the ship gave a lurch, and he grew sea-sick.)

### XX

'Sooner shall heaven kiss earth — (here he fell sicker)
  Oh, Julia! what is every other woe? —
(For God's sake let me have a glass of liquor;
  Pedro, Battista, help me down below.)

Julia my love! – (you rascal, Pedro, quicker) –
  Oh Julia! – (this curst vessel pitches so) –
Belovéd Julia, hear me still beseeching!'
  (Here he grew inarticulate with retching.)...


*The storm continues and passengers and crew are forced to take
to an open boat. Tossing on the sea, they run out of food and are
driven to eat first Juan's spaniel and then his tutor. Juan desists
from partaking of the latter, as he could hardly be expected to
'dine with them on his pastor and his master'. At last land is
sighted...*


### CIII

As they drew nigh the land, which now was seen
  Unequal in its aspect here and there,
They felt the freshness of its growing green,
  That waved in forest-tops, and smoothed the air,
And fell upon their glazed eyes like a screen
  From glistening waves, and skies so hot and bare –
Lovely seemed any object that should sweep
Away the vast, salt, dread, eternal deep.


### CIV

The shore looked wild, without a trace of man,
  And girt by formidable waves; but they
Were mad for land, and thus their course they ran,
  Though right ahead the roaring breakers lay:
A reef between them also now began
  To show its boiling surf and bounding spray,
But finding no place for their landing better,
They ran the boat for shore, – and overset her.

### CV

But in his native stream, the Guadalquivir,
  Juan to lave his youthful limbs was wont;
And having learnt to swim in that sweet river,
  Had often turned the art to some account:
A better swimmer you could scarce see ever,
  He could, perhaps, have passed the Hellespont,
As once (a feat on which ourselves we prided)
Leander, Mr Ekenhead, and I did.

### CVI

So here, though faint, emaciated, and stark,
  He buoyed his boyish limbs, and strove to ply
With the quick wave, and gain, ere it was dark,
  The beach which lay before him, high and dry:
The greatest danger here was from a shark,
  That carried off his neighbour by the thigh;
As for the other two, they could not swim,
So nobody arrived on shore but him.

### CVII

Nor yet had he arrived but for the oar,
  Which, providentially for him, was washed
Just as his feeble arms could strike no more,
  And the hard wave o'erwhelmed him as 'twas dashed
Within his grasp; he clung to it, and sore
  The waters beat while he thereto was lashed;
At last, with swimming, wading, scrambling, he
Rolled on the beach, half-senseless, from the sea:

### CVIII

There, breathless, with his digging nails he clung
  Fast to the sand, lest the returning wave,
From whose reluctant roar his life he wrung,
  Should suck him back to her insatiate grave:

And there he lay, full length, where he was flung,
  Before the entrance of a cliff-worn cave,
With just enough of life to feel its pain,
And deem that it was saved, perhaps, in vain.

### CIX

With slow and staggering effort he arose,
  But sunk again upon his bleeding knee
And quivering hand; and then he looked for those
  Who long had been his mates upon the sea;
But none of them appeared to share his woes,
  Save one, a corpse, from out the famished three,
Who died two days before, and now had found
An unknown barren beach for burial ground.

### CX

And as he gazed, his dizzy brain spun fast,
  And down he sunk; and as he sunk, the sand
Swam round and round, and all his senses passed:
  He fell upon his side, and his stretched hand
Drooped dripping on the oar (their jury-mast),
  And, like a withered lily, on the land
His slender frame and pallid aspect lay
As fair a thing as e'er was formed of clay.

### CXI

How long in his damp trance young Juan lay
  He knew not, for the earth was gone for him,
And Time had nothing more of night nor day
  For his congealing blood, and senses dim;
And how this heavy faintness passed away
  He knew not, till each painful pulse and limb,
And tingling vein, seemed throbbing back to life,
For Death, though vanquished, still retired with strife.

### CXII

His eyes he opened, shut, again unclosed,
  For all was doubt and dizziness; he thought
He still was in the boat, and had but dozed,
  And felt again with his despair o'erwrought,
And wished it death in which he had reposed,
  And then once more his feelings back were brought,
And slowly by his swimming eyes was seen
A lovely female face of seventeen.

### CXIII

'Twas bending close o'er his, and the small mouth
  Seemed almost prying into his for breath;
And chafing him, the soft warm hand of youth
  Recalled his answering spirits back from death;
And, bathing his chill temples, tried to soothe
  Each pulse to animation, till beneath
Its gentle touch and trembling care, a sigh
To these kind efforts made a low reply.

### CXIV

Then was the cordial poured, and mantle flung
  Around his scarce-clad limbs; and the fair arm
Raised higher the faint head which o'er it hung;
  And her transparent cheek, all pure and warm,
Pillow'd his death-like forehead; then she wrung
  His dewy curls, long drenched by every storm;
And watched with eagerness each throb that drew
A sigh from his heaved bosom – and hers, too.

### CXV

And lifting him with care into the cave,
  The gentle girl, and her attendant, – one
Young, yet her elder, and of brow less grave,
  And more robust of figure, – then begun

To kindle fire, and as the new flames gave
    Light to the rocks that roofed them, which the sun
Had never seen, the maid, or whatsoe'er
She was, appeared distinct, and tall, and fair.

### CXVI

Her brow was overhung with coins of gold,
    That sparkled o'er the auburn of her hair,
Her clustering hair, whose longer locks were rolled
    In braids behind; and though her stature were
Even of the highest for a female mould,
    They nearly reached her heel; and in her air
There was a something which bespoke command,
As one who was a lady in the land.

### CXVII

Her hair, I said, was auburn; but her eyes
    Were black as death, their lashes the same hue,
Of downcast length, in whose silk shadow lies
    Deepest attraction; for when to the view
Forth from its raven fringe the full glance flies,
    Ne'er with such force the swiftest arrow flew;
'Tis as the snake late coiled, who pours his length,
And hurls at once his venom and his strength.

### CXVIII

Her brow was white and low, her cheek's pure dye
    Like twilight rosy still with the set sun;
Short upper lip – sweet lips! that make us sigh
    Ever to have seen such; for she was one
Fit for the model of a statuary,
    (A race of mere impostors, when all's done –
I've seen much finer women, ripe and real,
Than all the nonsense of their stone ideal).

CXIX

I'll tell you why I say so, for 'tis just
   One should not rail without a decent cause:
There was an Irish lady, to whose bust
   I ne'er saw justice done, and yet she was
A frequent model; and if e'er she must
   Yield to stern Time and Nature's wrinkling laws,
They will destroy a face which mortal thought
Ne'er compassed, nor less mortal chisel wrought.

CXX

And such was she, the lady of the cave:
   Her dress was very different from the Spanish,
Simpler, and yet of colours not so grave;
   For, as you know, the Spanish women banish
Bright hues when out of doors, and yet, while wave
   Around them (what I hope will never vanish)
The basquina and the mantilla, they
Seem at the same time mystical and gay.

CXXI

But with our damsel this was not the case:
   Her dress was many-coloured, finely spun;
Her locks curled negligently round her face,
   But through them gold and gems profusely shone:
Her girdle sparkled, and the richest lace
   Flowed in her veil, and many a precious stone
Flashed on her little hand; but, what was shocking,
Her small snow feet had slippers, but no stocking.

CXXII

The other female's dress was not unlike,
   But of inferior materials: she
Had not so many ornaments to strike,
   Her hair had silver only, bound to be

Her dowry; and her veil, in form alike,
  Was coarser; and her air, though firm, less free;
Her hair was thicker, but less long; her eyes
As black, but quicker, and of smaller size.

### CXXIII

And these two tended him, and cheered him both
  With food and raiment, and those soft attentions,
Which are – (as I must own) – of female growth,
  And have ten thousand delicate inventions:
They made a most superior mess of broth,
  A thing which poesy but seldom mentions,
But the best dish that e'er was cooked since Homer's
Achilles ordered dinner for new comers.

### CXXIV

I'll tell you who they were, this female pair,
  Lest they should seem princesses in disguise;
Besides, I hate all mystery, and that air
  Of clap-trap, which your recent poets prize;
And so, in short, the girls they really were
  They shall appear before your curious eyes,
Mistress and maid; the first was only daughter
Of an old man, who lived upon the water.

### CXXV

A fisherman he had been in his youth,
  And still a sort of fisherman was he;
But other speculations were, in sooth,
  Added to his connection with the sea,
Perhaps not so respectable, in truth:
  A little smuggling, and some piracy,
Left him, at last, the sole of many masters
Of an ill-gotten million of piastres.

### CXXVI

A fisher, therefore, was he, – though of men,
  Like Peter the Apostle, – and he fished
For wandering merchant-vessels, now and then,
  And sometimes caught as many as he wished;
The cargoes he confiscated, and gain
  He sought in the slave-market too, and dished
Full many a morsel for that Turkish trade,
By which, no doubt, a good deal may be made.

### CXXVII

He was a Greek, and on his isle had built
  (One of the wild and smaller Cyclades)
A very handsome house from out his guilt,
  And there he lived exceedingly at ease;
Heaven knows what cash he got or blood he spilt,
  A sad old fellow was he, if you please;
But this I know, it was a spacious building,
Full of barbaric carving, paint, and gilding.

### CXXVIII

He had an only daughter, called Haidée,
  The greatest heiress of the Eastern Isles;
Besides, so very beautiful was she,
  Her dowry was as nothing to her smiles:
Still in her teens, and like a lovely tree
  She grew to womanhood, and between whiles
Rejected several suitors, just to learn
How to accept a better in his turn.

### CXXIX

And walking out upon the beach, below
  The cliff, towards sunset, on that day she found,
Insensible, – not dead, but nearly so, –
  Don Juan, almost famished, and half drowned;

But being naked, she was shocked, you know,
　　Yet deemed herself in common pity bound,
As far as in her lay, 'to take him in,
A stranger' dying, with so white a skin.

### CXXX

But taking him into her father's house
　　Was not exactly the best way to save,
But like conveying to the cat the mouse,
　　Or people in a trance into their grave;
Because the good old man had so much 'νους',
　　Unlike the honest Arab thieves so brave,
He would have hospitably cured the stranger,
And sold him instantly when out of danger.

### CXXXI

And therefore, with her maid, she thought it best
　　(A virgin always on her maid relies)
To place him in the cave for present rest:
　　And when, at last, he opened his black eyes,
Their charity increased about their guest;
　　And their compassion grew to such a size,
It opened half the turnpike-gates to heaven —
(St Paul says, 'tis the toll which must be given.)

### CXXXII

They made a fire, — but such a fire as they
　　Upon the moment could contrive with such
Materials as were cast up round the bay, —
　　Some broken planks, and oars, that to the touch
Were nearly tinder, since so long they lay
　　A mast was almost crumbled to a crutch;
But, by God's grace, here wrecks were in such plenty,
That there was fuel to have furnished twenty.

### CXXXIII

He had a bed of furs, and a pelisse,
    For Haidée stripped her sables off to make
His couch; and, that he might be more at ease,
    And warm, in case by chance he should awake,
They also gave a petticoat apiece,
    She and her maid, – and promised by daybreak
To pay him a fresh visit, with a dish
For breakfast, of eggs, coffee; bread, and fish.

### CXXXIV

And thus they left him to his lone repose:
    Juan slept like a top, or like the dead,
Who sleep at last, perhaps (God only knows),
    Just for the present; and in his lulled head
Not even a vision of his former woes
    Throbbed in accursèd dreams, which sometimes spread
Unwelcome visions of our former years,
Till the eye, cheated, opens thick with tears.

### CXXXV

Young Juan slept all dreamless: – but the maid,
    Who smoothed his pillow, as she left the den
Looked back upon him, and a moment stayed,
    And turned, believing that he called again.
He slumbered; yet she thought, at least she said
    (The heart will slip, even as the tongue and pen),
He had pronounced her name – but she forgot
That at this moment Juan knew it not.

### CXXXVI

And pensive to her father's house she went,
    Enjoining silence strict to Zoë, who
Better than her knew what, in fact, she meant,
    She being wiser by a year or two:

A year or two's an age when rightly spent,
   And Zoë spent hers, as most women do,
In gaining all that useful sort of knowledge
Which is acquired in Nature's good old college.

### CXXXVII

The morn broke, and found Juan slumbering still
   Fast in his cave, and nothing clashed upon
His rest; the rushing of the neighbouring rill,
   And the young beams of the excluded sun,
Troubled him not, and he might sleep his fill;
   And need he had of slumber yet, for none
Had suffered more – his hardships were comparative
To those related in my grand-dad's 'Narrative'.

### CXXXVIII

Not so Haidée: she sadly tossed and tumbled,
   And started from her sleep, and, turning o'er,
Dreamed of a thousand wrecks, o'er which she stumbled,
   And handsome corpses strewed upon the shore;
And woke her maid so early that she grumbled,
   And called her father's old slaves up, who swore
In several oaths – Armenian, Turk, and Greek –
They knew not what to think of such a freak.

### CXXXIX

But up she got, and up she made them get,
   With some pretence about the sun, that makes
Sweet skies just when he rises, or is set;
   And 'tis, no doubt, a sight to see when breaks
Bright Phoebus, while the mountains still are wet
   With mist, and every bird with him awakes,
And night is flung off like a mourning suit
Worn for a husband, – or some other brute.

### CXL

I say, the sun is a most glorious sight,
   I've seen him rise full oft, indeed of late
I have sat up on purpose all the night,
   Which hastens, as physicians say, one's fate;
And so all ye, who would be in the right
   In health and purse, begin your day to date
From daybreak, and when coffined at fourscore,
Engrave upon the plate, you rose at four.

### CXLI

And Haidée met the morning face to face;
   Her own was freshest, though a feverish flush
Had dyed it with the headlong blood, whose race
   From heart to cheek is curbed into a blush,
Like to a torrent which a mountain's base,
   That overpowers some Alpine river's rush,
Checks to a lake, whose waves in circles spread;
Or the Red Sea – but the sea is not red.

### CXLII

And down the cliff the island virgin came,
   And near the cave her quick light footsteps drew,
While the sun smiled on her with his first flame,
   And the young Aurora kissed her lips with dew,
Taking her for a sister; just the same
   Mistake you would have made on seeing the two,
Although the mortal, quite as fresh and fair,
Had all the advantage, too, of not being air.

### CXLIII

And when into the cavern Haidée stepped
   All timidly, yet rapidly, she saw
That like an infant Juan sweetly slept;
   And then she stopped, and stood as if in awe

(For sleep is awful), and on tiptoe crept
   And wrapt him closer, lest the air, too raw,
Should reach his blood, then o'er him still as death
Bent, with hushed lips, that drank his scarce-drawn breath.

### CXLIV

And thus like to an angel o'er the dying
   Who die in righteousness, she leaned; and there
All tranquilly the shipwrecked boy was lying,
   As o'er him lay the calm and stirless air:
But Zoë the meantime some eggs was frying,
   Since, after all, no doubt the youthful pair
Must breakfast, and betimes – lest they should ask it,
She drew out her provision from the basket.

### CXLV

She knew that the best feelings must have victual,
   And that a shipwrecked youth would hungry be;
Besides, being less in love, she yawned a little,
   And felt her veins chilled by the neighbouring sea;
And so, she cooked their breakfast to a tittle;
   I can't say that she gave them any tea,
But there were eggs, fruit, coffee, bread, fish, honey,
With Scio wine, – and all for love, not money.

### CXLVI

And Zoë, when the eggs were ready, and
   The coffee made, would fain have wakened Juan;
But Haidée stopped her with her quick small hand,
   And without word, a sign her finger drew on
Her lip, which Zoë needs must understand;
   And, the first breakfast spoilt, prepared a new one,
Because her mistress would not let her break
That sleep which seemed as it would ne'er awake.

### CXLVII

For still he lay, and on his thin worn cheek
   A purple hectic played like dying day
On the snow-tops of distant hills; the streak
   Of sufferance yet upon his forehead lay,
Where the blue veins looked shadowy, shrunk, and weak
   And his black curls were dewy with the spray,
Which weighed upon them yet, all damp and salt,
Mixed with the stony vapours of the vault.

### CXLVIII

And she bent o'er him, and he lay beneath,
   Hushed as the babe upon its mother's breast,
Drooped as the willow when no winds can breathe,
   Lulled like the depth of ocean when at rest.
Fair as the crowning rose of the whole wreath,
   Soft as the callow cygnet in its nest;
In short, he was a very pretty fellow,
Although his woes had turned him rather yellow.

### CXLIX

He woke and gazed, and would have slept again,
   But the fair face which met his eyes forbade
Those eyes to close, though weariness and pain
   Had further sleep a further pleasure made;
For woman's face was never formed in vain
   For Juan, so that even when he prayed
He turned from grisly saints, and martyrs hairy,
To the sweet portraits of the Virgin Mary.

### CL

And thus upon his elbow he arose,
   And looked upon the lady, in whose cheek
The pale contended with the purple rose,
   As with an effort she began to speak;

Her eyes were eloquent, her words would pose,
  Although she told him, in good modern Greek,
With an Ionian accent, low and sweet,
That he was faint, and must not talk, but eat.

### CLI

Now Juan could not understand a word,
  Being no Grecian; but he had an ear,
And her voice was the warble of a bird,
  So soft, so sweet, so delicately clear,
That finer, simpler music ne'er was heard;
  The sort of sound we echo with a tear,
Without knowing why – an overpowering tone,
Whence Melody descends as from a throne.

### CLII

And Juan gazed as one who is awoke
  By a distant organ, doubting if he be
Not yet a dreamer, till the spell is broke
  By the watchman, or some such reality,
Or by one's early valet's cursèd knock;
  At least it is a heavy sound to me,
Who like a morning slumber – for the night
Shows stars and women in a better light.

### CLIII

And Juan, too, was helped out from his dream,
  Or sleep, or whatsoe'er it was, by feeling
A most prodigious appetite: the steam
  Of Zoë's cookery no doubt was stealing
Upon his senses, and the kindling beam
  Of the new fire, which Zoë kept up, kneeling,
To stir her viands, made him quite awake
And long for food, but chiefly a beef-steak.

CLIV

But beef is rare within these oxless isles;
  Goat's flesh there is, no doubt, and kid, and mutton,
And, when a holiday upon them smiles,
  A joint upon their barbarous spits they put on:
But this occurs but seldom, between whiles,
  For some of these are rocks with scarce a hut on,
Others are fair and fertile, among which
This, though not large, was one of the most rich.

CLV

I say that beef is rare, and can't help thinking
  That the old fable of the Minotaur –
From which our modern morals, rightly shrinking,
  Condemn the royal lady's taste who wore
A cow's shape for a mask – was only (sinking
  The allegory) a mere type, no more,
That Pasiphaë promoted breeding cattle,
To make the Cretans bloodier in battle.

CLVI

For we all know that English people are
  Fed upon beef – I won't say much of beer,
Because 'tis liquor only, and being far
  From this my subject, has no business here;
We know, too, they are very fond of war,
  A pleasure – like all pleasures – rather dear;
So were the Cretans – from which I infer,
That beef and battles both were owing to her.

CLVII

But to resume. The languid Juan raised
  His head upon his elbow, and he saw
A sight on which he had not lately gazed,
  As all his latter meals had been quite raw,

Three or four things, for which the Lord he praised,
    And, feeling still the famished vulture gnaw,
He fell upon whate'er was offered, like
A priest, a shark, an alderman, or pike.

### CLVIII

He ate, and he was well supplied; and she,
    Who watched him like a mother, would have fed
Him past all bounds, because she smiled to see
    Such appetite in one she had deemed dead:
But Zoë, being older than Haidée,
    Knew (by tradition for she ne'er had read)
That famished people must be slowly nurst,
And fed by spoonfuls, else they always burst.

### CLIX

And so she took the liberty to state,
    Rather by deeds than words, because the case
Was urgent, that the gentleman, whose fate
    Had made her mistress quit her bed to trace
The sea-shore at this hour, must leave his plate,
    Unless he wished to die upon the place –
She snatched it, and refused another morsel,
Saying, he had gorged enough to make a horse ill.

### CLX

Next they – he being naked, save a tattered
    Pair of scarce decent trousers – went to work,
And in the fire his recent rags they scattered,
    And dressed him, for the present, like a Turk,
Or Greek – that is, although it not much mattered,
    Omitting turban, slippers, pistols, dirk, –
They furnished him, entire, except some stitches,
With a clean shirt, and very spacious breeches.

### CLXI

And then fair Haidée tried her tongue at speaking,
    But not a word could Juan comprehend,
Although he listened so that the young Greek in
    Her earnestness would ne'er have made an end;
And, as he interrupted not, went eking
    Her speech out to her protégé and friend,
Till pausing at the last her breath to take,
She saw he did not understand Romaic.

### CLXII

And then she had recourse to nods, and signs,
    And smiles, and sparkles of the speaking eye,
And read (the only book she could) the lines
    Of his fair face, and found, by sympathy,
The answer eloquent, where the soul shines
    And darts in one quick glance a long reply;
And thus in every look she saw exprest
A world of words, and things at which she guessed.

### CLXIII

And now, by dint of fingers and of eyes,
    And words repeated after her, he took
A lesson in her tongue; but by surmise,
    No doubt, less of her language than her look:
As he who studies fervently the skies
    Turns oftener to the stars than to his book,
Thus Juan learned his alpha beta better
From Haidée's glance than any graven letter.

### CLXIV

'Tis pleasing to be schooled in a strange tongue
    By female lips and eyes – that is, I mean,
When both the teacher and the taught are young,
    As was the case, at least, where I have been;

They smile so when one's right, and when one's wrong
   They smile still more, and then there intervene
Pressure of hands, perhaps even a chaste kiss; –
I learned the little that I know by this:

### CLXV

That is, some words of Spanish, Turk, and Greek,
   Italian not at all, having no teachers;
Much English I cannot pretend to speak,
   Learning that language chiefly from its preachers,
Barrow, South, Tillotson, whom every week
   I study, also Blair, the highest reachers
Of eloquence in piety and prose –
I hate your poets, so read none of those.

### CLXVI

As for the ladies, I have nought to say,
   A wanderer from the British world of fashion,
Where I, like other 'dogs, have had my day,'
   Like other men, too, may have had my passion –
But that, like other things, has passed away,
   And all her fools whom I *could* lay the lash on:
Foes, friends, men, women, now are nought to me,
But dreams of what has been, no more to be.

### CLXVII

Return we to Don Juan. He begun
   To hear new words, and to repeat them; but
Some feelings, universal as the sun,
   Were such as could not in his breast be shut
More than within the bosom of a nun:
   He was in love, – as you would be, no doubt,
With a young benefactress, – so was she,
Just in the way we very often see.

### CLXVIII

And every day by daybreak – rather early
　　For Juan, who was somewhat fond of rest –
She came into the cave, but it was merely
　　To see her bird reposing in his nest;
And she would softly stir his locks so curly,
　　Without disturbing her yet slumbering guest,
Breathing all gently o'er his cheek and mouth,
As o'er a bed of roses the sweet south.

### CLXIX

And every morn his colour freshlier came,
　　And every day helped on his convalescence;
'Twas well, because health in the human frame
　　Is pleasant, besides being true love's essence,
For health and idleness to passion's flame
　　Are oil and gunpowder; and some good lessons
Are also learnt from Ceres and from Bacchus,
Without whom Venus will not long attack us.

### CLXX

While Venus fills the heart, (without heart really
　　Love, though good always, is not quite so good,)
Ceres presents a plate of vermicelli, –
　　For love must be sustained like flesh and blood, –
While Bacchus pours out wine, or hands a jelly:
　　Eggs, oysters, too, are amatory food;
But who is their purveyor from above
Heaven knows, – it may be Neptune, Pan, or Jove.

### CLXXI

When Juan woke he found some good things ready,
　　A bath, a breakfast, and the finest eyes
That ever made a youthful heart less steady,
　　Besides her maid's, as pretty for their size;

But I have spoken of all this already –
 And repetition's tiresome and unwise, –
Well – Juan, after bathing in the sea,
Came always back to coffee and Haidée.

### CLXXII

Both were so young, and one so innocent,
 That bathing passed for nothing; Juan seemed
To her, as t'were, the kind of being sent,
 Of whom these two years she had nightly dreamed,
A something to be loved, a creature meant
 To be her happiness, and whom she deemed
To render happy; all who joy would win
Must share it – Happiness was born a twin.

### CLXXIII

It was such pleasure to behold him, such
 Enlargement of existence to partake
Nature with him, to thrill beneath his touch,
 To watch him slumbering, and to see him wake:
To live with him for ever were too much;
 But then the thought of parting made her quake;
He was her own, her ocean-treasure, cast
Like a rich wreck – her first love, and her last.

### CLXXIV

And thus a moon rolled on, and fair Haidée
 Paid daily visits to her boy, and took
Such plentiful precautions, that still he
 Remained unknown within his craggy nook;
At last her father's prows put out to sea,
 For certain merchantmen upon the look,
Not as of yore to carry off an Io,
But three Ragusan vessels, bound for Scio.

### CLXXV

Then came her freedom, for she had no mother,
    So that, her father being at sea, she was
Free as a married woman, or such other
    Female, as where she likes may freely pass,
Without even the incumbrance of a brother,
    The freest she that ever gazed on glass;
I speak of Christian lands in this comparison,
Where wives, at least, are seldom kept in garrison.

### CLXXVI

Now she prolonged her visits and her talk
    (For they must talk), and he had learnt to say
So much as to propose to take a walk, —
    For little had he wandered since the day
On which, like a young flower snapped from the stalk,
    Drooping and dewy on the beach he lay, —
And thus they walked out in the afternoon,
And saw the sun set opposite the moon.

### CLXXVII

It was a wild and breaker-beaten coast,
    With cliffs above, and a broad sandy shore,
Guarded by shoals and rocks as by an host,
    With here and there a creek, whose aspect wore
A better welcome to the tempest-tost;
    And rarely ceased the haughty billow's roar,
Save on the dead long summer days, which make
The outstretched ocean glitter like a lake.

### CLXXVIII

And the small ripple spilt upon the beach
    Scarcely o'erpassed the cream of your champagne,
When o'er the brim the sparkling bumpers reach,
    That spring-dew of the spirit! the heart's rain!

Few things surpass old wine; and they may preach
    Who please, – the more because they preach in vain, –
Let us have wine and women, mirth and laughter,
Sermons and soda-water the day after.

### CLXXIX

Man, being reasonable, must get drunk;
    The best of life is but intoxication:
Glory, the grape, love, gold, in these are sunk
    The hopes of all men, and of every nation;
Without their sap, how branchless were the trunk
    Of life's strange tree, so fruitful on occasion:
But to return, – get very drunk; and when
You wake with headache, you shall see what then.

### CLXXX

Ring for your valet – bid him quickly bring
    Some hock and soda-water, then you'll know
A pleasure worthy Xerxes the great king;
    For not the blest sherbet, sublimed with snow,
Nor the first sparkle of the desert-spring,
    Nor Burgundy in all its sunset glow,
After long travel, ennui, love, or slaughter,
Vie with that draught of hock and soda-water.

### CLXXXI

The coast – I think it was the coast that I
    Was just describing – Yes, it *was* the coast –
Lay at this period quiet as the sky,
    The sands untumbled, the blue waves untost,
And all was stillness, save the sea-bird's cry,
    And dolphin's leap, and little billow crost
By some low rock or shelve, that made it fret
Against the boundary it scarcely wet.

### CLXXXII

And forth they wandered, her sire being gone,
  As I have said, upon an expedition;
And mother, brother, guardian, she had none,
  Save Zoë, who, although with due precision
She waited on her lady with the sun,
  Thought daily service was her only mission,
Bringing warm water, wreathing her long tresses,
And asking now and then for cast-off dresses.

### CLXXXIII

It was the cooling hour, just when the rounded
  Red sun sinks down behind the azure hill,
Which then seems as if the whole earth it bounded,
  Circling all nature, hushed, and dim, and still,
With the far mountain-crescent half surrounded
  On one side, and the deep sea calm and chill
Upon the other, and the rosy sky
With one star sparkling through it like an eye.

### CLXXXIV

And thus they wandered forth, and hand in hand,
  Over the shining pebbles and the shells,
Glided along the smooth and hardened sand,
  And in the worn and wild receptacles
Worked by the storms, yet worked as it were planned,
  In hollow halls, with sparry roofs and cells,
They turned to rest; and, each clasped by an arm,
Yielded to the deep twilight's purple charm.

### CLXXXV

They looked up to the sky, whose floating glow
  Spread like a rosy ocean, vast and bright;
They gazed upon the glittering sea below,
  Whence the broad moon rose circling into sight;

They heard the waves' splash, and the wind so low,
  And saw each other's dark eyes darting light
Into each other – and, beholding this,
Their lips drew near, and clung into a kiss;

### CLXXXVI

A long, long kiss, a kiss of youth, and love,
  And beauty, all concentrating like rays
Into one focus, kindled from above;
  Such kisses as belong to early days,
Where heart, and soul, and sense, in concert move,
  And the blood's lava, and the pulse a blaze,
Each kiss a heart-quake, – for a kiss's strength,
I think, it must be reckoned by its length.

### CLXXXVII

By length I mean duration; theirs endured
  Heaven knows how long – no doubt they never reckoned;
And if they had, they could not have secured
  The sum of their sensations to a second:
They had not spoken; but they felt allured,
  As if their souls and lips each other beckoned,
Which, being joined, like swarming bees they clung –
Their hearts the flowers from whence the honey sprung.

### CLXXXVIII

They were alone, but not alone as they
  Who shut in chambers think it loneliness;
The silent ocean, and the starlight bay,
  The twilight glow, which momently grew less,
The voiceless sands, and dropping caves, that lay
  Around them, made them to each other press,
As if there were no life beneath the sky
Save theirs, and that their life could never die.

### CLXXXIX

They feared no eyes nor ears on that lone beach,
  They felt no terrors from the night; they were
All in all to each other: though their speech
  Was broken words, they *thought* a language there, –
And all the burning tongues the passions teach
  Found in one sigh the best interpreter
Of nature's oracle – first love – that all
Which Eve has left her daughters since her fall.

### CXC

Haidée spoke not of scruples, asked no vows,
  Nor offered any; she had never heard
Of plight and promises to be a spouse,
  Or perils by a loving maid incurred;
She was all which pure ignorance allows,
  And flew to her young mate like a young bird;
And, never, having dreamt of falsehood, she
Had not one word to say of constancy.

### CXCI

She loved, and was belovéd – she adored,
  And she was worshipped; after nature's fashion,
Their intense souls, into each other poured,
  If souls could die, had perished in that passion, –
But by degrees their senses were restored,
  Again to be o'ercome, again to dash on;
And, beating 'gainst *his* bosom, Haidée's heart
Felt as if never more to beat apart.

### CXCII

Alas! they were so young, so beautiful,
  So lonely, loving, helpless, and the hour
Was that in which the heart is always full,
  And, having o'er itself no further power,

Prompt deeds eternity can not annul,
    But pays off moments in an endless shower
Of hell-fire – all prepared for people giving
Pleasure or pain to one another living.

### CXCIII

Alas! for Juan and Haidée! they were
    So loving and so lovely – till then never,
Excepting our first parents, such a pair
    Had run the risk of being damned for ever:
And Haidée, being devout as well as fair,
    Had, doubtless, heard about the Stygian river,
And hell and purgatory – but forgot
Just in the very crisis she should not.

### CXCIV

They look upon each other, and their eyes
    Gleam in the moonlight; and her white arm clasps
Round Juan's head, and his around her lies
    Half buried in the tresses which it grasps;
She sits upon his knee, and drinks his sighs,
    He hers, until they end in broken gasps;
And thus they form a group that's quite antique,
Half naked, loving, natural, and Greek.

### CXCV

And when those deep and burning moments passed,
    And Juan sunk to sleep within her arms,
She slept not, but all tenderly, though fast,
    Sustained his head upon her bosom's charms;
And now and then her eye to heaven is cast,
    And then on the pale cheek her breast now warms,
Pillowed on her o'erflowing heart, which pants
With all it granted, and with all it grants.

### CXCVI

An infant when it gazes on a light,
　　A child the moment when it drains the breast,
A devotee when soars the Host in sight,
　　An Arab with a stranger for a guest,
A sailor when the prize has struck in fight,
　　A miser filling his most hoarded chest,
Feel rapture; but not such true joy are reaping
As they who watch o'er what they love while sleeping.

### CXCVII

For there it lies so tranquil, so beloved,
　　All that it hath of life with us is living;
So gentle, stirless, helpless, and unmoved,
　　And all unconscious of the joy 'tis giving;
All it hath felt, inflicted, passed, and proved,
　　Hushed into depths beyond the watcher's diving;
There lies the thing we love with all its errors
And all its charms, like death without its terrors.

### CXCVIII

The lady watched her lover – and that hour
　　Of love's, and night's, and ocean's solitude,
O'erflowed her soul with their united power;
　　Amidst the barren sand and rocks so rude
She and her wave-worn love had made their bower,
　　Where nought upon their passion could intrude,
And all the stars that crowded the blue space
Saw nothing happier than her glowing face.

### CXCIX

Alas! the love of women! it is known
　　To be a lovely and a fearful thing;
For all of theirs upon that die is thrown,
　　And if 'tis lost, life hath no more to bring

To them but mockeries of the past alone,
    And their revenge is as the tiger's spring,
Deadly, and quick, and crushing; yet, as real
Torture is theirs, what they inflict they feel.

### CC

They are right; for man, to man so oft unjust,
    Is always so to women; one sole bond
Awaits them, treachery is all their trust;
    Taught to conceal, their bursting hearts despond
Over their idol, till some wealthier lust
    Buys them in marriage – and what rests beyond?
A thankless husband, next a faithless lover,
Then dressing, nursing, praying, and all's over.

### CCI

Some take a lover, some take drams or prayers,
    Some mind their household, others dissipation,
Some run away, and but exchange their cares,
    Losing the advantage of a virtuous station;
Few changes e'er can better their affairs,
    Theirs being an unnatural situation,
From the dull palace to the dirty hovel:
Some play the devil, and then write a novel.

### CCII

Haidée was Nature's bride, and knew not this;
    Haidée was passion's child, born where the sun
Showers triple light, and scorches even the kiss
    Of his gazelle-eyed daughters; she was one
Made but to love, to feel that she was his
    Who was her chosen; what was said or done
Elsewhere was nothing. – She had nought to fear,
Hope, care, nor love, beyond, her heart beat *here*.

### CCIII

And oh! that quickening of the heart, that beat!
   How much it costs us! yet each rising throb
Is in its cause as its effect so sweet,
   That Wisdom, ever on the watch to rob
Joy of its alchemy, and to repeat
   Fine truths; even Conscience, too, has a tough job
To make us understand each good old maxim,
So good – I wonder Castlereagh don't tax 'em.

### CCIV

And now 'twas done – on the lone shore were plighted
   Their hearts; the stars, their nuptial torches, shed
Beauty upon the beautiful they lighted:
   Ocean their witness, and the cave their bed,
By their own feelings hallowed and united,
   Their priest was Solitude, and they were wed:
And they were happy, for to their young eyes
Each was an angel, and earth paradise.

### CCV

Oh, Love! of whom great Caesar was the suitor,
   Titus the master, Antony the slave,
Horace, Catullus, scholars, Ovid tutor,
   Sappho the sage blue-stocking, in whose grave
All those may leap who rather would be neuter –
   (Leucadia's rock still overlooks the wave) –
Oh, Love! thou art the very god of evil,
For, after all, we cannot call thee devil.

### CCVI

Thou makest the chaste connubial state precarious,
   And jestest with the brows of mightiest men:
Caesar and Pompey, Mahomet, Belisarius,
   Have much employed the muse of history's pen:

Their lives and fortunes were extremely various,
  Such worthies Time will never see again;
Yet to these four in three things the same luck holds,
They all were heroes, conquerors, and cuckolds.

### CCVII

Thou makest philosophers; there's Epicurus
  And Aristippus, a material crew!
Who to immoral courses would allure us
  By theories quite practicable too;
If only from the devil they would insure us,
  How pleasant were the maxim (not quite new),
'Eat, drink, and love, what can the rest avail us?'
So said the royal sage Sardanapalus.

### CCVIII

But Juan! had he quite forgotten Julia?
  And should he have forgotten her so soon?
I can't but say it seems to me most truly a
  Perplexing question; but, no doubt, the moon
Does these things for us, and whenever newly a
  Palpitation rises, 'tis her boon,
Else how the devil is it that fresh features
Have such a charm for us poor human creatures?

### CCIX

I hate inconstancy – I loathe, detest,
  Abhor, condemn, abjure the mortal made
Of such quicksilver clay that in his breast
  No permanent foundation can be laid;
Love, constant love, has been my constant guest,
  And yet last night, being at a masquerade,
I saw the prettiest creature, fresh from Milan,
Which gave me some sensations like a villain.

### CCX

But soon Philosophy came to my aid,
 And whispered, 'Think of every sacred tie!'
'I will, my dear Philosophy!' I said,
 'But then her teeth, and then, oh, Heaven! her eye!
I'll just inquire if she be wife or maid,
 Or neither – out of curiosity.'
'Stop!' cried Philosophy, with air so Grecian,
(Though she was masqued then as a fair Venetian;)

### CCXI

'Stop!' so I stopped. – But to return: that which
 Men call inconstancy is nothing more
Than admiration due where nature's rich
 Profusion with young beauty covers o'er
Some favoured object; and as in the niche
 A lovely statue we almost adore,
This sort of adoration of the real
Is but a heightening of the *beau ideal*.

### CCXII

'Tis the perception of the Beautiful,
 A fine extension of the faculties,
Platonic, universal, wonderful,
 Drawn from the stars, and filtered through the skies,
Without which life would be extremely dull;
 In short, it is the use of our own eyes,
With one or two small senses added, just
To hint that flesh is formed of fiery dust.

### CCXIII

Yet 'tis a painful feeling, and unwilling,
 For surely if we always could perceive
In the same object graces quite as killing
 As when she rose upon us like an Eve,

'Twould save us many a heartache, many a shilling,
   (For we must get them anyhow, or grieve,)
Whereas if one sole lady pleased for ever,
How pleasant for the heart, as well as liver!

#### CCXIV

The heart is like the sky, a part of heaven,
   But changes night and day, too, like the sky;
Now o'er it clouds and thunder must be driven,
   And darkness and destruction as on high:
But when it hath been scorched, and pierced, and riven,
   Its storms expire in water-drops; the eye
Pours forth at last the heart's blood turned to tears,
Which make the English climate of our years.

#### CCXV

The liver is the lazaret of bile,
   But very rarely executes its function,
For the first passion stays there such a while,
   That all the rest creep in and form a junction,
Like knots of vipers on a dunghill's soil,
   Rage, fear, hate, jealousy, revenge, compunction,
So that all mischiefs spring up from this entrail,
Like earthquakes from the hidden fire called 'central'.

#### CCXVI

In the mean time, without proceeding more
   In this anatomy, I've finished now
Two hundred and odd stanzas as before,
   That being about the number I'll allow
Each canto of the twelve, or twenty-four;
   And, laying down my pen, I make my bow,
Leaving Don Juan and Haidée to plead
For them and theirs with all who deign to read.

## *From Canto III*

### I

HAIL, Muse! *et cetera.* – We left Juan sleeping,
  Pillowed upon a fair and happy breast,
And watched by eyes that never yet knew weeping,
  And loved by a young heart, too deeply blest
To feel the poison through her spirit creeping,
  Or know who rested there, a foe to rest,
Had soiled the current of her sinless years,
And turned her pure heart's purest blood to tears!

### II

Oh, Love! what is it in this world of ours
  Which makes it fatal to be loved? Ah why
With cypress branches hast thou wreathed thy bowers,
  And made thy best interpreter a sigh?
As those who dote on odours pluck the flowers,
  And place them on their breast – but place to die –
Thus the frail beings we would fondly cherish
Are laid within our bosoms but to perish.

### III

In her first passion woman loves her lover,
  In all the others all she loves is love,
Which grows a habit she can ne'er get over,
  And fits her loosely – like an easy glove,
As you may find, whene'er you like to prove her:
  One man alone at first her heart can move;
She then prefers him in the plural number,
Not finding that the additions much encumber.

### IV

I know not if the fault be men's or theirs;
  But one thing's pretty sure; a woman planted
(Unless at once she plunge for life in prayers) –
  After a decent time must be gallanted;

Although, no doubt, her first of love affairs
   Is that to which her heart is wholly granted;
Yet there are some, they say, who have had *none*,
But those who have ne'er end with only *one*.

V

'Tis melancholy, and a fearful sign
   Of human frailty, folly, also crime,
That love and marriage rarely can combine,
   Although they both are born in the same clime;
Marriage from love, like vinegar from wine –
   A sad, sour, sober beverage – by time
Is sharpened from its high celestial flavour
Down to a very homely household savour.

VI

There's something of antipathy, as 'twere,
   Between their present and their future state;
A kind of flattery that's hardly fair
   Is used until the truth arrives too late –
Yet what can people do, except despair?
   The same things change their names at such a rate;
For instance – passion in a lover's glorious,
But in a husband is pronounced uxorious.

VII

Men grow ashamed of being so very fond;
   They sometimes also get a little tired
(But that, of course, is rare), and then despond:
   The same things cannot always be admired,
Yet 'tis 'so nominated in the bond',
   That both are tied till one shall have expired.
Sad thought! to lose the spouse that was adorning
Our days, and put one's servants into mourning.

### VIII

There's doubtless something in domestic doings
    Which forms, in fact, true love's antithesis;
Romances paint at full length people's wooings,
    But only give a bust of marriages;
For no one cares for matrimonial cooings,
    There's nothing wrong in a connubial kiss:
Think you, if Laura had been Petrarch's wife,
He would have written sonnets all his life?

### IX

All tragedies are finished by a death,
    All comedies are ended by a marriage;
The future states of both are left to faith,
    For authors fear description might disparage
The worlds to come of both, or fall beneath,
    And then both worlds would punish their miscarriage;
So leaving each their priest and prayer-book ready,
They say no more of death or of the lady.

### X

The only two that in my recollection,
    Have sung of heaven and hell, or marriage, are
Dante and Milton, and of both the affection
    Was hapless in their nuptials, for some bar
Of fault or temper ruined the connection
    (Such things, in fact, it don't ask much to mar);
But Dante's Beatrice and Milton's Eve
Were not drawn from their spouses, you conceive.

### XI

Some persons say that Dante meant theology
    By Beatrice, and not a mistress — I,
Although my opinion may require apology,
    Deem this a commentator's fantasy,

Unless indeed it was from his own knowledge he
   Decided thus, and showed good reason why;
I think that Dante's more abstruse ecstatics
Meant to personify the mathematics.

### XII

Haidée and Juan were not married, but
   The fault was theirs, not mine: it is not fair,
Chaste reader, then, in any way to put
   The blame on me, unless you wish they were;
Then if you'd have them wedded, please to shut
   The book which treats of this erroneous pair,
Before the consequences grow too awful;
'Tis dangerous to read of loves unlawful.

### XIII

Yet they were happy, – happy in the illicit
   Indulgence of their innocent desires;
But more imprudent grown with every visit,
   Haidée forgot the island was her sire's;
When we have what we like 'tis hard to miss it,
   At least in the beginning, ere one tires;
Thus she came often, not a moment losing,
Whilst her piratical papa was cruising.

### XIV

Let not his mode of raising cash seem strange,
   Although he fleeced the flags of every nation,
For into a prime minister but change
   His title, and 'tis nothing but taxation;
But he, more modest, took an humbler range
   Of life, and in an honester vocation
Pursued o'er the high seas his watery journey,
And merely practised as a sea-attorney.

XV

The good old gentleman had been detained
  By winds and waves, and some important captures;
And, in the hope of more, at sea remained,
  Although a squall or two had damped his raptures,
By swamping one of the prizes; he had chained
  His prisoners, dividing them like chapters
In numbered lots; they all had cuffs and collars,
And averaged each from ten to a hundred dollars.

XVI

Some he disposed of off Cape Matapan,
  Among his friends the Mainots; some he sold
To his Tunis correspondents, save one man
  Tossed overboard unsaleable (being old);
The rest – save here and there some richer one,
  Reserved for future ransom in the hold,
Were linked alike, as for the common people, he
Had a large order from the Dey of Tripoli.

XVII

The merchandise was served in the same way,
  Pieced out for different marts in the Levant,
Except some certain portions of the prey,
  Light classic articles of female want,
French stuffs, lace, tweezers, toothpicks, teapot, tray,
  Guitars and castanets from Alicant,
All which selected from the spoil he gathers,
Robbed for his daughter by the best of fathers.

XVIII

A monkey, a Dutch mastiff, a macaw,
  Two parrots, with a Persian cat and kittens,
He chose from several animals he saw –
  A terrier, too, which once had been a Briton's,

Who dying on the coast of Ithaca,
    The peasants gave the poor dumb thing a pittance:
These to secure in this strong blowing weather,
He caged in one huge hamper altogether.


### XIX

Then, having settled his marine affairs,
    Despatching single cruisers here and there,
His vessel having need of some repairs,
    He shaped his course to where his daughter fair
Continued still her hospitable cares;
    But that part of the coast being shoal and bare,
And rough with reefs which ran out many a mile,
His port lay on the other side o' the isle.


### XX

And there he went ashore without delay,
    Having no custom-house nor quarantine
To ask him awkward questions on the way,
    About the time and place where he had been:
He left his ship to be hove down next day,
    With orders to the people to careen;
So that all hands were busy beyond measure,
In getting out goods, ballast, guns, and treasure.


### XXI

Arriving at the summit of a hill
    Which overlooked the white walls of his home,
He stopped. — What singular emotions fill
    Their bosoms who have been induced to roam!
With fluttering doubts if all be well or ill —
    With love for many, and with fears for some;
All feelings which o'erleap the years long lost,
And bring our hearts back to their starting-post....

### LXI

Old Lambro passed unseen a private gate,
  And stood within his hall at eventide;
Meantime the lady and her lover sate
  At wassail in their beauty and their pride:
An ivory inlaid table spread with state
  Before them, and fair slaves on every side;
Gems, gold, and silver, formed the service mostly,
Mother of pearl and coral the less costly.

### LXII

The dinner made about a hundred dishes;
  Lamb and pistachio nuts – in short, all meats,
And saffron soups, and sweetbreads; and the fishes
  Were of the finest that e'er flounced in nets,
Drest to a Sybarite's most pampered wishes;
  The beverage was various sherbets
Of raisin, orange, and pomegranate juice,
Squeezed through the rind, which makes it best for use.

### LXIII

These were ranged round, each in its crystal ewer,
  And fruits, and date-bread loaves closed the repast,
And Mocha's berry, from Arabia pure,
  In small fine China cups, came in at last;
Gold cups of filigree made to secure
  The hand from burning underneath them placed,
Cloves, cinnamon and saffron too were boiled
Up with the coffee, which (I think) they spoiled.

### LXIV

The hangings of the room were tapestry, made
  Of velvet panels, each of different hue,
And thick with damask flowers of silk inlaid;
  And round them ran a yellow border too;

The upper border, richly wrought, displayed,
   Embroidered delicately o'er with blue,
Soft Persian sentences, in lilac letters,
From poets, or the moralists their betters.

### LXV

These Oriental writings on the wall,
   Quite common in those countries, are a kind
Of monitors adapted to recall,
   Like skulls at Memphian banquets, to the mind,
The words which shook Belshazzar in his hall,
   And took his kingdom from him: you will find,
Though sages may pour out their wisdom's treasure,
There is no sterner moralist than pleasure.

### LXVI

A beauty at the season's close grown hectic,
   A genius who has drunk himself to death,
A rake turned methodistic, or eclectic –
   (For that's the name they like to pray beneath) –
But most, an alderman struck apoplectic,
   Are things that really take away the breath, –
And show that late hours, wine, and love are able
To do not much less damage than the table.

### LXVII

Haidée and Juan carpeted their feet
   On crimson satin, bordered with pale blue;
Their sofa occupied three parts complete
   Of the apartment – and appeared quite new;
The velvet cushions (for a throne more meet) –
   Were scarlet, from whose glowing centre grew
A sun embossed in gold, whose rays of tissue,
Meridian-like, were seen all light to issue.

### LXVIII

Crystal and marble, plate and porcelain,
    Had done their work of splendour; Indian mats
And Persian carpets, which the heart bled to stain,
    Over the floors were spread; gazelles and cats,
And dwarfs and blacks, and such like things, that gain
    Their bread as ministers and favourites – that's
To say, by degradation – mingled there
As plentiful as in a court, or fair.

### LXIX

There was no want of lofty mirrors, and
    The tables, most of ebony inlaid
With mother of pearl or ivory, stood at hand,
    Or were of tortoise-shell or rare woods made,
Fretted with gold or silver: – by command,
    The greater part of these were ready spread
With viands and sherbets in ice – and wine –
Kept for all comers, at all hours to dine.

### LXX

Of all the dresses I select Haidée's:
    She wore two jelicks – one was of pale yellow;
Of azure, pink, and white was her chemise –
    'Neath which her breast heaved like a little billow;
With buttons formed of pearls as large as peas,
    All gold and crimson shone her jelick's fellow,
And the striped white gauze baracan that bound her,
Like fleecy clouds about the moon, flowed round her.

### LXXI

One large gold bracelet clasped each lovely arm,
    Lockless – so pliable from the pure gold
That the hand stretched and shut it without harm,
    The limb which it adorned its only mould

So beautiful – its very shape would charm,
   And clinging as if loath to lose its hold,
The purest ore enclosed the whitest skin
That e'er by precious metal was held in.

### LXXII

Around, as princess of her father's land,
   A like gold bar above her instep rolled,
Announced her rank; twelve rings were on her hand;
   Her hair was starred with gems; her veil's fine fold
Below her breast was fastened with a band
   Of lavish pearls, whose worth could scarce be told;
Her orange silk full Turkish trousers furled
Above the prettiest ankle in the world.

### LXXIII

Her hair's long auburn waves down to her heel
   Flowed like an Alpine torrent which the sun
Dyes with his morning light, – and would conceal
   Her person if allowed at large to run,
And still they seem resentfully to feel
   The silken fillet's curb, and sought to shun
Their bonds whene'er some Zephyr caught began
To offer his young pinion as her fan.

### LXXIV

Round her she made an atmosphere of life,
   The very air seemed lighter from her eyes,
They were so soft and beautiful, and rife
   With all we can imagine of the skies,
And pure as Psyche ere she grew a wife –
   Too pure even for the purest human ties;
Her overpowering presence made you feel
It would not be idolatry to kneel.

## LXXV

Her eyelashes, though dark as night, were tinged
 (It is the country's custom), but in vain;
For those large black eyes were so blackly fringed,
 The glossy rebels mocked the jetty stain,
And in their native beauty stood avenged:
 Her nails were touched with henna; but again
The power of art was turned to nothing, for
They could not look more rosy than before.

## LXXVI

The henna should be deeply dyed to make
 The skin relieved appear more fairly fair;
She had no need of this, day ne'er will break
 On mountain tops more heavenly white than her;
The eye might doubt if it were well awake,
 She was so like a vision; I might err,
But Shakespeare also says, 'tis very silly
'To gild refinéd gold, or paint the lily.'

## LXXVII

Juan had on a shawl of black and gold,
 But a white baracan, and so transparent
The sparkling gems beneath you might behold,
 Like small stars through the milky way apparent;
His turban, furled in many a graceful fold,
 An emerald aigrette with Haidée's hair in't
Surmounted, as its clasp, a glowing crescent,
Whose rays shone ever trembling, but incessant.

## LXXVIII

And now they were diverted by their suite,
 Dwarfs, dancing girls, black eunuchs, and a poet,
Which made their new establishment complete;
 The last was of great fame, and liked to show it:

His verses rarely wanted their due feet –
   And for his theme – he seldom sung below it,
He being paid to satirize or flatter,
As the psalm says, 'inditing a good matter'....

### LXXXIV

He had travelled 'mongst the Arabs, Turks, and Franks,
   And knew the self-loves of the different nations;
And having lived with people of all ranks,
   Had something ready upon most occasions –
Which got him a few presents and some thanks.
   He varied with some skill his adulations;
To 'do at Rome as Romans do' a piece
Of conduct was which he observed in Greece.

### LXXXV

Thus, usually, when he was asked to sing,
   He gave the different nations something national;
'Twas all the same to him – 'God save the king',
   Or 'Ça ira', according to the fashion all:
His muse made increment of any thing,
   From the high lyric down to the low rational;
If Pindar sang horse-races, what should hinder
Himself from being as pliable as Pindar?

### LXXXVI

In France, for instance, he would write a chanson;
   In England a six canto quarto tale;
In Spain, he'd make a ballad or romance on
   The last war – much the same in Portugal;
In Germany, the Pegasus he'd prance on
   Would be old Goethe's – (see what says De Staël);
In Italy he'd ape the 'Trecentisti';
In Greece, he'd sing some sort of hymn like this t'ye:

1

The isles of Greece, the isles of Greece!
    Where burning Sappho loved and sung,
Where grew the arts of war and peace,
    Where Delos rose, and Phoebus sprung!
Eternal summer gilds them yet,
But all, except their sun, is set.

2

The Scian and the Teian muse,
    The hero's harp, the lover's lute,
Have found the fame your shores refuse;
    Their place of birth alone is mute
To sounds which echo further west
Than your sires' 'Islands of the Blest'.

3

The mountains look on Marathon –
    And Marathon looks on the sea;
And musing there an hour alone,
    I dreamed that Greece might still be free;
For standing on the Persians' grave,
I could not deem myself a slave.

4

A king sate on the rocky brow
    Which looks o'er sea-born Salamis;
And ships, by thousands, lay below,
    And men in nations; – all were his!
He counted them at break of day –
And when the sun set where were they?

### 5

And where are they? and where art thou,
  My country? On thy voiceless shore
The heroic lay is tuneless now –
  The heroic bosom beats no more!
And must thy lyre, so long divine,
Degenerate into hands like mine?

### 6

'Tis something in the dearth of fame,
  Though linked among a fettered race,
To feel at least a patriot's shame,
  Even as I sing, suffuse my face;
For what is left the poet here?
For Greeks a blush – for Greece a tear.

### 7

Must *we* but weep o'er days more blest?
  Must *we* but blush? – Our fathers bled.
Earth! render back from out thy breast
  A remnant of our Spartan dead!
Of the three hundred grant but three,
To make a new Thermopylae!

### 8

What, silent still? and silent all?
  Ah! no; – the voices of the dead
Sound like a distant torrent's fall,
  And answer, 'Let one living head,
But one arise, – we come, we come!'
'Tis but the living who are dumb.

### 9

In vain — in vain; strike other chords;
  Fill high the cup with Samian wine!
Leave battles to the Turkish hordes,
  And shed the blood of Scio's vine!
Hark! rising to the ignoble call —
How answers each bold Bacchanal!

### 10

You have the Pyrrhic dance as yet,
  Where is the Pyrrhic phalanx gone?
Of two such lessons, why forget
  The nobler and the manlier one?
You have the letters Cadmus gave —
Think ye he meant them for a slave?

### 11

Fill high the bowl with Samian wine!
  We will not think of themes like these!
It made Anacreon's song divine:
  He served — but served Polycrates —
A tyrant; but our masters then
Were still, at least, our countrymen.

### 12

The tyrant of the Chersonese
  Was freedom's best and bravest friend;
*That* tyrant was Miltiades!
  Oh! that the present hour would lend
Another despot of the kind!
Such chains as his were sure to bind.

13

Fill high the bowl with Samian wine!
　　On Suli's rock, and Parga's shore,
Exists the remnant of a line
　　Such as the Doric mothers bore;
And there, perhaps, some seed is sown,
The Heracleidan blood might own.

14

Trust not for freedom to the Franks –
　　They have a king who buys and sells:
In native swords, and native ranks,
　　The only hope of courage dwells;
But Turkish force, and Latin fraud,
Would break your shield, however broad.

15

Fill high the bowl with Samian wine!
　　Our virgins dance beneath the shade –
I see their glorious black eyes shine;
　　But gazing on each glowing maid,
My own the burning tear-drop laves,
To think such breasts must suckle slaves.

16

Place me on Sunium's marbled steep,
　　Where nothing, save the waves and I,
May hear our mutual murmurs sweep;
　　There, swan-like, let me sing and die:
A land of slaves shall ne'er be mine –
Dash down yon cup of Samian wine!

### LXXXVII

Thus sung, or would, or could, or should have sung,
   The modern Greek, in tolerable verse;
If not like Orpheus quite, when Greece was young,
   Yet in these times he might have done much worse:
His strain displayed some feeling – right or wrong;
   And feeling, in a poet, is the source
Of others' feeling; but they are such liars,
And take all colours – like the hands of dyers....

### XCI

Milton's the prince of poets – so we say;
   A little heavy, but no less divine:
An independent being in his day –
   Learned, pious, temperate, in love and wine;
But, his life falling into Johnson's way,
   We're told this great high priest of all the Nine
Was whipt at college – a harsh sire – odd spouse,
For the first Mrs Milton left his house.

### XCII

All these are, *certes*, entertaining facts,
   Like Shakespeare's stealing deer, Lord Bacon's bribes;
Like Titus' youth, and Caesar's earliest acts;
   Like Burns (whom Doctor Currie well describes);
Like Cromwell's pranks; – but although truth exacts
   These amiable descriptions from the scribes,
As most essential to their hero's story,
They do not much contribute to his glory.

### XCIII

All are not moralists, like Southey, when
   He prated to the world of 'Pantisocrasy';
Or Wordsworth unexcised, unhired, who then
   Seasoned his pedlar poems with democracy;

Or Coleridge, long before his flighty pen
  Let to the Morning Post its aristocracy;
When he and Southey, following the same path,
Espoused two partners (milliners of Bath).

### XCIV

Such names at present cut a convict figure,
  The very Botany Bay in moral geography;
Their loyal treason, renegado rigour,
  Are good manure for their more bare biography;
Wordsworth's last quarto, by the way, is bigger
  Than any since the birthday of typography;
A drowsy frowsy poem, called the 'Excursion',
Writ in a manner which is my aversion.

### XCV

He there builds up a formidable dyke
  Between his own and others' intellect;
But Wordsworth's poem, and his followers, like
  Joanna Southcote's Shiloh, and her sect,
Are things which in this century don't strike
  The public mind, – so few are the elect;
And the new births of both their stale virginities
Have proved but dropsies, taken for divinities.

### XCVI

But let me to my story: I must own,
  If I have any fault, it is digression –
Leaving my people to proceed alone,
  While I soliloquize beyond expression;
But these are my addresses from the throne,
  Which put off business to the ensuing session:
Forgetting each omission is a loss to
The world, not quite so great as Ariosto.

### XCVII

I know that what our neighbours call 'longueurs',
   (We've not so good a *word*, but have the *thing*,
In that complete perfection which ensures
   An epic from Bob Southey every spring) –
Form not the true temptation which allures
   The reader; but 'twould not be hard to bring
Some fine examples of the *épopée*,
To prove its grand ingredient is *ennui*.

### XCVIII

We learn from Horace, 'Homer sometimes sleeps';
   We feel without him, Wordsworth sometimes wakes, –
To show with what complacency he creeps,
   With his dear '*Waggoners*', around his lakes.
He wishes for 'a boat' to sail the deeps –
   Of ocean? – No, of air; and then he makes
Another outcry for 'a little boat',
And drivels seas to set it well afloat.

### XCIX

If he must fain sweep o'er the ethereal plain,
   And Pegasus runs restive in his 'Waggon',
Could he not beg the loan of Charles's Wain?
   Or pray Medea for a single dragon?
Or if too classic for his vulgar brain,
   He feared his neck to venture such a nag on,
And he must needs mount nearer to the moon,
Could not the blockhead ask for a balloon?

### C

'Pedlars', and 'Boats', and 'Waggons!' Oh! ye shades
   Of Pope and Dryden, are we come to this?
That trash of such sort not alone evades
   Contempt, but from the bathos' vast abyss

Floats scumlike uppermost, and these Jack Cades
  Of sense and song above your graves may hiss –
The 'little boatman' and his 'Peter Bell'
Can sneer at him who drew 'Achitophel!'

### CI

T'our tale. – The feast was over, the slaves gone,
  The dwarfs and dancing girls had all retired;
The Arab lore and poet's song were done,
  And every sound of revelry expired;
The lady and her lover, left alone,
  The rosy flood of twilight's sky admired;–
Ave Maria! o'er the earth and sea,
That heavenliest hour of Heaven is worthiest thee!

### CII

Ave Maria! blessèd be the hour!
  The time, the clime, the spot, where I so oft
Have felt that moment in its fullest power
  Sink o'er the earth so beautiful and soft,
While swung the deep bell in the distant tower,
  Or the faint dying day-hymn stole aloft,
And not a breath crept through the rosy air,
And yet the forest leaves seemed stirred with prayer.

### CIII

Ave Maria! 'tis the hour of prayer!
  Ave Maria! 'tis the hour of love!
Ave Maria! may our spirits dare
  Look up to thine and to thy Son's above!
Ave Maria! oh that face so fair!
  Those downcast eyes beneath the Almighty dove –
What though 'tis but a pictured image? – strike –
That painting is no idol, – 'tis too like.

### CIV

Some kinder casuists are pleased to say
   In nameless print – that I have no devotion;
But set those persons down with me to pray,
   And you shall see who has the properest notion
Of getting into heaven the shortest way;
   My altars are the mountains and the ocean,
Earth, air, stars, – all that springs from the great Whole,
Who hath produced, and will receive the soul.

### CV

Sweet hour of twilight! – in the solitude
   Of the pine forest, and the silent shore
Which bounds Ravenna's immemorial wood,
   Rooted where once the Adrian wave flowed o'er,
To where the last Caesarean fortress stood,
   Evergreen forest! which Boccaccio's lore
And Dryden's lay made haunted ground to me,
How have I loved the twilight hour and thee!

### CVI

The shrill cicalas, people of the pine,
   Making their summer lives one ceaseless song,
Were the sole echoes, save my steed's and mine,
   And vesper bell's that rose the boughs along;
The spectre huntsman of Onesti's line,
   His hell-dogs, and their chase, and the fair throng
Which learned from this example not to fly
From a true lover, – shadowed my mind's eye.

### CVII

Oh, Hesperus! thou bringest all good things –
   Home to the weary, to the hungry cheer,
To the young bird the parent's brooding wings,
   The welcome stall to the o'erlaboured steer;

Whate'er of peace about our hearthstone clings,
　　Whate'er our household gods protect of dear,
Are gathered round us by thy look of rest;
Thou bringest the child, too, to the mother's breast.

## CVIII

Soft hour! which wakes the wish and melts the heart
　　Of those who sail the seas, on the first day
When they from their sweet friends are torn apart;
　　Or fills with love the pilgrim on his way
As the far bell of vesper makes him start,
　　Seeming to weep the dying day's decay;
Is this a fancy which our reason scorns?
Ah! surely nothing dies but something mourns!

## CIX

When Nero perished by the justest doom
　　Which ever the destroyer yet destroyed,
Amidst the roar of liberated Rome,
　　Of nations freed, and the world overjoyed,
Some hands unseen strewed flowers upon his tomb:
　　Perhaps the weakness of a heart not void
Of feeling for some kindness done, when power
Had left the wretch an uncorrupted hour.

## CX

But I'm digressing; what on earth has Nero,
　　Or any such like sovereign buffoons,
To do with the transactions of my hero,
　　More than such madmen's fellow man – the moon's?
Sure my invention must be down at zero,
　　And I grown one of many 'wooden spoons'
Of verse (the name with which we Cantabs please
To dub the last of honours in degrees).

### CXI

I feel this tediousness will never do –
 'Tis being *too* epic, and I must cut down
(In copying) this long canto into two;
 They'll never find it out, unless I own
The fact, excepting some experienced few;
 And then as an improvement 'twill be shown:
I'll prove that such the opinion of the critic is
From Aristotle *passim*. – See Ποιητικης.

   .   .   .

*The return of Haidée's father, the pirate Lambro, ends Juan and Haidée's happiness. She dies of grief and haemorrhage; and he is tied up, stowed under hatches, and shipped off to a slave market....*

### From Canto V

#### I

WHEN amatory poets sing their loves
 In liquid lines mellifluously bland,
And pair their rhymes as Venus yokes her doves,
 They little think what mischief is in hand;
The greater their success the worse it proves,
 As Ovid's verse may give to understand;
Even Petrarch's self, if judged with due severity,
Is the Platonic pimp of all posterity.

#### II

I therefore do denounce all amorous writing,
 Except in such a way as not to attract;
Plain – simple – short, and by no means inviting,
 But with a moral to each error tacked,

Formed rather for instructing than delighting,
   And with all passions in their turn attacked;
Now, if my Pegasus should not be shod ill,
This poem will become a moral model.

### III

The European with the Asian shore
   Sprinkled with palaces; the ocean stream
Here and there studded with a seventy-four;
   Sophia's cupola with golden gleam;
The cypress groves, Olympus high and hoar,
   The twelve isles, and the more than I could dream,
Far less describe, present the very view
Which charmed the charming Mary Montagu.

### IV

I have a passion for the name of 'Mary',
   For once it was a magic sound to me;
And still it half calls up the realms of fairy,
   Where I beheld what never was to be;
All feelings changed, but this was last to vary,
   A spell from which even yet I am not quite free:
But I grow sad – and let a tale grow cold,
Which must not be pathetically told.

### V

The wind swept down the Euxine, and the wave
   Broke foaming o'er the blue Symplegades;
'Tis a grand sight from off 'the Giant's Grave'
   To watch the progress of those rolling seas
Between the Bosphorus, as they lash and lave
   Europe and Asia, you being quite at ease;
There's not a sea the passenger e'er pukes in,
Turns up more dangerous breakers than the Euxine.

VI

'Twas a raw day of Autumn's bleak beginning,
  When nights are equal, but not so the days;
The Parcae then cut short the further spinning
  Of seamen's fates, and the loud tempests raise
The waters, and repentance for past sinning
  In all, who o'er the great deep take their ways:
They vow to amend their lives, and yet they don't;
Because if drowned, they can't – if spared, they won't.

VII

A crowd of shivering slaves of every nation,
  And age, and sex, were in the market ranged;
Each bevy with the merchant in his station:
  Poor creatures! their good looks were sadly changed.
All save the blacks seemed jaded with vexation,
  From friends, and home, and freedom far estranged;
The Negroes more philosophy displayed. –
Used to it, no doubt, as eels are to be flayed.

VIII

Juan was juvenile, and thus was full,
  As most at his age are, of hope and health;
Yet I must own, he looked a little dull,
  And now and then a tear stole down by stealth;
Perhaps his recent loss of blood might pull
  His spirit down; and then the loss of wealth,
A mistress, and such comfortable quarters,
To be put up for auction amongst Tartars,

IX

Were things to shake a stoic; ne'ertheless,
  Upon the whole his carriage was serene:
His figure, and the splendour of his dress,
  Of which some gilded remnants still were seen,

271

Drew all eyes on him, giving them to guess
    He was above the vulgar by his mien;
And then, though pale, he was so very handsome;
And then – they calculated on his ransom.


X

Like a backgammon board the place was dotted
    With whites and blacks, in groups on show for sale,
Though rather more irregularly spotted:
    Some bought the jet, while others chose the pale.
It chanced amongst the other people lotted,
    A man of thirty, rather stout and hale,
With resolution in his dark grey eye,
Next Juan stood, till some might choose to buy.


XI

He had an English look; that is, was square
    In make, of a complexion white and ruddy,
Good teeth, with curling rather dark brown hair,
    And, it might be from thought, or toil, or study,
An open brow a little marked with care:
    One arm had on a bandage rather bloody;
And there he stood with such sang-froid, that greater
Could scarce be shown even by a mere spectator.


XII

But seeing at his elbow a mere lad,
    Of a high spirit evidently, though
At present weighed down by a doom which had
    O'erthrown even men, he soon began to show
A kind of blunt compassion for the sad
    Lot of so young a partner in the woe,.
Which for himself he seemed to deem no worse
Than any other scrape, a thing of course.

272

### XIII

'My boy!' – said he, 'amidst this motley crew
  Of Georgians, Russians, Nubians, and what not,
All ragamuffins differing but in hue,
  With whom it is our luck to cast our lot,
The only gentlemen seem I and you;
  So let us be acquainted, as we ought:
If I could yield you any consolation,
'Twould give me pleasure. – Pray, what is your nation?'

### XIV

When Juan answered – 'Spanish!' he replied,
  'I thought, in fact, you could not be a Greek;
Those servile dogs are not so proudly eyed:
  Fortune has played you here a pretty freak,
But that's her way with all men, till they're tried;
  But never mind, – she'll turn, perhaps, next week;
She has served me also much the same as you,
Except that I have found it nothing new.'

### XV

'Pray, sir,' said Juan, 'if I may presume,
  *What* brought you here?' – 'Oh! nothing very rare –
Six Tartars and a drag-chain —' – 'To this doom
  But what conducted, if the question's fair,
Is that which I would learn.' – 'I served for some
  Months with the Russian army here and there,
And taking lately, by Suwarrow's bidding,
A town, was ta'en myself instead of Widdin.'

### XVI

'Have you no friends?' – 'I had – but, by God's blessing,
  Have not been troubled with them lately. Now
I have answered all your questions without pressing,
  And you an equal courtesy should show.'

'Alas!' said Juan, ''twere a tale distressing,
    And long besides.' – 'Oh! if 'tis really so,
You're right on both accounts to hold your tongue;
A sad tale saddens doubly, when 'tis long.

### XVII

'But droop not: Fortune at your time of life,
    Although a female moderately fickle,
Will hardly leave you (as she's not your wife)
    For any length of days in such a pickle.
To strive, too, with our fate were such a strife
    As if the corn-sheaf should oppose the sickle:
Men are the sport of circumstances, when
The circumstances seem the sport of men.'

### XVIII

''Tis not,' said Juan, 'for my present doom
    I mourn, but for the past; – I loved a maid': –
He paused, and his dark eye grew full of gloom;
    A single tear upon his eyelash staid
A moment, and then dropped; 'but to resume,
    'Tis not my present lot, as I have said,
Which I deplore so much; for I have borne
Hardships which have the hardiest overworn,

### XIX

'On the rough deep. But this last blow –' and here
    He stopped again, and turned away his face.
'Ay,' quoth his friend, 'I thought it would appear
    That there had been a lady in the case;
And these are things which ask a tender tear,
    Such as I, too, would shed if in your place:
I cried upon my first wife's dying day,
And also when my second ran away:

## XX

'My third —' – 'Your third!' quoth Juan, turning round;
　'You scarcely can be thirty: have you three?'
'No – only two at present above ground:
　Surely 'tis nothing wonderful to see
One person thrice in holy wedlock bound!'
　'Well, then, your third,' said Juan; 'what did she?
She did not run away, too, – did she, sir?'
'No, faith.' – 'What then?' – 'I ran away from her.'

## XXI

'You take things coolly, sir,' said Juan. 'Why,'
　Replied the other, 'what can a man do?
There still are many rainbows in your sky,
　But mine have vanished. All, when life is new,
Commence with feelings warm, and prospects high;
　But time strips our illusions of their hue,
And one by one in turn, some grand mistake
Casts off its bright skin yearly like the snake.

## XXII

''Tis true, it gets another bright and fresh,
　Or fresher, brighter; but the year gone through,
This skin must go the way, too, of all flesh,
　Or sometimes only wear a week or two; –
Love's the first net which spreads its deadly mesh;
　Ambition, avarice, vengeance, glory, glue
The glittering lime-twigs of our latter days,
Where still we flutter on for pence or praise.'

## XXIII

'All this is very fine, and may be true,'
　Said Juan; 'but I really don't see how
It betters present times with me or you.'
　'No?' quoth the other; 'yet you will allow

By setting things in their right point of view,
    Knowledge, at least, is gained; for instance, now,
We know what slavery is, and our disasters
May teach us better to behave when masters.'

### XXIV

'Would we were masters now, if but to try
    Their present lessons on our Pagan friends here,'
Said Juan, – swallowing a heart-burning sigh:
    'Heaven help the scholar whom his fortune sends here!'
'Perhap we shall be one day, by and by,'
    Rejoined the other, 'when our bad luck mends here;
Meantime (yon old black eunuch seems to eye us)
I wish to G–d that somebody would buy us.

### XXV

'But after all, what *is* our present state?
    'Tis bad, and may be better – all men's lot:
Most men are slaves, none more so than the great,
    To their own whims and passions, and what not;
Society itself, which should create
    Kindness, destroys what little we had got:
To feel for none is the true social art
Of the world's stoics – men without a heart.'

### XXVI

Just now a black old neutral personage
    Of the third sex stept up, and peering over
The captives seemed to mark their looks and age,
    And capabilities, as to discover
If they were fitted for the purposed cage:
    No lady e'er is ogled by a lover,
Horse by a blackleg, broadcloth by a tailor,
Fee by a counsel, felon by a jailor,

### XXVII

As is a slave by his intended bidder.
    'Tis pleasant purchasing our fellow-creatures;
And all are to be sold, if you consider
    Their passions, and are dext'rous; some by features
Are bought up, others by a warlike leader,
    Some by a place – as tend their years or natures;
The most by ready cash – but all have prices,
From crowns to kicks, according to their vices.

### XXVIII

The eunuch having eyed them o'er with care,
    Turned to the merchant, and begun to bid
First but for one, and after for the pair;
    They haggled, wrangled, swore, too – so they did!
As though they were in a mere Christian fair
    Cheapening an ox, an ass, a lamb, or kid;
So that their bargain sounded like a battle
For this superior yoke of human cattle.

### XXIX

At last they settled into simple grumbling,
    And pulling out reluctant purses, and
Turning each piece of silver o'er, and tumbling
    Some down, and weighing others in their hand,
And by mistake sequins with paras jumbling,
    Until the sum was accurately scanned,
And then the merchant giving change, and signing
Receipts in full, began to think of dining.

### XXX

I wonder if his appetite was good?
    Or, if it were, if also his digestion?
Methinks at meals some odd thoughts might intrude,
    And conscience asks a curious sort of question,

About the right divine how far we should
   Sell flesh and blood. When dinner has opprest one,
I think it is perhaps the gloomiest hour
Which turns up out of the sad twenty-four.


### XXXI

Voltaire says 'No': he tells you that Candide
   Found life most tolerable after meals;
He's wrong – unless man were a pig, indeed,
   Repletion rather adds to what he feels,
Unless he's drunk, and then no doubt he's freed
   From his own brain's oppression while it reels.
Of food I think with Philip's son, or rather
Ammon's (ill pleased with one world and one father);


### XXXII

I think with Alexander, that the act
   Of eating, with another act or two,
Makes us feel our mortality in fact
   Redoubled; when a roast and a ragout,
And fish, and soup, by some side dishes backed,
   Can give us either pain or pleasure, who
Would pique himself on intellects, whose use
Depends so much upon the gastric juice?


### XXXIII

The other evening ('twas on Friday last) –
   This is a fact, and no poetic fable –
Just as my great coat was about me cast,
   My hat and gloves still lying on the table,
I heard a shot – 'twas eight o'clock scarce past –
   And, running out as fast as I was able,
I found the military commandant
Stretched in the street, and able scarce to pant....

### XL

The purchaser of Juan and acquaintance
   Bore off his bargains to a gilded boat,
Embarked himself and them, and off they went thence
   As fast as oars could pull and water float;
They looked like persons being led to sentence,
   Wondering what next, till the caïque was brought
Up in a little creek below a wall
O'ertopped with cypresses, dark-green and tall.

### XLI

Here their conductor tapping at the wicket
   Of a small iron door, 'twas opened, and
He led them onward, first through a low thicket
   Flanked by large groves, which towered on either hand:
They almost lost their way, and had to pick it –
   For night was closing ere they came to land.
The eunuch made a sign to those on board,
Who rowed off, leaving them without a word.

### XLII

As they were plodding on their winding way
   Through orange bowers, and jasmine, and so forth:
(Of which I might have a good deal to say,
   There being no such profusion in the North
Of oriental plants, 'et cetera',
   But that of late your scribblers think it worth
Their while to rear whole hotbeds in *their* works,
Because *one* poet travelled 'mongst the Turks:)

### XLIII

As they were threading on their way, there came
   Into Don Juan's head a thought, which he
Whispered to his companion: – 'twas the same
   Which might have then occurred to you or me.

'Methinks,' — said he, — 'it would be no great shame
   If we should strike a stroke to set us free;
Let's knock that old black fellow on the head,
And march away — 'twere easier done than said.'

### XLIV

'Yes,' said the other, 'and when done, what then?
   How get out? how the devil got we in?
And when we once were fairly out, and when
   From Saint Bartholomew we have saved our skin,
Tomorrow'd see us in some other den,
   And worse off than we hitherto have been;
Besides, I'm hungry, and just now would take,
Like Esau, for my birthright a beef-steak.

### XLV

'We must be near some place of man's abode; —
   For the old Negro's confidence in creeping,
With his two captives, by so queer a road,
   Shows that he thinks his friends have not been sleeping:
A single cry would bring them all abroad:
   'Tis therefore better looking before leaping —
And there, you see, this turn has brought us through,
By Jove, a noble palace! — lighted too.'

### XLVI

It was indeed a wide extensive building
   Which opened on their view, and o'er the front
There seemed to be besprent a deal of gilding
   And various hues, as is the Turkish wont, —
A gaudy taste; for they are little skilled in
   The arts of which these lands were once the font:
Each villa on the Bosphorus looks a screen
New painted, or a pretty opera-scene.

### XLVII

And nearer as they came, a genial savour
  Of certain stews, and roast-meats, and pilaus,
Things which in hungry mortals' eyes find favour,
  Made Juan in his harsh intentions pause,
And put himself upon his good behaviour:
  His friend, too, adding a new saving clause,
Said, 'In Heaven's name let's get some supper now,
And then I'm with you, if you're for a row.'

### XLVIII

Some talk of an appeal unto some passion,
  Some to men's feelings, others to their reason;
The last of these was never much the fashion,
  For reason thinks all reasoning out of season.
Some speakers whine, and others lay the lash on,
  But more or less continue still to tease on,
With arguments according to their 'forte';
But no one ever dreams of being short. —

### XLIX

But I digress: of all appeals, — although
  I grant the power of pathos, and of gold,
Of beauty, flattery, threats, a shilling, — no
  Method's more sure at moments to take hold
Of the best feelings of mankind, which grow
  More tender, as we every day behold,
Than that all-softening, overpowering knell,
The tocsin of the soul — the dinner-bell.

### L

Turkey contains no bells, and yet men dine;
  And Juan and his friend, albeit they heard
No Christian knoll to table, saw no line
  Of lackeys usher to the feast prepared,

Yet smelt roast-meat, beheld a huge fire shine,
   And cooks in motion with their clean arms bared,
And gazed around them to the left and right,
With the prophetic eye of appetite.

### LI

And giving up all notions of resistance,
   They followed close behind their sable guide,
Who little thought that his own cracked existence
   Was on the point of being set aside:
He motioned them to stop at some small distance,
   And knocking at the gate, 'twas opened wide,
And a magnificent large hall displayed
The Asian pomp of Ottoman parade.

### LII

I won't describe; description is my forte,
   But every fool describes in these bright days
His wondrous journey to some foreign court,
   And spawns his quarto, and demands your praise –
Death to his publisher, to him 'tis sport;
   While Nature, tortured twenty thousand ways,
Resigns herself with exemplary patience
To guide-books, rhymes, tours, sketches, illustrations.

### LIII

Along this hall, and up and down, some, squatted
   Upon their hams, were occupied at chess;
Others in monosyllable talk chatted,
   And some seemed much in love with their own dress,
And divers smoked superb pipes decorated
   With amber mouths of greater price or less;
And several strutted, others slept, and some
Prepared for supper with a glass of rum.

### LIV

As the black eunuch entered with his brace
   Of purchased infidels, some raised their eyes
A moment without slackening from their pace;
   But those who sate, ne'er stirred in any wise:
One or two stared the captives in the face,
   Just as one views a horse to guess his price;
Some nodded to the Negro from their station,
But no one troubled him with conversation.

### LV

He leads them through the hall, and, without stopping,
   On through a farther range of goodly rooms,
Splendid but silent, save in one, where, dropping,
   A marble fountain echoes through the glooms
Of night, which robe the chamber, or where popping
   Some female head most curiously presumes
To thrust its black eyes through the door or lattice,
As wondering what the devil noise that is.

### LVI

Some faint lamps gleaming from the lofty walls
   Gave light enough to hint their farther way,
But not enough to show the imperial halls
   In all the flashing of their full array;
Perhaps there's nothing – I'll not say appals,
   But saddens more by night as well as day,
Than an enormous room without a soul
To break the lifeless splendour of the whole.

### LVII

Two or three seem so little, one seems nothing:
   In deserts, forests, crowds, or by the shore,
There solitude, we know, has her full growth in
   The spots which were her realms for evermore;

But in a mighty hall or gallery, both in
   More modern buildings and those built of yore,
A kind of death comes o'er us all alone,
Seeing what's meant for many with but one.

### LVIII

A neat, snug study on a winter's night,
   A book, friend, single lady, or a glass
Of claret, sandwich, and an appetite,
   Are things which make an English evening pass;
Though *certes* by no means so grand a sight
   As is a theatre lit up by gas.
I pass my evenings in long galleries solely;
And that's the reason I'm so melancholy....

### LXIV

At last they reached a quarter most retired,
   Where echo woke as if from a long slumber;
Though full of all things which could be desired,
   One wondered what to do with such a number
Of articles which nobody required;
   Here wealth had done its utmost to encumber
With furniture an exquisite apartment,
Which puzzled Nature much to know what Art meant.

### LXV

It seemed, however, but to open on
   A range or suite of further chambers, which
Might lead to heaven knows where: but in this one
   The moveables were prodigally rich:
Sofas 'twas half a sin to sit upon,
   So costly were they; carpets every stitch
Of workmanship so rare, they made you wish
You could glide o'er them like a golden fish.

### LXVI

The black, however, without hardly deigning
　A glance at that which wrapt the slaves in wonder,
Trampled what they scarce tród for fear of staining,
　As if the milky way their feet was under
With all its stars; and with a stretch attaining
　A certain press or cupboard niched in yonder –
In that remote recess which you may see –
Or if you don't the fault is not in me, –

### LXVII

I wish to be perspicuous – and the black,
　I say, unlocking the recess, pulled forth
A quantity of clothes fit for the back
　Of any Mussulman, whate'er his worth;
And of variety there was no lack –
　And yet, though I have said there was no dearth, –
He chose himself to point out what he thought
Most proper for the Christians he had bought.

### LXVIII

The suit he thought most suitable to each
　Was, for the elder and the stouter, first
A Candiote cloak, which to the knee might reach,
　And trousers not so tight that they would burst,
But such as fit an Asiatic breech;
　A shawl whose folds in Cashmire had been nurst,
Slippers of saffron, dagger rich and handy;
In short, all things which form a Turkish Dandy.

### LXIX

While he was dressing, Baba, their black friend,
　Hinted the vast advantages which they
Might probably attain both in the end,
　If they would but pursue the proper way

Which Fortune plainly seemed to recommend;
   And then he added, that he needs must say,
''Twould greatly tend to better their condition,
If they would condescend to circumcision.

### LXX

'For his own part, he really should rejoice
   To see them true believers, but no less
Would leave his proposition to their choice.'
   The other, thanking him for this excess
Of goodness, in thus leaving them a voice
   In such a trifle, scarcely could express
'Sufficiently' (he said) 'his approbation
Of all the customs of this polished nation.

### LXXI

'For his own share — he saw but small objection
   To so respectable an ancient rite;
And, after swallowing down a slight refection,
   For which he owned a present appetite,
He doubted not a few hours of reflection
   Would reconcile him to the business quite.'
'Will it?' said Juan, sharply: 'Strike me dead,
But they as soon shall circumcise my head!

### LXXII

'Cut off a thousand heads, before —' – 'Now, pray,'
   Replied the other, 'do not interrupt:
You put me out in what I had to say.
   Sir! – as I said, as soon as I have supt,
I shall perpend if your proposal may
   Be such as I can properly accept;
Provided always your great goodness still
Remits the matter to our own free-will.'

### LXXIII

Baba eyed Juan, and said, 'Be so good
　　As dress yourself –' and pointed out a suit
In which a Princess with great pleasure would
　　Array her limbs; but Juan standing mute,
As not being in a masquerading mood,
　　Gave it a slight kick with his Christian foot;
And when the old Negro told him to 'Get ready,'
Replied, 'Old gentleman, I'm not a lady.'

### LXXIV

'What you may be, I neither know nor care,'
　　Said Baba; 'but pray do as I desire:
I have no more time nor many words to spare.'
　　'At least,' said Juan, 'sure I may inquire
The cause of this odd travesty?' – 'Forbear,'
　　Said Baba, 'to be curious; 'twill transpire,
No doubt, in proper place, and time, and season:
I have no authority to tell the reason.'

### LXXV

'Then if I do,' said Juan, 'I'll be —' – 'Hold!'
　　Rejoined the Negro, 'pray be not provoking;
This spirit's well, but it may wax too bold,
　　And you will find us not too fond of joking.'
'What, sir!' said Juan, 'shall it e'er be told
　　That I unsexed my dress?' But Baba, stroking
The things down, said, 'Incense me, and I call
Those who will leave you of no sex at all.

### LXXVI

'I offer you a handsome suit of clothes:
　　A woman's, true; but then there is a cause
Why you should wear them.' – 'What, though my soul
　　　loathes
　　The effeminate garb?' – thus, after a short pause,

Sighed Juan, muttering also some slight oaths,
  'What the devil shall I do with all this gauze?'
Thus he profanely termed the finest lace
Which e'er set off a marriage-morning face.


### LXXVII

And then he swore; and, sighing, on he slipped
  A pair of trousers of flesh-coloured silk;
Next with a virgin zone he was equipped,
  Which girt a slight chemise as white as milk;
But tugging on his petticoat, he tripped,
  Which – as we say – or, as the Scotch say, *whilk*,
(The rhyme obliges me to this; sometimes
Monarchs are less imperative than rhymes) –


### LXXVIII

Whilk, which (or what you please), was owing to
  His garment's novelty, and his being awkward:
And yet at last he managed to get through
  His toilet, though no doubt a little backward:
The Negro Baba helped a little too,
  When some untoward part of raiment stuck hard;
And, wrestling both his arms into a gown,
He paused, and took a survey up and down.


### LXXIX

One difficulty still remained – his hair
  Was hardly long enough; but Baba found
So many false long tresses all to spare,
  That soon his head was most completely crowned,
After the manner then in fashion there;
  And this addition with such gems was bound
As suited the ensemble of his toilet,
While Baba made him comb his head and oil it.

### LXXX

And now being femininely all arrayed,
　With some small aid from scissors, paint, and tweezers,
He looked in almost all respects a maid,
　And Baba smilingly exclaimed, 'You see, sirs,
A perfect transformation here displayed;
　And now, then, you must come along with me, sirs,
That is – the Lady': clapping his hands twice,
Four blacks were at his elbow in a trice.

### LXXXI

'You, sir,' said Baba, nodding to the one,
　'Will please to accompany those gentlemen
To supper; but you, worthy Christian nun,
　Will follow me: no trifling, sir; for when
I say a thing, it must at once be done.
　What fear you? think you this a lion's den?
Why, 'tis a palace; where the truly wise
Anticipate the Prophet's paradise.

### LXXXII

'You fool! I tell you no one means you harm.'
　'So much the better,' Juan said, 'for them;
Else they shall feel the weight of this my arm,
　Which is not quite so light as you may deem.
I yield thus far; but soon will break the charm
　If any take me for that which I seem:
So that I trust for every body's sake,
That this disguise may lead to no mistake.'

### LXXXIII

'Blockhead! come on, and see,' quoth Baba; while
　Don Juan, turning to his comrade, who
Though somewhat grieved, could scarce forbear a smile
　Upon the metamorphosis in view, –

'Farewell!' they mutually exclaimed: 'this soil
  Seems fertile in adventures strange and new;
One's turned half Mussulman, and one a maid,
By this old black enchanter's unsought aid.

### LXXXIV

'Farewell!' said Juan: 'should we meet no more,
  I wish you a good appetite.' – 'Farewell!'
Replied the other; 'though it grieves me sore:
  When we next meet, we'll have a tale to tell:
We needs must follow when Fate puts from shore.
  Keep your good name; though Eve herself once fell.'
'Nay,' quoth the maid, 'the Sultan's self shan't carry me,
Unless his Highness promises to marry me.'

### LXXXV

And thus they parted, each by separate doors;
  Baba led Juan onward, room by room
Through glittering galleries, and o'er marble floors,
  Till a gigantic portal through the gloom,
Haughty and huge, along the distance lowers;
  And wafted far arose a rich perfume:
It seemed as though they came upon a shrine,
For all was vast, still, fragrant, and divine.

### LXXXVI

The giant door was broad, and bright, and high,
  Of gilded bronze, and carved in curious guise;
Warriors thereon were battling furiously;
  Here stalks the victor, there the vanquished lies;
There captives led in triumph droop the eye,
  And in perspective many a squadron flies:
It seems the work of times before the line
Of Rome transplanted fell with Constantine.

### LXXXVII

This massy portal stood at the wide close
   Of a huge hall, and on its either side
Two little dwarfs, the least you could suppose,
   Were sate, like ugly imps, as if allied
In mockery to the enormous gate which rose
   O'er them in almost pyramidic pride:
The gate so splendid was in all its features,
You never thought about those little creatures,

### LXXXVIII

Until you nearly trod on them, and then
   You started back in horror to survey
The wondrous hideousness of those small men,
   Whose colour was not black, nor white, nor grey,
But an extraneous mixture, which no pen
   Can trace, although perhaps the pencil may;
They were misshapen pigmies, deaf and dumb —
Monsters, who cost a no less monstrous sum.

### LXXXIX

Their duty was — for they were strong, and though
   They looked so little, did strong things at times —
To ope this door, which they could really do,
   The hinges being as smooth as Rogers' rhymes;
And now and then, with tough strings of the bow,
   As is the custom of those Eastern climes,
To give some rebel Pasha a cravat:
For mutes are generally used for that.

### XC

They spoke by signs — that is, not spoke at all;
   And looking like two incubi, they glared
As Baba with his fingers made them fall
   To heaving back the portal folds: it scared

Juan a moment, as this pair so small,
    With shrinking serpent optics on him stared;
It was as if their little looks could poison
Or fascinate whome'er they fixed their eyes on.

### XCI

Before they entered, Baba paused to hint
    To Juan some slight lessons as his guide:
'If you could just contrive,' he said, 'to stint
    That somewhat manly majesty of stride,
'Twould be as well, and, – (though there's not much in't)
    To swing a little less from side to side,
Which has at times an aspect of the oddest; –
And also could you look a little modest,

### XCII

' 'Twould be convenient; for these mutes have eyes
    Like needles, which may pierce those petticoats;
And if they should discover your disguise,
    You know how near us the deep Bosphorus floats;
And you and I may chance, ere morning rise,
    To find our way to Marmora without boats,
Stitched up in sacks – a mode of navigation
A good deal practised here upon occasion.'

### XCIII

With this encouragement, he led the way
    Into a room still nobler than the last;
A rich confusion formed a disarray
    In such sort, that the eye along it cast
Could hardly carry anything away,
    Object on object flashed so bright and fast;
A dazzling mass of gems, and gold, and glitter,
Magnificently mingled in a litter.

### XCIV

Wealth had done wonders – taste not much; such things
    Occur in Orient palaces, and even
In the more chastened domes of Western kings
    (Of which I have also seen some six or seven),
Where I can't say or gold or diamond flings
    Great lustre, there is much to be forgiven;
Groups of bad statues, tables, chairs, and pictures,
On which I cannot pause to make my strictures.

### XCV

In this imperial hall, at distance lay
    Under a canopy, and there reclined
Quite in a confidential queenly way,
    A lady; Baba stopped, and kneeling signed
To Juan, who though not much used to pray,
    Knelt down by instinct, wondering in his mind
What all this meant: while Baba bowed and bended
His head, until the ceremony ended.

### XCVI

The lady rising up with such an air
    As Venus rose with from the wave, on them
Bent like an antelope a Paphian pair
    Of eyes, which put out each surrounding gem;
And raising up an arm as moonlight fair,
    She signed to Baba, who first kissed the hem
Of her deep purple robe, and speaking low,
Pointed to Juan, who remained below.

### XCVII

Her presence was as lofty as her state;
    Her beauty of that overpowering kind,
Whose force description only would abate:
    I'd rather leave it much to your own mind,

Than lessen it by what I could relate
   Of forms and features; it would strike you blind
Could I do justice to the full detail;
So, luckily for both, my phrases fail.

### XCVIII

Thus much however I may add, – her years
   Were ripe, they might make six-and-twenty springs,
But there are forms which time to touch forbears,
   And turns aside his scythe to vulgar things,
Such as was Mary's, Queen of Scots; true – tears
   And love destroy; and sapping sorrow wrings
Charms from the charmer, yet some never grow
Ugly; for instance – Ninon de l'Enclos.

### XCIX

She spake some words to her attendants, who
   Composed a choir of girls, ten or a dozen,
And were all clad alike; like Juan, too,
   Who wore their uniform, by Baba chosen;
They formed a very nymph-like looking crew,
   Which might have called Diana's chorus 'cousin',
As far as outward show may correspond –
I won't be bail for anything beyond.

### C

They bowed obeisance and withdrew, retiring,
   But not by the same door through which came in
Baba and Juan, which last stood admiring,
   At some small distance, all he saw within
This strange saloon, much fitted for inspiring
   Marvel and praise; for both or none things win;
And I must say, I ne'er could see the very
Great happiness of the 'Nil Admirari'.

CI

'Not to admire is all the art I know
  (Plain truth, dear Murray, needs few flowers of speech)
To make men happy, or to keep them so';
  (So take it in the very words of Creech).
Thus Horace wrote we all know long ago;
  And thus Pope quotes the precept to re-teach
From his translation; but had *none admired*,
Would Pope have sung, or Horace been inspired?

CII

Baba, when all the damsels were withdrawn,
  Motioned to Juan to approach, and then
A second time desired him to kneel down,
  And kiss the lady's foot; which maxim when
He heard repeated, Juan with a frown
  Drew himself up to his full height again,
And said, 'It grieved him, but he could not stoop
To any shoe, unless it shod the Pope.'

CIII

Baba, indignant at this ill-timed pride,
  Made fierce remonstrances, and then a threat
He muttered (but the last was given aside)
  About a bow-string – quite in vain; not yet
Would Juan bend, though 'twere to Mahomet's bride:
  There's nothing in the world like etiquette
In kingly chambers or imperial halls,
As also at the race and county balls....

CVII

The lady eyed him o'er and o'er, and bade
  Baba retire, which he obeyed in style,
As if well used to the retreating trade;
  And taking hints in good part all the while,

He whispered Juan not to be afraid,
    And looking on him with a sort of smile,
Took leave, with such a face of satisfaction,
As good men wear who have done a virtuous action.

### CVIII

When he was gone, there was sudden change:
    I know not what might be the lady's thought,
But o'er her bright brow flashed a tumult strange,
    And into her clear cheek the blood was brought,
Blood-red as sunset summer clouds which range
    The verge of Heaven; and in her large eyes wrought,
A mixture of sensations might be scanned,
Of half voluptuousness and half command.

### CIX

Her form had all the softness of her sex,
    Her features all the sweetness of the devil,
When he put on the cherub to perplex
    Eve, and paved (God knows how) the road to evil;
The sun himself was scarce more free from specks
    Than she from aught at which the eye could cavil;
Yet, somehow, there was something somewhere wanting,
As if she rather *ordered* than was *granting*. –

### CX

Something imperial, or imperious, threw
    A chain o'er all she did; that is, a chain
Was thrown as 'twere about the neck of you –
    And rapture's self will seem almost a pain
With aught which looks like despotism in view:
    Our souls at least are free, and 'tis in vain
We would against them make the flesh obey –
The spirit in the end will have its way.

### CXI

Her very smile was haughty, though so sweet;
　　Her very nod was not an inclination;
There was a self-will even in her small feet,
　　As though they were quite conscious of her station –
They trod as upon necks; and to complete
　　Her state (it is the custom of her nation),
A poniard decked her girdle, as the sign
She was a sultan's bride, (thank Heaven, not mine!)

### CXII

'To hear and to obey' had been from birth
　　The law of all around her; to fulfil
All fantasies which yielded joy or mirth,
　　Had been her slaves' chief pleasure, as her will;
Her blood was high, her beauty scarce of earth:
　　Judge, then, if her caprices e'er stood still;
Had she but been a Christian, I've a notion
We should have found out the 'perpetual motion'.

### CXIII

Whate'er she saw and coveted was brought;
　　Whate'er she did *not* see, if she supposed
It might be seen, with diligence was sought,
　　And when 'twas found straightway the bargain closed:
There was no end unto the things she bought,
　　Nor to the trouble which her fancies caused;
Yet even her tyranny had such a grace,
The women pardoned all except her face.

### CXIV

Juan, the latest of her whims, had caught
　　Her eye in passing on his way to sale;
She ordered him directly to be bought,
　　And Baba, who had ne'er been known to fail

In any kind of mischief to be wrought,
　　At all such auctions knew how to prevail:
She had no prudence, but he had; and this
Explains the garb which Juan took amiss.


CXV

His youth and features favoured the disguise,
　　And, should you ask how she, a sultan's bride,
Could risk or compass such strange fantasies,
　　This I must leave sultanas to decide:
Emperors are only husbands in wives' eyes,
　　And kings and consorts oft are mystified,
As we may ascertain with due precision,
Some by experience, others by tradition.


CXVI

But to the main point, where we have been tending: –
　　She now conceived all difficulties past,
And deemed herself extremely condescending
　　When, being made her property at last,
Without more preface, in her blue eyes blending
　　Passion and power, a glance on him she cast,
And merely saying, 'Christian, canst thou love?'
Conceived that phrase was quite enough to move.


CXVII

And so it was, in proper time and place;
　　But Juan, who had still his mind o'erflowing
With Haidée's isle and soft Ionian face,
　　Felt the warm blood, which in his face was glowing,
Rush back upon his heart, which filled apace,
　　And left his cheeks as pale as snowdrops blowing:
These words went through his soul like Arab spears,
So that he spoke not, but burst into tears.

### CXVIII

She was a good deal shocked; not shocked at tears,
  For women shed and use them at their liking;
But there is something when man's eye appears
  Wet, still more disagreeable and striking:
A woman's tear-drop melts, a man's half sears,
  Like molten lead, as if you thrust a pike in
His heart to force it out, for (to be shorter)
To them 'tis a relief, to us a torture.

### CXIX

And she would have consoled, but knew not how:
  Having no equals, nothing which had e'er
Infected her with sympathy till now,
  And never having dreamt what 'twas to bear
Aught of a serious, sorrowing kind, although
  There might arise some pouting petty care
To cross her brow, she wondered how so near
Her eye another's eyes could shed a tear.

### CXX

But nature teaches more than power can spoil,
  And, when a strong although a strange sensation
Moves – female hearts are such a genial soil
  For kinder feelings, whatsoe'er their nation,
They naturally pour the 'wine and oil',
  Samaritans in every situation;
And thus Gulbeyaz, though she knew not why,
Felt an odd glistening moisture in her eye.

### CXXI

But tears must stop like all things else; and soon
  Juan, who for an instant had been moved
To such a sorrow by the intrusive tone
  Of one who dared to ask if 'he *had* loved',

Called back the stoic to his eyes, which shone
   Bright with the very weakness he reproved;
And although sensitive to beauty, he
Felt most indignant still at not being free.


CXXII

Gulbeyaz, for the first time in her days,
   Was much embarrassed, never having met
In all her life with aught save prayers and praise;
   And as she also risked her life to get
Him whom she meant to tutor in love's ways
   Into a comfortable tête-à-tête,
To lose the hour would make her quite a martyr,
And they had wasted now almost a quarter.


CXXIII

I also would suggest the fitting time,
   To gentlemen in any such like case,
That is to say in a meridian clime –
   With us there is more law given to the chase,
But here a small delay forms a great crime:
   So recollect that the extremest grace
Is just two minutes for your declaration –
A moment more would hurt your reputation.


CXXIV

Juan's was good; and might have been still better,
   But he had got Haidée into his head:
However strange, he could not yet forget her,
   Which made him seem exceedingly ill-bred.
Gulbeyaz, who looked on him as her debtor
   For having had him to her palace led,
Began to blush up to the eyes, and then
Grow deadly pale, and then blush back again.

### CXXV

At length, in an imperial way, she laid
   Her hand on his, and bending on him eyes
Which needed not an empire to persuade,
   Looked into his for love, where none replies:
Her brow grew black, but she would not upbraid,
   That being the last thing a proud woman tries;
She rose, and pausing one chaste moment, threw
Herself upon his breast, and there she grew.

### CXXVI

This was an awkward test, as Juan found,
   But he was steeled by sorrow, wrath, and pride:
With gentle force her white arms he unwound,
   And seated her all drooping by his side,
Then rising haughtily he glanced around,
   And looking coldly in her face, he cried,
'The prisoned eagle will not pair, nor I
Serve a sultana's sensual fantasy.

### CXXVII

'Thou ask'st, if I can love? be this the proof
   How much I *have* loved – that I love not *thee!*
In this vile garb, the distaff, web, and woof,
   Were fitter for me: love is for the free!
I am not dazzled by this splendid roof;
   Whate'er thy power, and great it seems to be,
Heads bow, knees bend, eyes watch around a throne,
And hands obey – our hearts are still our own.'

### CXXVIII

This was a truth to us extremely trite;
   Not so to her, who ne'er had heard such things:
She deemed her least command must yield delight,
   Earth being only made for queens and kings.

If hearts lay on the left side or the right
　　She hardly knew, to such perfection brings
Legitimacy its born votaries, when
Aware of their due royal rights o'er men....


### CXXXI

Suppose, — but you already have supposed,
　　The spouse of Potiphar, the Lady Booby,
Phaedra, and all which story has disclosed
　　Of good examples; pity that so few by
Poets and private tutors are exposed,
　　To educate — ye youth of Europe — you by!
But when you have supposed the few we know,
You can't suppose Gulbeyaz' angry brow....


### CXXXIX

Her first thought was to cut off Juan's head;
　　Her second, to cut only his — acquaintance;
Her third, to ask him where he had been bred;
　　Her fourth, to rally him into repentance;
Her fifth, to call her maids and go to bed;
　　Her sixth, to stab herself; her seventh, to sentence
The lash to Baba: — but her grand resource
Was to sit down again, and cry of course.


### CXL

She thought to stab herself, but then she had
　　The dagger close at hand, which made it awkward;
For Eastern stays are little made to pad,
　　So that a poniard pierces if 'tis stuck hard:
She thought of killing Juan — but, poor lad!
　　Though he deserved it well for being so backward,
The cutting off his head was not the art
Most likely to attain her aim — his heart.

### CXLI

Juan was moved: he had made up his mind
   To be impaled, or quartered as a dish
For dogs, or to be slain with pangs refined,
   Or thrown to lions, or made baits for fish,
And thus heroically stood resigned,
   Rather than sin – except to his own wish:
But all his great preparatives for dying
Dissolved like snow before a woman crying.

### CXLII

As through his palms Bob Acres' valour oozed,
   So Juan's virtue ebbed, I know not how;
And first he wondered why he had refused;
   And then, if matters could be made up now;
And next his savage virtue he accused,
   Just as a friar may accuse his vow,
Or as a dame repents her of her oath,
Which mostly ends in some small breach of both.

### CXLIII

So he began to stammer some excuses;
   But words are not enough in such a matter,
Although you borrowed all that e'er the muses
   Have sung, or even a Dandy's dandiest chatter,
Or all the figures Castlereagh abuses;
   Just as a languid smile began to flatter
His peace was making, but before he ventured
Further, old Baba rather briskly entered.

### CXLIV

'Bride of the Sun! and Sister of the Moon!'
   ('Twas thus he spake,) 'and Empress of the Earth!
Whose frown would put the spheres all out of tune
   Whose smile makes all the planets dance with mirth,

Your slave brings tidings – he hopes not too soon –
   Which your sublime attention may be worth:
The Sun himself has sent me like a ray,
To hint that he is coming up this way.'

### CXLV

'Is it,' exclaimed Gulbeyaz, 'as you say?
   I wish to heaven he would not shine till morning!
But bid my women form the milky way.
   Hence, my old comet! give the stars due warning –
And, Christian! mingle with them as you may,
   And as you'd have me pardon your past scorning –'
Here they were interrupted by a humming
Sound, and then by a cry, 'The Sultan's coming!'

### CXLVI

First came her damsels, a decorous file,
   And then his Highness' eunuchs, black and white;
The train might reach a quarter of a mile:
   His majesty was always so polite
As to announce his visits a long while
   Before he came, especially at night;
For being the last wife of the Emperor,
She was of course the favourite of the four.

### CXLVII

His Highness was a man of solemn port,
   Shawled to the nose, and bearded to the eyes,
Snatched from a prison to preside at court,
   His lately bowstrung brother caused his rise;
He was as good a sovereign of the sort
   As any mentioned in the histories
Of Cantemir, or Knōllĕs, where few shine
Save Solyman, the glory of their line.

### CXLVIII

He went to mosque in state, and said his prayers
    With more than 'Oriental scrupulosity';
He left to his vizier all state affairs,
    And showed but little royal curiosity;
I know not if he had domestic cares —
    No process proved connubial animosity;
Four wives, and twice five hundred maids, unseen,
Were ruled as calmly as a Christian queen.

### CXLIX

If now and then there happened a slight slip,
    Little was heard of criminal or crime;
The story scarcely passed a single lip —
    The sack and sea had settled all in time,
From which the secret nobody could rip:
    The public knew no more than does this rhyme;
No scandals made the daily press a curse —
Morals were better, and the fish no worse....

### CLIV

His Majesty saluted his fourth spouse
    With all the ceremonies of his rank,
Who cleared her sparkling eyes and smoothed her brows,
    As suits a matron who has played a prank;
These must seem doubly mindful of their vows,
    To save the credit of their breaking bank:
To no men are such cordial greetings given,
As those whose wives have made them fit for heaven.

### CLV

His Highness cast around his great black eyes,
    And looking, as he always looked, perceived
Juan amongst the damsels in disguise,
    At which he seemed no whit surprised nor grieved,

But just remarked with air sedate and wise,
  While still a fluttering sigh Gulbeyaz heaved,
'I see you've bought another girl; 'tis pity
That a mere Christian should be half so pretty.'

### CLVI

This compliment, which drew all eyes upon
  The new-bought virgin, made her blush and shake.
Her comrades, also, thought themselves undone:
  Oh! Mahomet! that his Majesty should take
Such notice of a giaour, while scarce to one
  Of them his lips imperial ever spake!
There was a general whisper, toss, and wriggle,
But etiquette forbade them all to giggle.

### CLVII

The Turks do well to shut — at least, sometimes —
  The women up — because, in sad reality,
Their chastity in these unhappy climes
  Is not a thing of that astringent quality,
Which in the North prevents precocious crimes,
  And makes our snow less pure than our morality;
The sun, which yearly melts the polar ice,
Has quite the contrary effect on vice.

### CLVIII

Thus in the East they are extremely strict,
  And wedlock and a padlock mean the same;
Excepting only when the former's picked
  It ne'er can be replaced in proper frame;
Spoilt, as a pipe of claret is when pricked:
  But then their own polygamy's to blame;
Why don't they knead two virtuous souls for life
Into that moral centaur, man and wife?

### CLIX

Thus far our chronicle; and now we pause,
　　Though not for want of matter; but 'tis time,
According to the ancient epic laws,
　　To slacken sail, and anchor with our rhyme.
Let this fifth canto meet with due applause,
　　The sixth shall have a touch of the sublime;
Meanwhile, as Homer sometimes sleeps, perhaps
You'll pardon to my muse a few short naps.

## From Canto VI

### XXIV

Gulbeyaz and her lord were sleeping, or
　　At least one of them! – Oh, the heavy night,
When wicked wives, who love some bachelor,
　　Lie down in dudgeon to sigh for the light
Of the grey morning, and look vainly for
　　Its twinkle through the lattice dusky quite –
To toss, to tumble, doze, revive, and quake
Lest their too lawful bed-fellow should wake!

### XXV

These are beneath the canopy of heaven,
　　Also beneath the canopy of beds,
Four-posted and silk-curtained, which are given
　　For rich men and their brides to lay their heads
Upon, in sheets white as what bards call 'driven
　　Snow'. Well! 'tis all haphazard when one weds.
Gulbeyaz was an empress, but had been
Perhaps as wretched if a peasant's quean.

### XXVI

Don Juan in his feminine disguise,
　　With all the damsels in their long array,
Had bowed themselves before th' imperial eyes,
　　And at the usual signal ta'en their way

Back to their chambers, those long galleries
   In the seraglio, where the ladies lay
Their delicate limbs; a thousand bosoms there
Beating for love, as the caged bird's for air.

### XXVII

I love the sex, and sometimes would reverse
   The tyrant's wish, 'that mankind only had
One neck, which he with one fell stroke might pierce':
   My wish is quite as wide, but not so bad,
And much more tender on the whole than fierce;
   It being (not *now*, but only while a lad)
That womankind had but one rosy mouth,
To kiss them all at once from North to South.

### XXVIII

Oh, enviable Briareus! with thy hands
   And heads, if thou hadst all things multiplied
In such proportion! – But my Muse withstands
   The giant thought of being a Titan's bride,
Or travelling in Patagonian lands;
   So let us back to Lilliput, and guide
Our hero through the labyrinth of love,
In which we left him several lines above.

### XXIX

He went forth with the lovely Odalisques,
   At the given signal joined to their array;
And though he certainly ran many risks,
   Yet he could not at times keep, by the way,
(Although the consequences of such frisks
   Are worse than the worst damages men pay
In moral England, where the thing's a tax,)
From ogling all their charms from breasts to backs.

### XXX

Still he forgot not his disguise: – along
　　The galleries from room to room they walked,
A virgin-like and edifying throng,
　　By eunuchs flanked; while at their head there stalked
A dame who kept up discipline among
　　The female ranks, so that none stirred or talked,
Without her sanction on their she-parades:
Her title was 'the Mother of the Maids'.

### XXXI

Whether she was a 'mother', I know not,
　　Or whether they were 'maids' who called her mother;
But this is her seraglio title, got
　　I know not how, but good as any other;
So Cantemir can tell you, or De Tott:
　　Her office was to keep aloof or smother
All bad propensities in fifteen hundred
Young women, and correct them when they blundered.

### XXXII

A goodly sinecure, no doubt! but made
　　More easy by the absence of all men –
Except his majesty, – who, with her aid,
　　And guards, and bolts, and walls, and now and then
A slight example, just to cast a shade
　　Along the rest, contrived to keep this den
Of beauties cool as an Italian convent,
Where all the passions have, alas! but one vent.

### XXXIII

And what is that? Devotion, doubtless – how
　　Could you ask such a question? – but we will
Continue. As I said, this goodly row
　　Of ladies of all countries at the will

Of one good man, with stately march and slow,
   Like water-lilies floating down a rill –
Or rather lake – for rills do not run slowly, –
Paced on most maiden-like and melancholy.

### XXXIV

But when they reached their own apartments, there,
   Like birds, or boys, or bedlamites broke loose,
Waves at spring-tide, or women anywhere
   When freed from bonds (which are of no great use
After all), or like Irish at a fair,
   Their guards being gone, and as it were a truce
Established between them and bondage, they
Began to sing, dance, chatter, smile, and play.

### XXXV

Their talk, of course, ran most on the new comer;
   Her shape, her hair, her air, her everything:
Some thought her dress did not so much become her,
   Or wondered at her ears without a ring;
Some said her years were getting nigh their summer,
   Others contended they were but in spring;
Some thought her rather masculine in height,
While others wished that she had been so quite.

### XXXVI

But no one doubted on the whole, that she
   Was what her dress bespoke, a damsel fair,
And fresh, and 'beautiful exceedingly',
   Who with the brightest Georgians might compare:
They wondered how Gulbeyaz, too, could be
   So silly as to buy slaves who might share
(If that his Highness wearied of his bride)
Her throne and power, and every thing beside.

### XXXVII

But what was strangest in this virgin crew,
  Although her beauty was enough to vex,
After the first investigating view,
  They all found out as few, or fewer, specks
In the fair form of their companion new,
  Than is the custom of the gentle sex,
When they survey, with Christian eyes or heathen,
In a new face, 'the ugliest creature breathing'.

### XXXVIII

And yet they had their little jealousies,
  Like all the rest; but upon this occasion,
Whether there are such things as sympathies
  Without our knowledge or our approbation,
Although they could not see through his disguise,
  All felt a soft kind of concatenation,
Like magnetism, or devilism, or what
You please – we will not quarrel about that:

### XXXIX

But certain 'tis they all felt for their new
  Companion something newer still, as 'twere
A sentimental friendship through and through,
  Extremely pure, which made them all concur
In wishing her their sister, save a few
  Who wished they had a brother just like her,
Whom, if they were at home in sweet Circassia,
They would prefer to Padisha or Pacha.

### XL

Of those who had most genius for this sort
  Of sentimental friendship, there were three,
Lolah, Katinka, and Dudù – in short,
  (To save description) fair as fair can be

Were they, according to the best report,
    Though differing in stature and degree,
And clime and time, and country and complexion;
They all alike admired their new connection.

### XLI

Lolah was dusk as India and as warm;
    Katinka was a Georgian, white and red,
With great blue eyes, a lovely hand and arm,
    And feet so small they scarce seemed made to tread,
But rather skim the earth; while Dudù's form
    Looked more adapted to be put to bed,
Being somewhat large, and languishing, and lazy,
Yet of a beauty that would drive you crazy.

### XLII

A kind of sleepy Venus seemed Dudù,
    Yet very fit to 'murder sleep' in those
Who gazed upon her cheek's transcendent hue,
    Her Attic forehead, and her Phidian nose:
Few angles were there in her form, 'tis true,
    Thinner she might have been, and yet scarce lose;
Yet, after all, 'twould puzzle to say where
It would not spoil some separate charm to pare.

### XLIII

She was not violently lively, but
    Stole on your spirit like a May-day breaking;
Her eyes were not too sparkling, yet, half-shut,
    They put beholders in a tender taking;
She looked (this simile's quite new) just cut
    From marble, like Pygmalion's statue waking,
The mortal and the marble still at strife,
And timidly expanding into life.

### XLIV

Lolah demanded the new damsel's name –
  'Juanna.' – Well, a pretty name enough.
Katinka asked her also whence she came –
  'From Spain.' – 'But where *is* Spain?' – 'Don't ask
    such stuff,
Nor show your Georgian ignorance – for shame!'
  Said Lolah, with an accent rather rough,
To poor Katinka: 'Spain's an island near
Morocco, betwixt Egypt and Tangier.'

### XLV

Dudù said nothing, but sat down beside
  Juanna, playing with her veil or hair;
And looking at her steadfastly, she sighed,
  As if she pitied her for being there,
A pretty stranger, without friend or guide,
  And all abashed, too, at the general stare
Which welcomes hapless strangers in all places,
With kind remarks upon their mien and faces.

### XLVI

But here the Mother of the Maids drew near,
  With, 'Ladies, it is time to go to rest.
I'm puzzled what to do with you, my dear,'
  She added to Juanna, their new guest:
'Your coming has been unexpected here,
  And every couch is occupied; you had best
Partake of mine; but by tomorrow early
We will have all things settled for you fairly.'

### XLVII

Here Lolah interposed – 'Mamma, you know
  You don't sleep soundly, and I cannot bear
That anybody should disturb you so;
  I'll take Juanna; we're a slenderer pair

313

Than you would make the half of; – don't say no;
   And I of your young charge will take due care.'
But here Katinka interfered, and said,
'She also had compassion and a bed.'

### XLVIII

'Besides, I hate to sleep alone,' quoth she.
   The matron frowned: 'Why so?' – 'For fear of ghosts,'
Replied Katinka; 'I am sure I see
   A phantom upon each of the four posts;
And then I have the worst dreams that can be,
   Of Guebres, Giaours, and Ginns, and Gouls in hosts.'
The dame replied, 'Between your dreams and you,
I fear Juanna's dreams would be but few.

### XLIX

'You, Lolah, must continue still to lie
   Alone, for reasons which don't matter; you
The same, Katinka, until by and by;
   And I shall place Juanna with Dudù,
Who's quiet, inoffensive, silent, shy,
   And will not toss and chatter the night through.
What say you, child?' – Dudù said nothing, as
Her talents were of the more silent class;

### L

But she rose up, and kissed the matron's brow
   Between the eyes, and Lolah on both cheeks,
Katinka, too; and with a gentle bow
   (Curt'sies are neither used by Turks nor Greeks)
She took Juanna by the hand to show
   Their place of rest, and left to both their piques,
The others pouting at the matron's preference
Of Dudù, though they held their tongues from deference.

### LI

It was a spacious chamber (Oda is
 The Turkish title), and ranged round the wall
Were couches, toilets – and much more than this
 I might describe, as I have seen it all,
But it suffices – little was amiss;
 'Twas on the whole a nobly furnished hall,
With all things ladies want, save one or two,
And even those were nearer than they knew.

### LII

Dudù, as has been said, was a sweet creature,
 Not very dashing, but extremely winning,
With the most regulated charms of feature,
 Which painters cannot catch like faces sinning
Against proportion – the wild strokes of nature
 Which they hit off at once in the beginning,
Full of expression, right or wrong, that strike,
And pleasing, or unpleasing, still are like.

### LIII

But she was a soft landscape of mild earth,
 Where all was harmony, and calm, and quiet,
Luxuriant, budding; cheerful without mirth,
 Which, if not happiness, is much more nigh it
Than are your mighty passions and so forth,
 Which some call 'the sublime': I wish they'd try it:
I've seen your stormy seas and stormy women,
And pity lovers rather more than seamen.

### LIV

But she was pensive more than melancholy,
 And serious more than pensive, and serene,
It may be, more than either – not unholy
 Her thoughts, at least till now, appear to have been.

The strangest thing was, beauteous, she was wholly
Unconscious, albeit turned of quick seventeen,
That she was fair, or dark, or short, or tall;
She never thought about herself at all.

### LV

And therefore was she kind and gentle as
   The Age of Gold (when gold was yet unknown,
By which its nomenclature came to pass;
   Thus most appropriately has been shown
'Lucus a *non* lucendo,' *not* what *was*,
   But what *was not*; a sort of style that's grown
Extremely common in this age, whose metal
The devil may decompose, but never settle:

### LVI

I think it may be of 'Corinthian Brass',
   Which was a mixture of all metals, but
The brazen uppermost). Kind reader! pass
   This long parenthesis: I could not shut
It sooner for the soul of me, and class
   My faults even with your own! which meaneth, put
A kind construction upon them and me:
But *that* you won't – then don't – I am not less free.

### LVII

'Tis time we should return to plain narration,
   And thus my narrative proceeds: – Dudù,
With every kindness short of ostentation,
   Showed Juan, or Juanna, through and through
This labyrinth of females, and each station
   Described – what's strange – in words extremely few:
I have but one simile, and that's a blunder,
For wordless woman, which is *silent* thunder.

### LVIII

And next she gave her (I say *her*, because
　The gender still was epicene, at least
In outward show, which is a saving clause)
　An outline of the customs of the East,
With all their chaste integrity of laws,
　By which the more a harem is increased,
The stricter doubtless grow the vestal duties
Of any supernumerary beauties.

### LIX

And then she gave Juanna a chaste kiss:
　Dudù was fond of kissing – which I'm sure
That nobody can ever take amiss,
　Because 'tis pleasant, so that it be pure,
And between females means no more than this –
　That they have nothing better near, or newer.
'Kiss' rhymes to 'bliss' in fact as well as verse –
I wish it never led to something worse.

### LX

In perfect innocence she then unmade
　Her toilet, which cost little, for she was
A child of Nature, carelessly arrayed:
　If fond of a chance ogle at her glass,
'Twas like the fawn, which, in the lake displayed,
　Beholds her own shy, shadowy image pass,
When first she starts, and then returns to peep,
Admiring this new native of the deep.

### LXI

And one by one her articles of dress
　Were laid aside; but not before she offered
Her aid to fair Juanna, whose excess
　Of modesty declined the assistance proffered:

Which passed well off – as she could do no less;
  Though by this politesse she rather suffered,
Pricking her fingers with those cursed pins,
Which surely were invented for our sins, –

### LXII

Making a woman like a porcupine,
  Not to be rashly touched. But still more dread,
Oh ye! whose fate it is, as once 'twas mine,
  In early youth, to turn a lady's maid; –
I did my very boyish best to shine
  In tricking her out for a masquerade:
The pins were placed sufficiently, but not
Stuck all exactly in the proper spot.

### LXIII

But these are foolish things to all the wise,
  And I love wisdom more than she loves me;
My tendency is to philosophize
  On most things, from a tyrant to a tree;
But still the spouseless virgin Knowledge flies.
  What are we? and whence came we? what shall be
Our ultimate existence? what's our present?
Are questions answerless, and yet incessant.

### LXIV

There was deep silence in the chamber: dim
  And distant from each other burned the lights,
And slumber hovered o'er each lovely limb
  Of the fair occupants: if there be sprites,
They should have walked there in their sprightliest trim,
  By way of change from their sepulchral sites,
And shown themselves as ghosts of better taste
Than haunting some old ruin or wild waste.

### LXV

Many and beautiful lay those around,
  Like flowers of different hue, and clime, and root,
In some exotic garden sometimes found,
  With cost, and care, and warmth induced to shoot.
One with her auburn tresses lightly bound,
  And fair brows gently drooping, as the fruit
Nods from the tree, was slumbering with soft breath,
And lips apart, which showed the pearls beneath.

### LXVI

One with her flushed cheek laid on her white arm,
  And raven ringlets gathered in dark crowd
Above her brow, lay dreaming soft and warm;
  And smiling through her dream, as through a cloud
The moon breaks, half unveiled each further charm,
  As, slightly stirring in her snowy shroud,
Her beauties seized the unconscious hour of night
All bashfully to struggle into light.

### LXVII

This is no bull, although it sounds so; for
  'Twas night, but there were lamps, as hath been said.
A third's all pallid aspect offered more
  The traits of sleeping sorrow, and betrayed
Through the heaved breast the dream of some far shore
  Belovéd and deplored; while slowly strayed
(As night-dew, on a cypress glittering, tinges
The black bough) tear-drops through her eyes' dark
    fringes.

### LXVIII

A fourth as marble, statue-like and still,
  Lay in a breathless, hushed, and stony sleep;
White, cold, and pure, as looks a frozen rill,
  Or the snow minaret on an Alpine steep,

Or Lot's wife done in salt, – or what you will; –
   My similes are gathered in a heap,
So pick and choose – perhaps you'll be content
With a carved lady on a monument.

### LXIX

And lo! a fifth appears; – and what is she?
   A lady of a 'certain age', which means
Certainly agéd – what her years might be
   I know not, never counting past their teens;
But there she slept, not quite so fair to see,
   As ere that awful period intervenes
Which lays both men and women on the shelf,
To meditate upon their sins and self.

### LXX

But all this time how slept, or dreamed, Dudù?
   With strict inquiry I could ne'er discover,
And scorn to add a syllable untrue;
   But ere the middle watch was hardly over,
Just when the fading lamps waned dim and blue,
   And phantoms hovered, or might seem to hover,
To those who like their company, about
The apartment, on a sudden she screamed out:

### LXXI

And that so loudly, that upstarted all
   The Oda, in a general commotion:
Matron and maids, and those whom you may call
   Neither, came crowding like the waves of ocean,
One on the other, throughout the whole hall,
   All trembling, wondering, without the least notion
More than I have myself of what could make
The calm Dudù so turbulently wake.

### LXXII

But wide awake she was, and round her bed,
  With floating draperies and with flying hair,
With eager eyes, and light but hurried tread,
  And bosoms, arms, and ankles glancing bare,
And bright as any meteor ever bred
  By the North Pole, – they sought her cause of care,
For she seemed agitated, flushed, and frightened,
Her eye dilated and her colour heightened.

### LXXIII

But what is strange – and a strong proof how great
  A blessing is sound sleep – Juanna lay
As fast as ever husband by his mate
  In holy matrimony snores away.
Not all the clamour broke her happy state
  Of slumber, ere they shook her, – so they say
At least, – and then she, too, unclosed her eyes,
And yawned a good deal with discreet surprise.

### LXXIV

And now commenced a strict investigation,
  Which, as all spoke at once, and more than once
Conjecturing, wondering, asking a narration,
  Alike might puzzle either wit or dunce
To answer in a very clear oration.
  Dudù had never passed for wanting sense,
But, being 'no orator as Brutus is',
Could not at first expound what was amiss.

### LXXV

At length she said, that in a slumber sound
  She dreamed a dream, of walking in a wood –
A 'wood obscure', like that where Dante found
  Himself in at the age when all grow good;

Life's half-way house, where dames with virtue crowned
   Run much less risk of lovers turning rude;
And that this wood was full of pleasant fruits,
And trees of goodly growth and spreading roots;

### LXXVI

And in the midst a golden apple grew, –
   A most prodigious pippin – but it hung
Rather too high and distant; that she threw
   Her glances on it, and then, longing, flung
Stones and whatever she could pick up, to
   Bring down the fruit, which still perversely clung
To its own bough, and dangled yet in sight,
But always at a most provoking height; –

### LXXVII

That on a sudden, when she least had hope,
   It fell down of its own accord before
Her feet; that her first movement was to stoop
   And pick it up, and bite it to the core;
That just as her young lip began to ope
   Upon the golden fruit the vision bore,
A bee flew out, and stung her to the heart,
And so – she awoke with a great scream and start.

### LXXVIII

All this she told with some confusion and
   Dismay, the usual consequence of dreams
Of the unpleasant kind, with none at hand
   To expound their vain and visionary gleams.
I've known some odd ones which seemed really planned
   Prophetically, or that which one deems
A 'strange coincidence', to use a phrase
By which such things are settled now-a-days.

### LXXIX

The damsels, who had thoughts of some great harm,
  Began, as is the consequence of fear,
To scold a little at the false alarm
  That broke for nothing on their sleeping ear.
The matron, too, was wroth to leave her warm
  Bed for the dream she had been obliged to hear,
And chafed at poor Dudù, who only sighed,
And said, that she was sorry she had cried.

### LXXX

'I've heard of stories of a cock and bull;
  But visions of an apple and a bee,
To take us from our natural rest, and pull
  The whole Oda from their beds at half-past three,
Would make us think the moon is at its full.
  You surely are unwell, child! we must see,
Tomorrow, what his Highness's physician
Will say to this hysteric of a vision.

### LXXXI

'And poor Juanna, too, the child's first night
  Within these walls, to be broke in upon
With such a clamour – I had thought it right
  That the young stranger should not lie alone,
And, as the quietest of all, she might
  With you, Dudù, a good night's rest have known;
But now I must transfer her to the charge
Of Lolah – though her couch is not so large.'

### LXXXII

Lolah's eyes sparkled at the proposition;
  But poor Dudù, with large drops in her own,
Resulting from the scolding or the vision,
  Implored that present pardon might be shown

For this first fault, and that on no condition
  (She added in a soft and piteous tone)
Juanna should be taken from her, and
Her future dreams should all be kept in hand.

### LXXXIII

She promised never more to have a dream,
  At least to dream so loudly as just now;
She wondered at herself how she could scream –
  'Twas foolish, nervous, as she must allow,
A fond hallucination, and a theme
  For laughter – but she felt her spirits low,
And begged they would excuse her; she'd get over
This weakness in a few hours, and recover.

### LXXXIV

And here Juanna kindly interposed,
  And said she felt herself extremely well
Where she then was, as her sound sleep disclosed,
  When all around rang like a tocsin bell;
She did not find herself the least disposed
  To quit her gentle partner, and to dwell
Apart from one who had no sin to show,
Save that of dreaming once 'mal-à-propos'.

### LXXXV

As thus Juanna spoke, Dudù turned round
  And hid her face within Juanna's breast;
Her neck alone was seen, but that was found
  The colour of a budding rose's crest.
I can't tell why she blushed, nor can expound
  The mystery of this rapture of their rest;
All that I know is, that the facts I state
Are true as truth has ever been of late.

### LXXXVI

And so good night to them, – or, if you will,
   Good morrow – for the cock had crown, and light
Began to clothe each Asiatic hill,
   And the mosque crescent struggled into sight
Of the long caravan, which in the chill
   Of dewy dawn wound slowly round each height
That stretches to the stony belt, which girds
Asia, where Kaff looks down upon the Kurds....

*The canto ends with Juan and Dudù being threatened with a
dipping....*

### CXX

I leave them for the present with good wishes,
   Though doubts of their well doing, to arrange
Another part of history; for the dishes
   Of this our banquet we must sometimes change;
And trusting Juan may escape the fishes,
   Although his situation now seems strange,
And scarce secure, as such digressions *are* fair,
The Muse will take a little touch at warfare.

### *From Canto VII*

### XIV

The Russians now were ready to attack;
   But oh, ye goddesses of war and glory!
How shall I spell the name of each Cossacque
   Who were immortal, could one tell their story?
Alas! what to their memory can lack?
   Achilles' self was not more grim and gory
Than thousands of this new and polished nation,
Whose names want nothing but – pronunciation.

### XV

Still I'll record a few, if but to increase
  Our euphony: there was Strongenoff, and Strokonoff,
Meknop, Serge Lwow, Arsniéw of modern Greece,
  And Tschitsshakoff, and Roguenoff, and Chokenoff,
And others of twelve consonants apiece;
  And more might be found out, if I could poke enough
Into gazettes; but Fame (capricious strumpet),
It seems, has got an ear as well as trumpet,

### XVI

And cannot tune those discords of narration,
  Which may be names at Moscow, into rhyme;
Yet there were several worth commemoration,
  As e'er was virgin of a nuptial chime;
Soft words, too, fitted for the peroration
  Of Londonderry drawling against time,
Ending in 'ischskin', 'ousckin', 'iffskchy', 'ouski',
Of whom we can insert but Rousamouski,

### XVII

Scherematoff and Chrematoff, Koklophti,
  Koclobski, Kourakin, and Mouskin Pouskin,
All proper men of weapons, as e'er scoffed high
  Against a foe, or ran a sabre through skin:
Little cared they for Mahomet or Mufti,
  Unless to make their kettle-drums a new skin
Out of their hides, if parchment had grown dear,
And no more handy substitute been near.

### XVIII

Then there were foreigners of much renown,
  Of various nations, and all volunteers;
Not fighting for their country or its crown,
  But wishing to be one day brigadiers:

Also to have the sacking of a town;
   A pleasant thing to young men at their years.
'Mongst them were several Englishmen of pith,
Sixteen called Thomson, and nineteen named Smith.

### XIX

Jack Thomson and Bill Thomson; – all the rest
   Had been called '*Jemmy*', after the great bard;
I don't know whether they had arms or crest,
   But such a godfather's as good a card.
Three of the Smiths were Peters; but the best
   Amongst them all, hard blows to inflict or ward,
Was *he*, since so renowned 'in country quarters
At Halifax'; but now he served the Tartars.

### XX

The rest were Jacks and Gills and Wills and Bills,
   But when I've added that the elder Jack Smith
Was born in Cumberland among the hills,
   And that his father was an honest blacksmith,
I've said all *I* know of a name that fills
   Three lines of the despatch in taking 'Schmacksmith',
A village of Moldavia's waste, wherein
He fell, immortal in a bulletin.

### XXI

I wonder (although Mars no doubt's a god I
   Praise) if a man's name in a *bulletin*
May make up for a *bullet in* his body?
   I hope this little question is no sin,
Because, though I am but a simple noddy,
   I think one Shakespeare puts the same thought in
The mouth of some one in his plays so doting,
Which many people pass for wits by quoting.

### XXII

Then there were Frenchmen, gallant, young, and gay:
  But I'm too great a patriot to record
Their Gallic names upon a glorious day;
  I'd rather tell ten lies than say a word
Of truth; — such truths are treason; they betray
  Their country; and as traitors are abhorred
Who name the French in English, save to show
How Peace should make John Bull the Frenchman's foe.

### XXIII

The Russians, having built two batteries on
  An isle near Ismail, had two ends in view,
The first was to bombard it, and knock down
  The public buildings and the private too,
No matter what poor souls might be undone.
  The city's shape suggested this, 'tis true;
Formed like an amphitheatre, each dwelling
Presented a fine mark to throw a shell in.

### XXIV

The second object was to profit by
  The moment of the general consternation,
To attack the Turks' flotilla, which lay nigh
  Extremely tranquil, anchored at its station:
But a third motive was as probably
  To frighten them into capitulation;
A fantasy which sometimes seizes warriors,
Unless they are game as bull-dogs and fox-terriers.

### XXV

A habit rather blameable, which is
  That of despising those we combat with,
Common in many cases, was in this
  The cause of killing Tchitchitzkoff and Smith;

One of the valorous 'Smiths' whom we shall miss
   Out of those nineteen who late rhymed to 'pith';
But 'tis a name so spread o'er 'Sir' and 'Madam',
That one would think the first who bore it 'Adam'.

### XXVI

The Russian batteries were incomplete,
   Because they were constructed in a hurry;
Thus the same cause which makes a verse want feet,
   And throws a cloud o'er Longman and John Murray,
When the sale of new books is not so fleet
   As they who print them think is necessary,
May likewise put off for a time what story
Sometimes calls 'murder', and at others 'glory'.

### XXVII

Whether it was their engineer's stupidity,
   Their haste or waste, I neither know nor care,
Or some contractor's personal cupidity,
   Saving his soul by cheating in the ware
Of homicide, but there was no solidity
   In the new batteries erected there;
They either missed, or they were never missed,
And added greatly to the missing list.

### XXVIII

A sad miscalculation about distance
   Made all their naval matters incorrect;
Three fireships lost their amiable existence
   Before they reached a spot to take effect:
The match was lit too soon, and no assistance
   Could remedy this lubberly defect;
They blew up in the middle of the river,
While, though 'twas dawn, the Turks slept fast as ever.

### XXIX

At seven they rose, however, and surveyed
   The Russ flotilla getting under way;
'Twas nine, when still advancing undismayed,
   Within a cable's length their vessels lay
Off Ismail, and commenced a cannonade,
   Which was returned with interest, I may say,
And by a fire of musketry and grape,
And shells and shot of every size and shape.

### XXX

For six hours bore they without intermission
   The Turkish fire, and, aided by their own
Land batteries, worked their guns with great precision:
   At length they found mere cannonade alone
By no means would produce the town's submission,
   And made a signal to retreat at one.
One bark blew up, a second near the works
Running aground, was taken by the Turks.

### XXXI

The Moslem, too, had lost both ships and men;
   But when they saw the enemy retire,
Their Delhis manned some boats, and sailed again,
   And galled the Russians with a heavy fire,
And tried to make a landing on the main;
   But here the effect fell short of their desire:
Count Damas drove them back into the water
Pell-mell, and with a whole gazette of slaughter....

### XLII

Our friends the Turks, who with loud 'Allahs' now
   Began to signalize the Russ retreat,
Were damnably mistaken; few are slow
   In thinking that their enemy is beat,

(Or *beaten*, if you insist on grammar, though
   I never think about it in a heat,)
But here I say the Turks were much mistaken,
Who hating hogs, yet wished to save their bacon.

### XLIII

For, on the sixteenth, at full gallop, drew
   In sight two horsemen, who were deemed Cossacques
For some time, till they came in nearer view.
   They had but little baggage at their backs,
For there were but *three* shirts between the two;
   But on they rode upon two Ukraine hacks,
Till, in approaching, were at length descried
In this plain pair, Suwarrow and his guide....

### XLVI

But to the tale; – great joy unto the camp!
   To Russian, Tartar, English, French, Cossacque,
O'er whom Suwarrow shone like a gas lamp,
   Presaging a most luminous attack;
Or like a wisp along the marsh so damp,
   Which leads beholders on a boggy walk,
He flitted to and fro a dancing light,
Which all who saw it followed, wrong or right.

### XLVII

But, certes, matters took a different face;
   There was enthusiasm and much applause,
The fleet and camp saluted with great grace,
   And all presaged good fortune to their cause.
Within a cannon-shot length of the place
   They drew, constructed ladders, repaired flaws
In former works, made new, prepared fascines,
And all kinds of benevolent machines.

### XLVIII

'Tis thus the spirit of a single mind
   Makes that of multitudes take one direction,
As roll the waters to the breathing wind,
   Or roams the herd beneath the bull's protection;
Or as a little dog will lead the blind,
   Or a bell-wether form the flock's connection
By tinkling sounds, when they go forth to victual;
Such is the sway of your great men o'er little.

### XLIX

The whole camp rung with joy; you would have thought
   That they were going to a marriage feast
(This metaphor, I think, holds good as aught,
   Since there is discord after both at least):
There was not now a luggage boy but sought
   Danger and spoil with ardour much increased;
And why? because a little – odd – old man,
Stript to his shirt, was come to lead the van.

### L

But so it was; and every preparation
   Was made with all alacrity: the first
Detachment of three columns took its station,
   And waited but the signal's voice to burst
Upon the foe: the second's ordination
   Was also in three columns, with a thirst
For glory gaping o'er a sea of slaughter:
The third, in columns two, attacked by water.

### LI

New batteries were erected, and was held
   A general council, in which unanimity,
That stranger to most councils, here prevailed,
   As sometimes happens in a great extremity;

And every difficulty being dispelled,
    Glory began to dawn with due sublimity,
While Souvaroff, determined to obtain it,
Was teaching his recruits to use the bayonet.

### LII

It is an actual fact, that he, commander
    In chief, in proper person deigned to drill
The awkward squad, and could afford to squander
    His time, a corporal's duty to fulfil;
Just as you'd break a sucking salamander
    To swallow flame, and never take it ill:
He showed them how to mount a ladder (which
Was not like Jacob's) or to cross a ditch.

### LIII.

Also he dressed up, for the nonce, fascines
    Like men with turbans, scimitars, and dirks,
And made them charge with bayonet these machines,
    By way of lesson against actual Turks;
And when well practised in these mimic scenes,
    He judged them proper to assail the works;
At which your wise men sneered in phrases witty:
He made no answer; but he took the city.

### LIV

Most things were in this posture on the eve
    Of the assault, and all the camp was in
A stern repose; which you would scarce conceive;
    Yet men resolved to dash through thick and thin
Are very silent when they once believe
    That all is settled: – there was little din,
For some were thinking of their home and friends,
And others of themselves and latter ends.

### LV

Suwarrow chiefly was on the alert,
   Surveying, drilling, ordering, jesting, pondering;
For the man was, we safely may assert,
   A thing to wonder at beyond most wondering;
Here, buffoon, half-demon, and half-dirt,
   Praying, instructing, desolating, plundering –
Now Mars, now Momus – and when bent to storm
A fortress, Harlequin in uniform.

### LVI

The day before the assault, while upon drill –
   For this great conqueror played the corporal –
Some Cossacques, hovering like hawks round a hill,
   Had met a party towards the twilight's fall,
One of whom spoke their tongue – or well or ill,
   'Twas much that he was understood at all;
But whether from his voice, or speech, or manner,
They found that he had fought beneath their banner.

### LVII

Whereon immediately at his request
   They brought him and his comrades to headquarters;
Their dress was Moslem, but you might have guessed
   That these were merely masquerading Tartars,
And that beneath each Turkish-fashioned vest
   Lurked Christianity; which sometimes barters
Her inward grace for outward show, and makes
It difficult to shun some strange mistakes.

### LVIII

Suwarrow, who was standing in his shirt
   Before a company of Calmucks, drilling,
Exclaiming, fooling, swearing at the inert,
   And lecturing on the noble art of killing, –

For deeming human clay but common dirt
  This great philosopher was thus instilling
His maxims, which to martial comprehension
Proved death in battle equal to a pension; –

LIX

Suwarrow, when he saw this company
  Of Cossacques and their prey, turned round and cast
Upon them his slow brow and piercing eye: –
  'Whence come ye?' – 'From Constantinople last,
Captives just now escaped,' was the reply.
  'What are ye?' – 'What you see us.' Briefly passed
This dialogue; for he who answered knew
To whom he spoke, and made his words but few.

LX

'Your names?' – 'Mine's Johnson, and my comrade's Juan;
  The other two are women, and the third
Is neither man nor woman.' The chief threw on
  The party a slight glance, then said, 'I have heard
*Your* name before, the second is a new one:
  To bring the other three here was absurd:
But let that pass: – I think I have heard your name
In the Nikolaiew regiment?' – 'The same.'

LXI

'You served at Widdin?' – 'Yes.' – 'You led the attack?'
  'I did.' – 'What next?' – 'I really hardly know.'
'You were the first i' the breach?' – 'I was not slack
  At least to follow those who might be so.'
'What followed?' – 'A shot laid me on my back,
  And I became a prisoner to the foe.'
'You shall have vengeance, for the town surrounded
Is twice as strong as that where you were wounded.

335

LXII

'Where will you serve?' – 'Where'er you please.' – 'I know
   You like to be the hope of the forlorn,
And doubtless would be foremost on the foe
   After the hardships you've already borne.
And this young fellow – say what can he do?
   He with the beardless chin and garments torn?' –
'Why, general, if he hath no greater fault
In war than love, he had better lead the assault.' –

LXIII

'He shall if that he dare.' Here Juan bowed
   Low as the compliment deserved. Suwarrow
Continued: 'Your old regiment's allowed,
   By special providence, to lead tomorrow,
Or, it may be tonight, the assault: I have vowed
   To several saints, that shortly plough or harrow
Shall pass o'er what was Ismail, and its tusk
Be unimpeded by the proudest mosque.

LXIV

'So now, my lads, for glory!' – Here he turned
   And drilled away in the most classic Russian,
Until each high, heroic bosom burned
   For cash and conquest, as if from a cushion
A preacher had held forth (who nobly spurned
   All earthly goods save tithes) and bade them push on
To slay the pagans who resisted, battering
The armies of the Christian Empress Catherine.

LXV

Johnson, who knew by this long colloquy
   Himself a favourite, ventured to address
Suwarrow, though engaged with accents high
   In his resumed amusement. 'I confess

My debt in being thus allowed to die
   Among the foremost; but if you'd express
Explicitly our several posts, my friend
And self would know what duty to attend.'

### LXVI

'Right! I was busy, and forgot. Why, you
   Will join your former regiment, which should be
Now under arms. Ho! Katskoff, take him to –'
   (Here he called up a Polish orderly)
'His post, I mean the regiment Nikolaiew:
   The stranger stripling may remain with me;
He's a fine boy. The women may be sent
To the other baggage, or to the sick tent.'

### LXVII

But here a sort of scene began to ensue:
   The ladies, – who by no means had been bred
To be disposed of in a way so new,
   Although their harem education led
Doubtless to that of doctrines the most true,
   Passive obedience, – now raised up the head
With flashing eyes and starting tears, and flung
Their arms, as hens their wings about their young,

### LXVIII

O'er the promoted couple of brave men
   Who were thus honoured by the greatest chief
That ever peopled hell with heroes slain,
   Or plunged a province or a realm in grief.
Oh, foolish mortals! Always taught in vain!
   Oh, glorious laurel! since for one sole leaf
Of thine imaginary deathless tree,
Of blood and tears must flow the unebbing sea.

### LXIX

Suwarrow, who had small regard for tears,
    And not much sympathy for blood, surveyed
The women with their hair about their ears
    And natural agonies, with a slight shade
Of feeling: for however habit sears
    Men's hearts against whole millions, when their trade
Is butchery, sometimes a single sorrow
Will touch even heroes – and such was Suwarrow.

### LXX

He said, – and in the kindest Calmuck tone, –
    'Why, Johnson, what the devil do you mean
By bringing women here? They shall be shown
    All the attention possible, and seen
In safety to the waggons, where alone
    In fact they can be safe. You should have been
Aware this kind of baggage never thrives:
Save wed a year, I hate recruits with wives.' –

### LXXI

'May it please your excellency,' thus replied
    Our British friend, 'these are the wives of others,
And not our own. I am too qualified
    By service with my military brothers
To break the rules by bringing one's own bride
    Into a camp: I know that nought so bothers
The hearts of the heroic on a charge,
As leaving a small family at large.

### LXXII

'But these are but two Turkish ladies, who
    With their attendant aided our escape,
And afterwards accompanied us through
    A thousand perils in this dubious shape.

To me this kind of life is not so new;
  To them, poor things, it is an awkward scrape.
I therefore, if you wish me to fight freely,
Request that they may both be used genteelly.'

### LXXIII

Meantime these two poor girls, with swimming eyes,
  Looked on as if in doubt if they could trust
Their own protectors; nor was their surprise
  Less than their grief (and truly not less just)
To see an old man, rather wild than wise
  In aspect, plainly clad, besmeared with dust,
Stript to his waistcoat, and that not too clean,
More feared than all the sultans ever seen.

### LXXIV

For every thing seemed resting on his nod,
  As they could read in all eyes. Now to them,
Who were accustomed, as a sort of god,
  To see the sultan, rich in many a gem,
Like an imperial peacock stalk abroad
  (That royal bird, whose tail's a diadem,)
With all the pomp of power, it was a doubt
How power could condescend to do without.

### LXXV

John Johnson, seeing their extreme dismay,
  Though little versed in feelings oriental,
Suggested some slight comfort in his way:
  Don Juan, who was much more sentimental,
Swore they should see him by the dawn of day,
  Or that the Russian army should repent all:
And, strange to say, they found some consolation
In this – for females like exaggeration.

### LXXVI

And then with tears, and sighs, and some slight kisses,
    They parted for the present – these to await,
According to the artillery's hits or misses,
    What sages call Chance, Providence, or Fate –
(Uncertainty is one of many blisses,
    A mortgage on humanity's estate) –
While their beloved friends began to arm,
To burn a town which never did them harm....

### LXXXVI

Hark! through the silence of the cold, dull night,
    The hum of armies gathering rank on rank!
Lo! dusky masses steal in dubious sight
    Along the leaguered wall and bristling bank
Of the armed river, while with straggling light
    The stars peep through the vapours dim and dank,
Which curl in various wreaths: – how soon the smoke
Of Hell shall pall them in a deeper cloak!

### LXXXVII

Here pause we for the present – as even then
    That awful pause, dividing life from death,
Struck for an instant on the hearts of men,
    Thousands of whom were drawing their last breath!
A moment – and all will be life again!
    The march! the charge! the shouts of either faith!
Hurrah! and Allah! and – one moment more –
The death-cry drowning in the battle's roar.

*The war continues, and in the course of it Juan rescues a little
Moslem girl from 'the flashing eyes and weapons' of two villain-
ous Cossacques – 'and Juan wept, and made a vow to shield her,
which he kept'....*

## *From Canto IX*

### XXIX

Don Juan, who had shone in the late slaughter,
   Was left upon his way with the despatch,
Where blood was talked of as we would of water;
   And carcasses that lay as thick as thatch
O'er silenced cities, merely served to flatter
   Fair Catherine's pastime – who looked on the match
Between these nations as a main of cocks,
Wherein she liked her own to stand like rocks.

### XXX

And there in a *kibitka* he rolled on,
   (A curséd sort of carriage without springs,
Which on rough roads leaves scarcely a whole bone,)
   Pondering on glory, chivalry, and kings,
And orders, and on all that he had done –
   And wishing that post-horses had the wings
Of Pegasus, or at the least post-chaises
Had feathers, when a traveller on deep ways is.

### XXXI

At every jolt – and they were many – still
   He turned his eyes upon his little charge,
As if he wished that she should fare less ill
   Than he, in these sad highways left at large
To ruts, and flints, and lovely nature's skill,
   Who is no paviour, nor admits a barge
On *her* canals, where God takes sea and land,
Fishery and farm, both into his own hand....

### XLII

So on I ramble, now and then narrating,
   Now pondering: – it is time we should narrate.
I left Don Juan, with his horses baiting –
   Now we'll get o'er the ground at a great rate:

I shall not be particular in stating
   His journey, we've so many tours of late:
Suppose him then at Petersburgh; suppose
That pleasant capital of painted snows;

### XLIII

Supposed him in a handsome uniform;
   A scarlet coat, black facings, a long plume,
Waving, like sails new shivered in a storm,
   Over a cocked hat in a crowded room,
And brilliant breeches, bright as a Cairngorm
   Of yellow casimire we may presume,
White stockings drawn uncurdled as new milk
O'er limbs whose symmetry set off the silk;

### XLIV

Suppose him sword by side, and hat in hand,
   Made up by youth, fame, and an army tailor –
That great enchanter, at whose rod's command
   Beauty springs forth, and nature's self turns paler,
Seeing how art can make her work more grand
   (When she don't pin men's limbs in like a gaoler), –
Behold him placed as if upon a pillar! He
Seems Love turned a lieutenant of artillery.

### XLV

His bandage slipped down into a cravat;
   His wings subdued to epaulettes; his quiver
Shrunk to a scabbard, with his arrows at
   His side as a small sword, but sharp as ever;
His bow converted into a cocked hat;
   But still so like, that Psyche were more clever
Than some wives (who make blunders no less stupid),
If she had not mistaken him for Cupid.

### XLVI

The courtiers stared, the ladies whispered, and
    The empress smiled: the reigning favourite frowned –
I quite forget which of them was in hand
    Just then; as they are rather numerous found,
Who took by turns that difficult command,
    Since first her majesty was singly crowned:
But they were mostly nervous six-foot fellows,
All fit to make a Patagonian jealous.

### XLVII

Juan was none of these, but slight and slim,
    Blushing and beardless; and yet ne'ertheless
There was a something in his turn of limb,
    And still more in his eye, which seemed to express,
That though he looked like one of the seraphim,
    There lurked a man beneath the spirit's dress.
Besides, the empress sometimes liked a boy,
And had just buried the fair-faced Lanskoi.

### XLVIII

No wonder then that Yermoloff, or Momonoff,
    Or Scherbatoff, or any other *off*
Or *on*, might dread her majesty had not room enough
    Within her bosom (which was not too tough)
For a new flame; a thought to cast of gloom enough
    Along the aspect, whether smooth or rough,
Of him who, in the language of his station,
Then held that 'high official situation'....

### LII

And thus I supplicate your supposition,
    And mildest, matron-like interpretation,
Of the imperial favourite's condition.
    'Twas a high place, the highest in the nation

In fact, if not in rank; and the suspicion
   Of any one's attaining to his station,
No doubt gave pain, where each new pair of shoulders,
If rather broad, made stocks rise and their holders.


### LIII

Juan, I said, was a most beauteous boy,
   And had retained his boyish look beyond
The usual hirsute seasons which destroy,
   With beards and whiskers, and the like, the fond
Parisian aspect, which upset old Troy
   And founded Doctors' Commons: – I have conned
The history of divorces, which, though chequered,
Calls Ilion's the first damages on record.


### LIV

And Catherine, who loved all things, (save her lord,
   Who was gone to his place,) and passed for much,
Admiring those (by dainty dames abhorred)
   Gigantic gentlemen, yet had a touch
Of sentiment; and he she most adored
   Was the lamented Lanskoi, who was such
A lover as had cost her many a tear,
And yet but made a middling grenadier. . . .


### LXVII

Her majesty looked down, the youth looked up –
   And so they fell in love; – she with his face,
His grace, his God–knows–what: for Cupid's cup
   With the first draught intoxicates apace,
A quintessential laudanum or 'black drop',
   Which makes one drunk at once, without the base
Expedient of full bumpers; for the eye
In love drinks all life's fountains (save tears) dry.

LXVIII

He, on the other hand, if not in love,
    Fell into that no less imperious passion
Self-love – which, when some sort of thing above
    Ourselves, a singer, dancer, much in fashion,
Or duchess, princess, empress, 'deigns to prove'
    ('Tis Pope's phrase) a great longing, though a rash one,
For one especial person out of many,
Makes us believe ourselves as good as any.

LXIX

Besides, he was of that delighted age
    Which makes all female ages equal – when
We don't much care with whom we may engage,
    As bold as Daniel in the lion's den,
So that we can our native sun assuage
    In the next ocean, which may flow just then,
To make a twilight in, just as Sol's heat is
Quenched in the lap of the salt sea, or Thetis.

LXX

And Catherine (we must say thus much for Catherine),
    Though bold and bloody, was the kind of thing
Whose temporary passion was quite flattering,
    Because each lover looked a sort of king,
Made up upon an amatory pattern,
    A royal husband in all save the ring –
Which, being the damn'dest part of matrimony,
Seemed taking out the sting to leave the honey.

LXXI

And when you add to this, her womanhood
    In its meridian, her blue eyes or grey –
(The last, if they have soul, are quite as good,
    Or better, as the best examples say:

Napoleon's, Mary's (queen of Scotland), should
　　Lend to that colour a transcendent ray;
And Pallas also sanctions the same hue,
Too wise to look through optics black or blue) –

### LXXII

Her sweet smile, and her then majestic figure,
　　Her plumpness, her imperial condescension,
Her preference of a boy to men much bigger
　　(Fellows whom Messalina's self would pension),
Her prime of life, just now in juicy vigour,
　　With other extras, which we need not mention, –
All these, or any one of these, explain
Enough to make a stripling very vain.

### LXXIII

And that's enough, for love is vanity,
　　Selfish in its beginning as its end,
Except where 'tis a mere insanity,
　　A maddening spirit which would strive to blend
Itself with beauty's frail inanity,
　　On which the passion's self seems to depend:
And hence some heathenish philosophers
Make love the main-spring of the universe.

### LXXIV

Besides Platonic love, besides the love
　　Of God, the love of sentiment, the loving
Of faithful pairs – (I needs must rhyme with dove,
　　That good old steam-boat which keeps verses moving
'Gainst reason – Reason ne'er was hand-and-glove
　　With rhyme, but always leant less to improving
The sound than sense) – besides all these pretences
To love, there are those things which words name senses;

### LXXV

Those movements, those improvements in our bodies
   Which make all bodies anxious to get out
Of their own sand-pits, to mix with a goddess,
   For such all women are at first no doubt.
How beautiful that moment! and how odd is
   That fever which precedes the languid rout
Of our sensations! What a curious way
The whole thing is of clothing souls in clay!

### LXXVI

The noblest kind of love is love Platonical,
   To end or to begin with; the next grand
Is that which may be christened love canonical,
   Because the clergy take the thing in hand;
The third sort to be noted in our chronicle
   As flourishing in every Christian land,
Is, when chaste matrons to their other ties
Add what may be called *marriage in disguise*.

### LXXVII

Well, we won't analyse – our story must
   Tell for itself: the sovereign was smitten,
Juan much flattered by her love, or lust; –
   I cannot stop to alter words once written,
And the two are so mixed with human dust,
   That he who names one, both perchance may hit on:
But in such matters Russia's mighty empress
Behaved no better than a common sempstress.

### LXXVIII

The whole court melted into one wide whisper,
   And all lips were applied unto all ears!
The elder ladies' wrinkles curled much crisper
   As they beheld; the younger cast some leers

On one another, and each lovely lisper
    Smiled as she talked the matter o'er; but tears
Of rivalship rose in each clouded eye
Of all the standing army who stood by.

### LXXIX

All the ambassadors of all the powers
    Inquired, Who was this very new young man,
Who promised to be great in some few hours?
    Which is full soon (though life is but a span).
Already they beheld the silver showers
    Of rubles rain, as fast as specie can,
Upon his cabinet, besides the presents
Of several ribands, and some thousand peasants.

### LXXX

Catherine was generous, – all such ladies are:
    Love, that great opener of the heart and all
The ways that lead there, be they near or far,
    Above, below, by turnpikes great or small, –
Love – (though she had a curséd taste for war,
    And was not the best wife, unless we call
Such Clytemnestra, though perhaps 'tis better
That one should die, than two drag on the fetter) –

### LXXXI

Love had made Catherine make each lover's fortune,
    Unlike our own half-caste Elizabeth,
Whose avarice all disbursements did importune,
    If history, the grand liar, ever saith
The truth; and though grief her old age might shorten,
    Because she put a favourite to death,
Her vile, ambiguous method of flirtation,
And stinginess, disgrace her sex and station.

### LXXXII

But when the levee rose, and all was bustle
  In the dissolving circle, all the nations'
Ambassadors began as 'twere to hustle
  Round the young man with their congratulations.
Also the softer silks were heard to rustle
  Of gentle dames, among whose recreations
It is to speculate on handsome faces,
Especially when such lead to high places.

### LXXXIII

Juan, who found himself, he knew not how,
  A general object of attention, made
His answers with a very graceful bow,
  As if born for the ministerial trade.
Though modest, on his unembarrassed brow
  Nature had written 'gentleman'. He said
Little, but to the purpose; and his manner
Flung hovering graces o'er him like a banner.

### LXXXIV

An order from her majesty consigned
  Our young lieutenant to the genial care
Of those in office: all the world looked kind,
  As it will look sometimes with the first stare,
Which youth would not act ill to keep in mind,
  As also did Miss Protasoff then there,
Named from her mystic office 'l'Eprouveuse',
A term inexplicable to the Muse.

### LXXXV

With *her* then, as in humble duty bound,
  Juan retired, – and so will I, until
My Pegasus shall tire of touching ground.
  We have just lit on a 'heaven-kissing hill',

So lofty that I feel my brain turn round,
   And all my fancies whirling like a mill;
Which is a signal to my nerves and brain,
To take a quiet ride in some green lane.

## From Canto X

### XXXVII

The gentle Juan flourished, though at times
   He felt like other plants called sensitive,
Which shrink from touch, as monarchs do from rhymes,
   Save such as Southey can afford to give.
Perhaps he longed in bitter frosts for climes
   In which the Neva's ice would cease to live
Before May-day: perhaps, despite his duty,
In royalty's vast arms he sighed for beauty:

### XXXVIII

Perhaps – but, sans perhaps, we need not seek
   For causes young or old: the canker-worm
Will feed upon the fairest, freshest cheek,
   As well as further drain the withered form:
Care, like a housekeeper, brings every week
   His bills in, and however we may storm,
They must be paid: though six days smoothly run,
The seventh will bring blue devils or a dun.

### XXXIX

I don't know how it was, but he grew sick:
   The empress was alarmed, and her physician
(The same who physicked Peter) found the tick
   Of his fierce pulse betoken a condition
Which augured of the dead, however *quick*
   Itself, and showed a feverish disposition;
At which the whole court was extremely troubled,
The sovereign shocked, and all his medicines doubled.

### XL

Low were the whispers, manifold the rumours:
    Some said he had been poisoned by Potemkin;
Others talked learnedly of certain tumours,
    Exhaustion, or disorders of the same kin;
Some said 'twas a concoction of the humours,
    Which with the blood too readily will claim kin;
Others again were ready to maintain,
'"Twas only the fatigue of last campaign.'...

### XLIII

Juan demurred at this first notice to
    Quit; and though death had threatened an ejection,
His youth and constitution bore him through,
    And sent the doctors in a new direction.
But still his state was delicate: the hue
    Of health but flickered with a faint reflection
Along his wasted cheek, and seemed to gravel
The faculty – who said that he must travel.

### XLIV

The climate was too cold, they said, for him,
    Meridian-born, to bloom in. This opinion
Made the chaste Catherine look a little grim,
    Who did not like at first to lose her minion:
But when she saw his dazzling eye wax dim,
    And drooping like an eagle's with clipt pinion,
She then resolved to send him on a mission,
But in a style becoming his condition.

### XLV

There was just then a kind of a discussion,
    A sort of treaty or negotiation
Between the British cabinet and Russian,
    Maintained with all the due prevarication

With which great states such things are apt to push on;
    Something about the Baltic's navigation,
Hides, train-oil, tallow, and the rights of Thetis,
Which Britons deem their 'uti possidetis'.


### XLVI

So Catherine, who had a handsome way
    Of fitting out her favourites, conferred
This secret charge on Juan, to display
    At once her royal splendour, and reward
His services. He kissed hands the next day,
    Received instructions how to play his card,
Was laden with all kinds of gifts and honours,
Which showed what great discernment was the donor's.


*Juan set off for England, travelling through Poland, Germany, and Holland....*


### LXIV

Here he embarked, and with a flowing sail
    Went bounding for the island of the free,
Towards which the impatient wind blew half a gale;
    High dashed the spray, the bows dipped in the sea,
And sea-sick passengers turned somewhat pale;
    But Juan, seasoned, as he well might be,
By former voyages, stood to watch the skiffs
Which passed, or catch the first glimpse of the cliffs.


### LXV

At length they rose, like a white wall along
    The blue sea's border; and Don Juan felt –
What even young strangers feel a little strong
    At the first sight of Albion's chalky belt –

A kind of pride that he should be among
   Those haughty shopkeepers, who sternly dealt
Their goods and edicts out from pole to pole,
And made the very billows pay them toll.

### LXVI

I've no great cause to love that spot of earth,
   Which holds what *might have been* the noblest nation;
But though I owe it little but my birth,
   I feel a mixed regret and veneration
For its decaying fame and former worth.
   Seven years (the usual term of transportation)
Of absence lay one's old resentments level,
When a man's country's going to the devil.

### LXVII

Alas! could she but fully, truly, know
   How her great name is now throughout abhorred;
How eager all the earth is for the blow
   Which shall lay bare her bosom to the sword;
How all the nations deem her their worst foe,
   That worse than worst of foes, the once adored
False friend, who held out freedom to mankind,
And now would chain them, to the very mind; –

### LXVIII

Would she be proud, or boast herself the free,
   Who is but first of slaves? The nations are
In prison, – but the gaoler, what is he?
   No less a victim to the bolt and bar.
Is the poor privilege to turn the key
   Upon the captive, freedom? He's as far
From the enjoyment of the earth and air
Who watches o'er the chain, as they who wear.

### LXIX

Don Juan now saw Albion's earliest beauties,
  Thy cliffs, dear Dover! harbour, and hotel;
Thy custom-house, with all its delicate duties;
  Thy waiters running mucks at every bell;
Thy packets, all whose passengers are booties
  To those who upon land or water dwell;
And last, not least, to strangers uninstructed,
Thy long, long bills, whence nothing is deducted.

### LXX

Juan, though careless, young, and magnifique,
  And rich in rubles, diamonds, cash, and credit,
Who did not limit much his bills per week,
  Yet stared at this a little, though he paid it, –
(His Maggior Duomo, a smart, subtle Greek,
  Before him summoned the awful scroll and read it:)
But doubtless as the air, though seldom sunny,
Is free, the respiration's worth the money.

### LXXI

On with the horses! Off to Canterbury!
  Tramp, tramp o'er pebble, and splash, splash through
      puddle;
Hurrah! how swiftly speeds the post so merry!
  Not like slow Germany, wherein they muddle
Along the road, as if they went to bury
  Their fare; and also pause besides, to fuddle,
With 'schnapps' – sad dogs! whom 'Hundsfot', or 'Ver-
      flucter',
Affect no more than lightning a conductor.

### LXXII

Now there is nothing gives a man such spirits,
  Leavening his blood as cayenne doth a curry,
As going at full speed – no matter where its
  Direction be, so 'tis but in a hurry,

And merely for the sake of its own merits;
   For the less cause there is for all this flurry,
The greater is the pleasure in arriving
At the great end of travel – which is driving.

### LXXIII

They saw at Canterbury the cathedral;
   Black Edward's helm, and Becket's bloody stone,
Were pointed out as usual by the bedral,
   In the same quaint, uninterested tone: –
There's glory again for you, gentle reader! All
   Ends in a rusty casque and dubious bone,
Half-solved into these sodas or magnesias,
Which form that bitter draught, the human species.

### LXXIV

The effect on Juan was of course sublime:
   He breathed a thousand Cressys, as he saw
That casque, which never stooped except to time.
   Even the bold Churchman's tomb excited awe,
Who died in the then great attempt to climb
   O'er kings, who now at least must talk of law
Before they butcher. Little Leila gazed,
And asked why such a structure had been raised:

### LXXV

And being told it was 'God's house', she said
   He was well lodged, but only wondered how
He suffered infidels in his homestead,
   The cruel Nazarenes, who had laid low
His holy temples in the lands which bred
   The true believers; – and her infant brow
Was bent with grief that Mahomet should resign
A mosque so noble, flung like pearls to swine.

### LXXVI

On! on! through meadows, managed like a garden,
  A paradise of hops and high production;
For after years of travel by a bard in
  Countries of greater heat, but lesser suction,
A green field is a sight which makes him pardon
  The absence of that more sublime construction;
Which mixes up vines, olives, precipices,
Glaciers, volcanoes, oranges, and ices.

### LXXVII

And when I think upon a pot of beer —
  But I won't weep! — and so drive on, postilions!
As the smart boys spurred fast in their career,
  Juan admired these highways of free millions;
A country in all senses the most dear
  To foreigner or native, save some silly ones,
Who 'kick against the pricks' just at this juncture,
And for their pains get only a fresh puncture.

### LXXVIII

What a delightful thing's a turnpike road!
  So smooth, so level, such a mode of shaving
The earth, as scarce the eagle in the broad
  Air can accomplish, with his wide wings waving.
Had such been cut in Phaeton's time, the god
  Had told his son to satisfy his craving
With the York mail; — but onward as we roll,
'Surgit amari aliquid' — the toll!

### LXXIX

Alas! how deeply painful is all payment!
  Take lives, take wives, take aught except men's purses
As Machiavel shows those in purple raiment,
  Such is the shortest way to general curses.

They hate a murderer much less than a claimant
  On that sweet ore which every body nurses. –
Kill a man's family, and he may brook it,
But keep your hands out of his breeches' pocket:

### LXXX

So said the Florentine: ye monarchs, hearken
  To your instructor. Juan now was borne,
Just as the day began to wane and darken,
  O'er the high hill, which looks with pride or scorn
Toward the great city. – Ye who have a spark in
  Your veins of Cockney spirit, smile or mourn
According as you take things well or ill; –
Bold Britons, we are now on Shooter's Hill!

### LXXXI

The sun went down, the smoke rose up, as from
  A half-unquenched volcano, o'er a space
Which well beseemed the 'Devil's drawing-room',
  As some have qualified that wondrous place;
But Juan felt, though not approaching home,
  As one who, though he were not of the race,
Revered the soil, of those true sons the mother,
Who butchered half the earth, and bullied t'other.

### LXXXII

A mighty mass of brick, and smoke, and shipping,
  Dirty and dusky, but as wide as eye
Could reach, with here and there a sail just skipping
  In sight, then lost amidst the forestry
Of masts; a wilderness of steeples peeping
  On tiptoe through their sea-coal canopy;
A huge, dun cupola, like a foolscap crown
On a fool's head – and there is London Town!...

## From Canto XI

### XLVII

But Juan was a bachelor – of arts,
   And parts, and hearts: he danced and sung, and had
An air as sentimental as Mozart's
   Softest of melodies; and could be sad
Or cheerful, without any 'flaws or starts',
   Just at the proper time; and though a lad,
Had seen the world – which is a curious sight,
And very much unlike what people write.

### XLVIII

Fair virgins blushed upon him; wedded dames
   Bloomed also in less transitory hues;
For both commodities dwell by the Thames,
   The painting and the painted; youth, ceruse,
Against his heart preferred their usual claims,
   Such as no gentleman can quite refuse:
Daughters admired his dress, and pious mothers
Inquired his income, and if he had brothers.

### XLIX

The milliners who furnish 'drapery Misses'
   Throughout the season, upon speculation
Of payment ere the honey-moon's last kisses
   Have waned into a crescent's coruscation,
Thought such an opportunity as this is,
   Of a rich foreigner's initiation,
Not to be overlooked – and gave such credit,
That future bridegrooms swore, and sighed, and paid it.

### L

The Blues, that tender tribe, who sigh o'er sonnets,
   And with the pages of the last Review
Line the interior of their heads or bonnets,
   Advanced in all their azure's highest hue:

They talked bad French or Spanish, and upon its
    Late authors asked him for a hint or two;
And which was softest, Russian or Castilian?
And whether in his travels he saw Ilion?

LI

Juan, who was a little superficial,
    And not in literature a great Drawcansir,
Examined by this learnéd and especial
    Jury of matrons, scarce knew what to answer:
His duties warlike, loving or official,
    His steady application as a dancer,
Had kept him from the brink of Hippocrene,
Which now he found was blue instead of green.

LII

However, he replied at hazard, with
    A modest confidence and calm assurance,
Which lent his learnéd lucubrations pith,
    And passed for arguments of good endurance.
That prodigy, Miss Araminta Smith
    (Who at sixteen translated 'Hercules Furens'
Into as furious English), with her best look,
Set down his sayings in her common-place book.

LIII

Juan knew several languages – as well
    He might – and brought them up with skill, in time
To save his fame with each accomplished belle,
    Who still regretted that he did not rhyme.
There wanted but this requisite to swell
    His qualities (with them) into sublime:
Lady Fitz-Frisky, and Miss Maevia Mannish,
Both longed extremely to be sung in Spanish.

### LIV

However, he did pretty well, and was
    Admitted as an aspirant to all
The coteries, and, as in Banquo's glass,
    At great assemblies or in parties small,
He saw ten thousand living authors pass,
    That being about their average numeral;
Also the eighty 'greatest living poets',
As every paltry magazine can show it's....

### LXIV

My Juan, whom I left in deadly peril
    Amongst live poets and blue ladies, past
With some small profit through that field so sterile.
    Being tired in time, and neither least nor last,
Left it before he had been treated very ill;
    And henceforth found himself more gaily classed
Amongst the higher spirits of the day,
The sun's true son, no vapour, but a ray.

### LXV

His morns he passed in business – which dissected,
    Was like all business, a laborious nothing
That leads to lassitude, the most infected
    And Centaur Nessus garb of mortal clothing,
And on our sofas makes us lie dejected,
    And talk in tender horrors of our loathing
All kinds of toil, save for our country's good –
Which grows no better, though 'tis time it should.

### LXVI

His afternoons he passed in visits, luncheons,
    Lounging, and boxing; and the twilight hour
In riding round those vegetable puncheons
    Called 'Parks', where there is neither fruit nor flower

Enough to gratify a bee's slight munchings;
　　But after all it is the only 'bower',
(In Moore's phrase) where the fashionable fair
Can form a slight acquaintance with fresh air.

### LXVII

Then dress, then dinner, then awakes the world!
　　Then glare the lamps, then whirl the wheels, then roar
Through street and square fast flashing chariots hurled
　　Like harnessed meteors; then along the floor
Chalk mimics painting; then festoons are twirled;
　　Then roll the brazen thunders of the door,
Which opens to the thousand happy few
An earthly paradise of 'Or Molu'.

### LXVIII

There stands the noble hostess, nor shall sink
　　With the three-thousandth curtsy; there the waltz,
The only dance which teaches girls to think,
　　Makes one in love even with its very faults.
Saloon, room, hall, o'erflow beyond their brink,
　　And long the latest of arrivals halts,
'Midst royal dukes and dames condemned to climb,
And gain an inch of staircase at a time.

### LXIX

Thrice happy he who, after a survey
　　Of the good company, can win a corner,
A door that's in or boudoir out of the way,
　　Where he may fix himself like small 'Jack Horner',
And let the Babel round run as it may,
　　And look on as a mourner, or a scorner,
Or an approver, or a mere spectator,
Yawning a little as the night grows later.

### LXX

But this won't do, save by and by; and he
 Who, like Don Juan, takes an active share,
Must steer with care through all that glittering sea
 Of gems and plumes and pearls and silks, to where
He deems it is his proper place to be;
 Dissolving in the waltz to some soft air,
Or proudlier prancing with mercurial skill,
Where Science marshals forth her own quadrille.

### LXXI

Or, if he dance not, but hath higher views
 Upon an heiress or his neighbour's bride,
Let him take care that that which he pursues
 Is not at once too palpably descried.
Full many an eager gentleman oft rues
 His haste: impatience is a blundering guide
Amongst a people famous for reflection,
Who like to play the fool with circumspection.

### LXXII

But, if you can contrive, get next at supper;
 Or if, forestalled, get opposite and ogle: –
Oh, ye ambrosial moments! always upper
 In mind, a sort of sentimental bogle,
Which sits for ever upon memory's crupper,
 The ghost of vanished pleasures once in vogue! Ill
Can tender souls relate the rise and fall
Of hopes and fears which shake a single ball. . . .

### LXXXVI

But 'carpe diem', Juan, 'carpe, carpe!'
 Tomorrow sees another race as gay
And transient, and devoured by the same harpy.
 'Life's a poor player,' – then 'play out the play,

Ye villains!' and above all keep a sharp eye
    Much less on what you do than what you say:
By hypocritical, be cautious, be
Not what you seem, but always what you see.

### LXXXVII

But how shall I relate in other cantos
    Of what befell our hero in the land,
Which 'tis the common cry and lie to vaunt as
    A moral country? But I hold my hand —
For I disdain to write an Atalantis;
    But 'tis as well at once to understand,
You are not a moral people, and you know it,
Without the aid of too sincere a poet.

### LXXXVIII

What Juan saw and underwent shall be
    My topic, with of course the due restriction
Which is required by proper courtesy;
    And recollect the work is only fiction,
And that I sing of neither mine nor me,
    Though every scribe, in some slight turn of diction,
Will hint allusions never meant. Ne'er doubt
*This* — when I speak, I don't hint, but speak out.

### LXXXIX

Whether he married with the third or fourth
    Offspring of some sage husband-hunting countess,
Or whether with some virgin of more worth
    (I mean in Fortune's matrimonial bounties)
He took to regularly peopling Earth,
    Of which your lawful, awful wedlock fount is, —
Or whether he was taken in for damages,
For being too excursive in his homages, —

### XC

Is yet within the unread events of time.
 Thus far, go forth, thou lay, which I will back
Against the same given quantity of rhyme,
 For being as much the subject of attack
As ever yet was any work sublime,
 By those who love to say that white is black.
So much the better! – I may stand alone,
But would not change my free thoughts for a throne....

*The concluding cantos of the poem are devoted to Juan's association with Lady Adeline Amundeville.*

## INDEX OF FIRST LINES OF
## SHORTER POEMS

# FOR THE BEST IN PAPERBACKS, LOOK FOR THE 🐧

In every corner of the world, on every subject under the sun, Penguin represents quality and variety – the very best in publishing today.

For complete information about books available from Penguin – including Puffins, Penguin Classics and Arkana – and how to order them, write to us at the appropriate address below. Please note that for copyright reasons the selection of books varies from country to country.

---

**In the United Kingdom:** Please write to *Dept E.P., Penguin Books Ltd, Harmondsworth, Middlesex, UB7 0DA.*

If you have any difficulty in obtaining a title, please send your order with the correct money, plus ten per cent for postage and packaging, to *PO Box No 11, West Drayton, Middlesex*

**In the United States:** Please write to *Dept BA, Penguin, 299 Murray Hill Parkway, East Rutherford, New Jersey 07073*

**In Canada:** Please write to *Penguin Books Canada Ltd, 2801 John Street, Markham, Ontario L3R 1B4*

**In Australia:** Please write to the *Marketing Department, Penguin Books Australia Ltd, P.O. Box 257, Ringwood, Victoria 3134*

**In New Zealand:** Please write to the *Marketing Department, Penguin Books (NZ) Ltd, Private Bag, Takapuna, Auckland 9*

**In India:** Please write to *Penguin Overseas Ltd, 706 Eros Apartments, 56 Nehru Place, New Delhi, 110019*

**In the Netherlands:** Please write to *Penguin Books Netherlands B.V., Postbus 195, NL–1380AD Weesp*

**In West Germany:** Please write to *Penguin Books Ltd, Friedrichstrasse 10–12, D–6000 Frankfurt/Main 1*

**In Spain:** Please write to *Longman Penguin España, Calle San Nicolas 15, E–28013 Madrid*

**In Italy:** Please write to *Penguin Italia s.r.l., Via Como 4, I-20096 Pioltello (Milano)*

**In France:** Please write to *Penguin Books Ltd, 39 Rue de Montmorency, F-75003 Paris*

**In Japan:** Please write to *Longman Penguin Japan Co Ltd, Yamaguchi Building, 2–12–9 Kanda Jimbocho, Chiyoda-Ku, Tokyo 101*